© Copyright 2020 by Paula W. Millet
All rights reserved.

This book or any portion thereof may not be reproduced or used in any manner whatsoever without the express written permission of the publisher except for the use of brief quotations in a book review.

Printed in the United States of America
Second Chapter Publishing
First Printing, 2020
ISBN 978-0-9976677-6-9

Cover art Courtesy National Gallery of Art, Washington
Cover photo – Lisa Ann Hughes Photography

This is a work of fiction. All incidents and dialogue, and all characters with the exception of some well-known historical and public figures, are products of the author's imagination and are not to be construed as real. Where real-life historical or public figures appear, the situations, incidents, and dialogues concerning those persons are entirely fictional and are not intended to depict actual events or to change the entirely fictional nature of the work. In all other respects, any resemblance to persons living or dead is entirely coincidental.

Angelique's Legacy

TABLE OF CONTENTS

Chapter One 1

Chapter Two..9

Chapter Three..13

Chapter Four 19

Chapter Five 25

Chapter Six 28

Chapter Seven 34

Chapter Eight 39

Chapter Nine 42

Chapter Ten 47

Chapter Eleven..50

Chapter Twelve...53

Chapter Thirteen...57

Chapter Fourteen 61

Chapter Fifteen...66

Chapter Sixteen 69

Chapter Seventeen 72

Chapter Eighteen 79

Chapter Nineteen 83

Chapter Twenty 89

Chapter Twenty-one 93

Chapter Twenty-two 97

Chapter Twenty-three 102

Chapter Twenty-four 106

Chapter Twenty-five 110

Chapter Twenty-six 114

Chapter Twenty-seven 117

Chapter Twenty-eight 121

Chapter Twenty-nine 125

Chapter Thirty 129

Chapter Thirty-one 134

Chapter Thirty-two 136

Chapter Thirty-three 140

Chapter Thirty-four 142

Chapter Thirty-five 145

Chapter Thirty-six 153

Chapter Thirty-seven 157

Chapter Thirty-eight 167

Chapter Thirty-nine 172

Chapter Forty 178

Chapter Forty-one 183

Chapter Forty-two 187

Chapter Forty-three 193

Chapter Forty-four 197

Chapter Forty-five 200

Chapter Forty-six 206

Chapter Forty-seven 208

Chapter Forty-eight 211

Chapter Forty-nine 216

Chapter Fifty 219

Chapter Fifty-one 222

Chapter Fifty-two 227

Chapter Fifty-three 230

Chapter Fifty-four 234

Chapter Fifty-five 239

Chapter Fifty-six 241

Chapter Fifty-seven 247

Chapter Fifty-eight 252

Chapter Fifty-nine 257

Chapter Sixty 261

Chapter Sixty-one 265

Chapter Sixty-two 269

Chapter Sixty-three 272

Chapter Sixty-four 277

Chapter Sixty-five 282

Chapter Sixty-six 286

Chapter Sixty-seven 290

Chapter Sixty-eight 294

Chapter Sixty-nine 298

Chapter Seventy 304

Chapter Seventy-one 306

Chapter Seventy-two 309

Epilogue 314

Author's Notes 320

CHAPTER ONE

SPRING, 1875

Aimee exhaled, the sound of it echoing through the silent room. She concentrated on her breathing, a technique she had often employed as she assisted Franklin in surgery during those moments when the gruesome sight of blood and infection was too much to bear. And with each lungful, she willed herself to calm her runaway emotions, as the sound of her heart beat so loudly that she was sure the others heard it as well. It seemed like hours had passed since they had first gathered in the parlor, and she had taken her place on the crimson velvet settee, but it had only been a few minutes, fifteen at the most. Time has a way of playing tricks on the mind at such times, she thought.

Her mother, Angelique, had insisted that this, the best room in the house, be reserved for company and important occasions, so when she appeared with the fancy china coffee pot and delicate cups loaded onto a silver tray and invited them to sit, both Aimee and Franklin knew that something significant was about to happen. But something significant had already happened that day and the one which had proceeded it. Uncle Gaston, the man who had once stolen her, ripped her from the busy streets of Charleston as though she was the pocket book belonging to a fancy lady, had resurfaced. Although the passing years had done much to erase the memories, she still had occasional nightmares, moments when she was once again that helpless five-year-old child kidnapped by a stranger. His arrival at the clinic had seemed like an uncanny coincidence, a cruel twist of fate, and as he slept, she gazed at his scarred face, the cracked lips of his mouth twitching with the pain. She mentally practiced the speech, the words that as a grown woman, she wanted him to hear. And she was ready to deliver it, anxious to do so. But Franklin, always her protector, had shielded her from him, and the loathsome man had passed away far too quickly for her to get the closure she didn't even realize she needed. Aimee wrung her hands. Gaston was gone and never able to hurt her again, but her mother's implication that there was more to the story than neither she nor Franklin knew gave her pause. Obviously, he was not her brother as he had once claimed. That was a ploy to gain Aimee's trust. She couldn't imagine what secrets connected her charming, elegant mother and that wretched creature, but her intuition, honed from years of nursing, told her that it couldn't be good. She closed her eyes and prepared to hear the truth.

The china clock on the mantle began its melodious song, marking the half hour. Angelique carefully poured the coffee and cream, then dropped a cube of sugar into the cups. Her hands shook as she handed one to each of them before moving to the chair opposite to where Aimee and Franklin sat. She looked first to Andrew, her husband and father of her children, searching his face, her eyes filled with tears. He had always been her greatest supporter and an ever-present source of comfort. She reached over to take his hand. He nodded and then offered a weak smile. Angelique cleared her throat. There was a long pause, and Aimee thought it odd, that her mother, always so poised and prepared, seemed to be at a loss for words.

"Just tell us what you think we need to know, Mother," Franklin said, "We are not children, certainly."

"Whatever it is, we will understand. You have shown us that the tie that binds our family is strong. We have weathered some difficulties, of course, but as you were always quick to point out, together we can face whatever may befall us. It is one of the first lessons you taught me as a child," Aimee said.

Angelique sighed. "My beautiful, brave children. You do honor me with your loyalty. However painful it is to tell, you deserve to know the story of the life your mother lived before this one with all of you. As you will soon see, it is quite the tale."

"Before Poppa, you mean?" Aimee asked.

"Long before then, when I was a young girl, living on Chauvin Plantation and the years which followed."

Franklin took a sip of coffee and shifted his weight. She had his full attention.

"I met him one night at a dance held at a neighboring plantation. He was older, brazen in his attempts to get my attention. But there was something mysterious and interesting about him as well, and he swept me off my feet in a matter of weeks. The courtship was brief; the marriage came quickly. As a young bride I adored him, and the baby girl who came into our lives shortly thereafter."

Angelique swallowed hard. She knew that there was more, much more, to tell, and once the box which carefully secured the memories had been unsealed, she would have no choice but to relive them. The moments rolled through her mind like tumbleweed in the desert.

"Life changed when our sweet Josephina went to live with the angels, claimed by the fever. It was as though she was the one who bound us as a couple." Angelique paused, remembering. She wiped away a tear. "Without her, little remained between us. I locked myself away, lost in my grief, and despair. He fell deep into the arms of the devil."

"The devil?" Franklin asked, his eyes growing wide.

"It undoubtedly seemed that way," Angelique said. "I had no idea that he was a gambler, even in those early years together, but as time passed, it became the center of his life. He courted Lady Luck as he would a lover, and she ultimately jilted him. Within a short period of time, the debts became overwhelming, he grew so desperate that he faked his death, staged an elaborate hunting accident just to escape the financial penalties of his misdeeds. He simply disappeared, swallowed up by a big world, leaving me penniless and alone to sort through the mess he had created. Because of him, I lost Chauvin Plantation and everything else we owned, a tragedy that altered my life."

"And that got you to the island where you met Poppa." Aimee added. She cleared her throat. "I am so sorry, Momma. Now I understand why getting your home back was important. How sad for you. How utterly unfair to be burdened by the consequences of another's choices." She hesitated. The story had triggered a recollection she herself had fought to forget. "Uncle Gaston. He gambled, too. Every single day. I didn't understand at the time what playing cards meant. I was so little, and it was hard to sit and wait while he spent hours at the tables. But I remember that some days he would be sad and happy on others. I guess it was tied to his winning."

Franklin furrowed his brow. He remembered the first time he saw Aimee, perched on a high stool as she waited patiently for her uncle to finish his game, finally releasing her. She was so innocent, so fearful. His heart clenched. Those images of little Aimee haunted him, too, but this raised bigger questions in his mind. "Is that why you recognized Uncle Gaston? Did he know the gambler you married, the one who vanished? And did you ever find him? Was he still alive and did you divorce him? I assume you must have in order to have married Poppa."

Angelique took a deep breath. This was the moment of truth. Jean Paul seemed to have been unstoppable, a man resurrected from the dead over and over again. She certainly had believed the men who had carried what she assumed to be his lifeless body home so many years ago. And she thought he was dead for the second time after he rowed away into the raging winds of the hurricane. But the evil one had lived, and once again shattered her life when he stole her precious child, breaking her motherly heart into a million pieces. She had no knowledge of what might have happened to him in the years which followed, but it appeared that he had lived a hard life, reaping the consequences for his reckless decisions. That was justice. But now, he was truly gone, and she had watched him take his last breath earlier that morning. After all that happened, all of the pain and sorrow, it was time that he was finally buried, laid to rest once and for all.

"Gaston is a name he bestowed upon himself, an alias, a change in identity to hide who he really was. In truth, he was Jean Paul LaTour. And he was once my husband."

The silence was deafening, the air in the room suddenly thick and heavy.

Aimee stared into the delicate cup filled with cold coffee. Her mind was reeling, replaying the months spent with the man who had claimed to be her mother's brother, but actually was her husband. "I don't understand," she whispered.

"I know it is confusing, Aimee. And there is more to tell, of course. But for now, let me say that I truly believed him to be dead when I met your poppa. When our paths crossed again on Last Island, I thought we had engaged in a final show down and that he had perished in the storm that had claimed so many. It wasn't until we met Franklin in the park that I learned the truth, his identity confirmed by the tell-tale scar he bore."

Franklin winced at the memory, which had changed his life as well. "I'm not sure who rescued whom that day, but I am glad that I could help."

"You were our hero, Franklin. And most recently, you have proved that still to be true."

"So that means I had an older sister?" Aimee asked.

"Half-sister. But yes, and she was beautiful just like you girls."

"One more question, Momma," Aimee said.

"Of course. Ask anything."

"Were you not going to tell us the truth? Did you not think we deserved to know?"

Tears filled Angelique's eyes as she searched for the words, the justification for concealing something so important. She swallowed hard, unable to speak.

Andrew, who felt that it was not his story to tell, had patiently listened as the drama unfolded, but sensing his wife's discomfort, finally spoke. "Once your momma found you that's all that mattered to her, Aimee, to both of us. Besides, we figured that he was still in Charleston, or perhaps had gone to France. We had determined that it was best for our family to leave his existence in the past."

Aimee nodded in understanding. She looked to her mother, who seemed to be intent on saying all that was on her mind.

Angelique sat quietly, her hands folded as though in prayer. "There is one more thing." She took a deep breath. "Since this is a confession, you should probably know that I was prepared to kill him as he lay in your clinic. And I would have done it with little consideration as to the value of his life. Somehow, I thought that doing so would erase the history, his role in my story. But that was foolish. I suppose. I imagined that with him gone, I would never have to face this moment, one I have dreaded for years."

"Telling us, you mean?" Franklin asked.

"Yes, of course. But I learned something important as I sat at his bedside. Unless we can face the demons of our past, we seek revenge rather than truly feeling what has happened to us and all of the subsequent pain it has caused. And that only begets more sorrow. To turn judgment into compassion and vengeance into forgiveness is powerful. And truly difficult. But that's when true healing begins."

Franklin placed his cup on the tray and moved to his mother's side. He offered a hug. "You are strong and brave." He turned to Aimee. "Now we know the truth. It is finally over."

She nodded. "The truth," she repeated.

"The undertaker is on his way to claim the body and transport it to the cemetery. Jean Paul will be laid to rest next to our daughter, since that place was prepared for him many years ago. I will be there when they seal the tomb, certainly not from any sense of loyalty, but because everybody, even those who have hurt us deeply, deserves a proper burial."

"We will come, too. You shouldn't have to face this alone."

"Thank you, my children. I won't refuse your kindness."

"What about Aida?" Aimee asked. "Certainly you will tell her when she arrives next week."

"Indeed. Your sister should know as well. I hope it won't overshadow her happy mood. We have a wedding to plan," Angelique said.

"Aida will be fine," Franklin said. "She really had no contact with Gaston, I mean, Jean Paul, as we did. Besides, we know that she will be so involved in bridal details that it will be no more than a passing story to her. She does love to be the center of attention."

Angelique chuckled. "You know her very well," she said, grateful for a bit of levity.

But before Angelique could even clear the coffee tray, Aimee had excused herself, retreating to the quiet of her bedroom. She paused in the doorway, studying the shadows cast by the afternoon sun. The curtains moved gently in the breeze as she crossed the room and knelt at the foot of her bed. She carefully opened the wooden trunk, casting aside the books and old clothing until she reached the bottom, her fingers searching until she found it, an old doll with matted hair, a faded calico dress. She clutched it to her bosom as she began to cry. "Sarah," she whispered. "Oh, Sarah."

CHAPTER TWO

Aimee stood on the dock, her eyes searching for the first glimpse of the steamer as it rounded the bend.

"Do you see it?" Angelique asked.

"Not yet," Aimee replied, standing on her tip toes to get a better look.

The crowd grew thicker. People intent on welcoming a friend or loved one, who had been away, lined the wooden wharf that led to the debarkation area. Dirty-faced children weaved among the throng, and gentlemen held onto their coats, having been forewarned of the likelihood of pickpockets. Ladies opened bedecked parasols to shade their fair skin from the scorching Louisiana sun. Waiting carriages took their place on the cobblestone street as the horses struggled against the harnesses, their lips pursed for a drink. Farmers and shopkeepers had their wagons poised, ready to be loaded with cargo that had taken months to deliver. The day the boat from New York arrived, was always an exciting one.

"Look there!" a voice cried out. There rose a collective cheer as the ship slowly made its way to where they stood.

Within minutes, the longshoremen had secured the massive ropes to the iron cleats and lowered the gangway. Aida was among the first to emerge, waving enthusiastically when she spotted them.

"Sissy," Aida screamed as she fell into Aimee's arms. "And Mother. I have missed you so."

"We have missed you, too. It feels like you have been gone forever," Aimee said.

"Just two months. But I must admit that although New York is the most exciting city on earth, I have longed for home. And family."

Angelique smiled, examining her fashionable daughter who handed an elaborate hatbox to a porter as she gave him instructions for procuring her luggage. The young woman who stood before her was very different from the one who had left. Aida appeared to be much more sophisticated, more worldly, the result, no doubt, of being in the company of the Count and his family, living in the most progressive city in America, one that had not suffered the ravages of war as New Orleans had.

Aida adjusted her bonnet, a stylish creation of silk and linen with delicate ribbon rosettes along the crown, which mimicked the same detail along the bodice of her emerald-green gown. This was no traveling dress thought Angelique; she knew that Aida had chosen it carefully just to impress them.

"What you are wearing is beautiful," Aimee remarked as though reading her mother's mind. It amused her to think that although they were identical twins, alike in every way except for the burn scar that still marred Aimee's forearm, their taste in clothing made them as different as salt and pepper. Aimee, always the practical one, had worn her best day dress, a plain frock made of beige cotton. Her bonnet was straw, adorned only by the black grosgrain ribbon, which outlined the brim. Nobody would have a difficult time telling them apart like when they were children.

Aida smiled, pleased that the outfit had elicited the anticipated response. "Thank you. You can't begin to imagine the stores in New York. Anything you can conceive can so easily be custom made for you in a matter of days. They get silks from the Orient that are so colorful, your eyes have a difficult time taking in the sight. The brocades and velvets and tassels are breathtaking. I am afraid that Michel and his family totally spoiled me while I was there."

"As well they should have," Angelique said. "They took my daughter away from me for so long, while I worried sick about her welfare."

Aida laughed. "I know that you were just fine, Momma, although I suppose that life was quite boring without me around to liven things up a bit."

Aimee rolled her eyes. Her sister had not changed one bit. "Somehow we managed to survive."

"How is Poppa? Franklin?"

"They survived your absence, too, if that's what you mean." Aimee said, stifling a giggle.

"No, it is not what I meant. I was simply inquiring about their health. I am disappointed that they didn't come with you to meet me."

"You do forget that both Poppa and Franklin are busy men with demanding careers," Aimee said. "Goodness, Aida, you will see them tonight at dinner and every day which follows, leading up to your wedding day."

Aida paused, her lip quivering for a moment before raising her gloved hand to signal the porter. She turned to her mother. "Shall we go now? Lead the way."

Aida continued to chatter about the excitement of being in New York for the entire carriage ride home. When they arrived, Aimee breathed a sigh of relief and ran upstairs to change into her nursing dress. As she was securing the starched white apron, she met Aida in the hall, who was half carrying, half dragging a heavy tapestry satchel.

"Come, Sissy. Let me show you what I brought you."

"Not now. I am afraid that I am expected at the hospital. Unlike you, I don't have a titled fiancé. I am expected to work for a living."

Aida stood as through rooted to the spot. Just a few months earlier, she had considered herself to be a progressive woman, with her sights set on a career of her own. More than anything, she wanted to practice law, to be a champion for the downtrodden and to prove that a woman could accomplish anything a man could. Now, she was no more than a porcelain figurine, all wrapped up in feathers and finery. Worse than that, she had become defined by her relationship with a man. She wondered how it had happened, how her resolve had been so easily discarded. Women, she thought, are expected to sacrifice everything for love. And so, it seems, she had.

The front door closed with a loud thud, signaling Aimee's departure. Aida swallowed hard, suddenly overcome by emotion. They had always been so close, especially after the nightmare of her sister's kidnapping, but the time apart, coupled by the different paths into adulthood they had each taken, seemed to separate them. Aida loved Michel, truly, and she looked forward to becoming his wife. He was an educated man, handsome and strong. She considered herself fortunate to be marrying into a family of rank and privilege, and she knew that there would be many adventures in her future because of it. But standing there in the wide hall of her family home, she felt unsettled, uncertain in her choices. As crazy as it seemed, she was envious of her sister and her career among the sick and dying. It was not the homecoming she expected. Not at all.

CHAPTER THREE

Angelique peered out of the window. It appeared to be a lovely day, but she was unable to embrace it. Something hard and heavy stood between her eyes and her heart. She rubbed her temples. Her head ached, pounded with an unyielding pain. A wave of nausea swept over her, as she took a deep breath, willing herself to a place of calm. Down the hall, she could hear Aida crying. She wondered if her timing had been poor, that perhaps she should have waited to have the conversation about her life with Jean Paul. But they had been alone in the house, which provided an opportune moment, and besides, she feared that Aimee or Franklin might say something, revealing the secret to their sister before she could speak with her. No, she had made the right decision in telling her. But Aida's weeping was surprising. After all, she had never met the man, had no interest in him other than knowing he was the villain who had separated her from her beloved sister when they were so very young. Why was she inconsolable? Panic rose in Angelique's mind as she considered the possibility that Aida thought her mother irrational and foolish to have married a man capable of such terrible acts. She worried that Aida might never view her in the same way, that somehow their relationship had been diminished. If that was true for Aida, then, might it be true of Aimee and Franklin as well? Had Jean Paul's final offense been to separate her children from her, weakening the bond they had spent a lifetime building? The thought of it was more than she could bear.

She took a deep breath before tentatively knocking on the door of Aida's room. "May I come in?"

Aida nodded, wiping away the tears with the back of her hand.

"I am so sorry to have hurt you, honey. I had no idea that you would react this way. This happened a long time ago, before I met your Poppa, when I was young and so very naive. I had no idea that the man I was marrying was capable of doing such evil. But please know that my mistakes haven't defined me, even though the consequences of my life with Jean Paul have wreaked havoc on our family. But more importantly, this has not changed my love for you and Aimee and Franklin one bit. You must believe that."

There was a long moment of silence between them. Angelique's heart was breaking, the sadness filling the room. "Talk to me. Tell me what you are thinking," she said.

"I'm sorry, Momma. I don't wish to make you feel melancholy," Aida said. "I understand why you needed to share. I am glad that you did, truly, especially since Aida and Franklin already know. How dreadful to have been so deceived. It is hard to imagine that this is the same man that took Aimee from us. Truly, it all seems like a nightmare."

"Indeed, it does. But we are awake now. It is over. He can never hurt us again."

Aida nodded and began to cry once more.

"What is wrong, my precious girl. Why are you weeping?"

"You are the smartest woman I know, Momma. You have survived a hurricane, regained your plantation and turned it into a thriving business. You started an orphanage, helped so many motherless children. I have always been in awe of your strength and courage."

Angelique reached for her daughter's hand. "Your words flatter me."

"I have always wanted to be just like you. People admire you because you change things, you make the world a better place."

"Someday you will, too."

"That has always been my greatest wish. But Momma, if you made such a big mistake by giving your heart away to a scoundrel, if you married, thinking that life was to be beautiful and instead it was horrible, then, how am I to trust my own judgment? How do I know that Michel will always be good and kind? How can I be sure that I am not making an error in judgment, like you did, by marrying him?"

Angelique sighed. "Aida, every person feels a bit of doubt on their wedding day. You think because you have courted someone you know them, but people tend to be on their best behavior when they are motivated to get something or someone they want. It isn't until later, when time has rewritten the love story that you come to understand the person to whom you have pledged your life."

"What does that mean exactly?"

"You think you truly know another human being, but in reality, you don't. You can't. It is one of the great truths of life. There will always be something held back, some secret locked away. It often feels like mystery you are unable to solve."

"Then are we all doomed? Should I cancel this wedding because I fear what he may become, what we may become?"

Angelique smiled. "No, of course not. Faith is having confidence in that which we cannot see. We trust that what our heart tells us to be true simply is. There is no certainty in this life, but we wake each day, confident that the choices we make of what we do with the hours that lie before us will be good ones. If we didn't believe, then, we wouldn't know joy. Life is a risk, but you can't live in fear of what might happen. Look, I made a terrible mistake by marrying Jean Paul, but I definitely made the right choice with your father. I think that evens the score."

"Ah yes, you and Poppa are most surely a good match, a real partnership. I have watched you all of my life, and I have been inspired by your devotion to each other. I suppose you are right," Aida said.

"Love is the most amazingly wonderful thing that will ever happen to you. Do not let fear hold you back from all of the magic that awaits you and Michel as you begin your life together. In this great big world, you two have managed to find each other. I think that is pretty remarkable, don't you? Besides, you both have a pretty powerful angel looking out for you."

"Angel? Who?"

"The Countess, of course!!"

"Ah yes, Michel never knew her, but she lives on in the stories his father tells as well as your days with her. She must have been quite something."

"Indeed. Your husband-to-be's grandmother was the most remarkable woman I have ever known. Her kindness and wit were legendary, but she was also sensible and fair. Trust me, your union will be blessed."

Aida moved to hug her mother. "Thank you for this, for everything, really. I am so grateful to have your wisdom."

"I may not have all the answers, but I will always have a sympathetic ear. I am here for you whenever you need me. Now, how about you come and help me prepare dinner. We have a lot to celebrate tonight."

"Sure. And Momma?"

"Yes, Aida?"

"It truly is good to be home."

The family had all taken their seats at the dinner table when Aida appeared wearing a diamond tiara, along with her cotton housedress.

"Well, well, if it isn't Princess Aida," Franklin joked. "Glad that you could grace us with your presence."

Aida laughed. "Consider yourself graced."

Aimee rolled her eyes. "Where did you get the crown, Sissy? Or should I just guess."

"Well, it actually came from Michel's mother. It was hers when she married his father, and she wants me to wear it on my wedding day as well."

"Then, she must like you, Aida," Angelique said. "You know; a mother-in-law can be difficult if she feels threatened by the woman who is taking her place in her son's life. You should consider it an honor to receive such a gift."

"Well, of course I do. At first, I refused to take it. I had my own ideas of what to wear. But she looked hurt. She was quick to point out that I was marrying into an aristocratic family so there would be bits of protocol that I would have to learn."

"Sounds like a lot of pressure to me," Aimee said.

Aida stabbed at the green beans on her plate with a fork. "I thought that as well, but it will also be an amazing opportunity. Think of the good I can do, Aimee. Michel's family name will open doors that might otherwise be closed for me. I can also continue to help with the fund raising for the orphanage."

"I am grateful for that, "Angelique added. "Your fancy friends from New York have made it possible for us to stay afloat financially over the past few months. I was also able to add some much-needed supplies for the school."

"Good. Some of those folks are full of themselves, so I don't mind convincing them to part with their money. Besides, I have ideas for things I want to accomplish as Michel's wife. I will have privilege, but I won't forget that you raised us to think of others, Momma. I will do my best."

"I know you will," Andrew said, "Your mother and I have the utmost faith in your ability to change the world."

"Maybe not the whole world, Poppa, but I would be happy with changing just a little part of it."

"Your dreams of being a lawyer?" Aimee asked.

"Deferred," Aida said. "I still want to go to law school, but it continues to be a closed door to women, even for those who think they have the key."

"Well, if anybody can unlock it, you can," Aimee said.

Franklin raised his glass. "To having our family together again, even if it only for a short while."

"To my family," Andrew said, "the most important people in my life."

CHAPTER FOUR

The house was quiet as Aida lay in her childhood bed contemplating her impending wedding. To the casual observer, she was one lucky girl, betrothed to a handsome viscount, who could offer her the world. But in spite of her undeniable love for him, her overwhelming desire to be his wife, she couldn't shake her misgivings, the unrelenting churning in the pit of her stomach.

"You know, my dear, there are unspoken concessions that we women have to make when marrying a nobleman," her future mother-in-law had whispered the previous week when they were alone in the parlor. They had often spent afternoons together, working on sewing projects or sorting names for the wedding guest list. Aida knew that she was being schooled, with a test most surely to follow.

Aida smiled. "Like decorum, you mean? I figure that I will have to keep my rather strong opinions to myself at times. I absolutely want to be a positive representative of your family."

"Well, yes, of course, that, but as the word implies, titled gentry believe themselves to be entitled to certain liberties, allowances, if you will. Men in power are accustomed to having their way, and they expect their wives to look the other way if they transgress."

"Transgress?" Aida asked, confused. "In what way?"

The Countess cleared her throat as she reached for Aida's hand. "No need to concern yourself with that now, dear. I know that you will be a patient, loving wife to my son. That's all I could ever want."

She had wanted to ask for clarification, but deemed it unwise when the Countess had so quickly changed the subject. Nevertheless, Aida replayed the conversation over and over again in her mind, wondering why it seemed so important to Michel's mother to warn her. And yet, she was so cryptic with her words, that all it did was plant a very large seed of doubt in Aida's mind, one that had grown rampantly in the days which followed. She needed some reassurance, some clarification before making the most important promise of her life. She knew just where to get it.

She grabbed her cape and bonnet and set out for a walk. The fresh air lifted her spirits momentarily, and she raised her face to the sun, feeling its warmth on her cheeks. She tried to quieten her mind, which continued to spin first in one direction, then another as she studied the street names, hoping to remember the route. She had only been there once and that was as an impetuous teenager, who thought it might be fun to discover what awaited her young life. But the woman had been non-committal, far too vague with her predictions. When Aida and her friend giggled through the reading, she readily dismissed the girls, determining that their intentions were strictly frivolous. But she hadn't forgotten the power she felt in the old woman's presence, and she hoped that the visit would provide her with the answers. She needed them more than anything.

Aida took a deep breath and counted the numbers, until she was relatively sure she had reached her destination. The building was non-descript, blending in with the other row houses. It stood on brick pilings which elevated it from the street, but there was nothing which distinguished it as special, no placard or sign. In fact, the peeling paint, revealing the raw cypress underneath, made it appear vulnerable, brutally exposed to the harsh South Louisiana elements. But then, she spied it. The number on the door, unlike the others, was written in French, the fancy black script *trois* designating it as number three. She marveled that she was able to remember such a small detail.

She paused before knocking, examining her impulsive decision to visit this place. Her mother would disapprove. So would Aimee. For a moment, she considered turning and running away. But as the doubts nagged at her, it strengthened her resolve. Perhaps it was an unwise thing to do, but she had always been one to leap first, asking questions later. She could sort it all out afterwards, perhaps even finding some truth in the experience.

The old woman opened the door a few inches. Aida tried to peek into the darkness, but she could see nothing but piercing blue eyes staring into hers. "Yes? Can I help you, girl?"

"I, uh, came to learn of my fortune," Aida said, her voice trembling.

The door opened a bit more and the old woman stepped closer. She grinned, revealing her missing two front teeth. "Your fortune, eh? And what makes you think that I can help you with that?"

Aida tried not to panic. It had been such a long time. Had she miscalculated, knocked on the wrong door? She decided to simply be honest and apologize if she had been wrong. "I am filled with many questions, Madame. I had hoped that you might help me find answers."

"Really? How should I do that?"

The old woman was toying with her, testing her fortitude. Aida was up for the challenge. "I do believe that you have the gift of foresight, that you are able to see into a person's life and know their destiny. If I am wrong, I will gladly offer my humblest apologies." She turned toward the street, poised to leave.

"Wait," the woman said, holding up her hand. "What have you to offer me in return for my gift?"

Aida had been prepared for the negotiation. She held up a five-dollar gold coin, determining it was best to offer her highest bid first.

The old woman snatched the coin from Aida's hand with one quick move and opened the door wide as she invited her to enter. The room was dark with the shutters closed, the faded velvet curtains drawn shut. Aida paused a moment, waiting for her eyes to adjust. A kerosene lantern illuminated part of the room, while flickering candles cast an eerie glow upon the rose-colored walls. Aida struggled to breathe in the oppressive heat, and braced herself against the wall, fearing that she would faint. The woman motioned to a round wooden table in the center of the room, and Aida sat in the straight back chair. Although she tried, willed herself to be calm, she was unable to control the shaking.

"Now then," the woman said. "Let us begin. Give me your hands."

Aida reluctantly offered her palms as the woman examined them. "Hmmm," she said, and then paused, her eyes fixed toward the heavens. "You give your heart so freely. Guard and protect it from those who are near and dear to you."

"Who might that be?" Aida asked, determined to get more specific answers.

"We shall see." The old woman took the cards from the tarnished sliver box and handed them to Aida. "Choose."

Aida reached into the deck, handed over the card and waited. "Ah, it is the king."

Aida gasped, placing her hand over her racing heart. "Who?"

The old woman held the card up for inspection. "The King. Usually it represents a significant man in your life. I assume you know who that might be. Shall we continue?" Aida nodded.

"Choose another."

Aida selected the second card.

"And the Queen."

So far, the old woman had revealed no secrets. It had been the luck of the draw, Aida thought.

She shuffled the remaining cards and dealt them one-by one. "I see it clearly now," the old woman mumbled as she carefully studied each.

"What?"

"Patience, child. Ah, yes, there are roses."

Aida folded her arms. "Flowers?"

"Or perhaps something more. Time will disclose the significance."

Aida tried to hide her annoyance. She hadn't paid for a riddle. "I am afraid this is far too ambiguous for me."

"The truth is often shrouded in mystery, my dear. We are only meant to see what the cards suggest to us. What is revealed is what we are meant to know. You do understand that, do you not?

Aida shrugged.

"Shall I continue?"

"Yes," Aida whispered.

"There will be great pain in your life, sadness, loss, and despair, but you will triumph, overcome it all. You are destined for greatness, but only through struggle will you learn to be strong."

Aida exhaled. It all seemed a little too noncommittal to her. Certainly, this could be said about anyone. "Is that all?" she asked. She was angry with herself for thinking that she would find answers here with this fraud.

"No, my dear. My final message to you is this. Tread softly and with care, for someone you love will break your heart. The questions that you ask are being answered, but you must be still and listen."

The room was spinning and Aida felt as though she would surely die in that very spot. A week ago, she was the happiest young woman in the world, giddy and in love, hopeful for the future. It was true that questions only begat more questions. The one which loomed the largest in her mind was what would she do next.

Aida was in no hurry to get home. She needed time to think, to process all that the old woman had said. "Someone you love" could apply to a number of people. There was Aimee and Franklin, of course, her parents, and Michel's family, whom she had grown to care for as well. She had a few close friends, too. Besides, she rationalized, loving always comes with the risk of heartbreak., which makes it all the more precious. By the time she had reached the front door of her mother's house, she had convinced herself that the old crone was a con artist, with no more clairvoyant powers than she had. Laughing at the folly of her visit, she vowed never to tell a soul how she had spent the afternoon. As she climbed the stairs to her bedroom, she determined that if nothing else, the experience had removed her doubts, strengthening her resolve to become Michel's devoted wife.

CHAPTER FIVE

Angelique looked forward to the mornings she spent at the orphanage. The children, always bubbling with energy and excitement, never failed to delight her. It was a happy place, filled with laughter, and any problems she might have had always fell away as soon as she crossed the threshold into the lobby where she was greeted by the smiling face of some precious boy or girl. Establishing Countess Maria Children's Home had been the most important work of her life and nothing, not even regaining Chauvin Plantation, would surpass the pride she had felt when she had welcomed the first child.

There had been some surprises along the way. Using the money left to her by her generous mentor and friend to renovate the old structure meant that the Countess' family had been part of that grand opening celebration, which in turn brought Michel into Aida's life. There are no coincidences, she thought, only divine plans which unfold before us, taking our breath away with their timing and their magic.

When Angelique had finished her breakfast and sent the last of the children off to the school room, she retreated to her office. There was always something that required her attention, supplies to be ordered and the budget to be balanced. Occasionally, she would receive a letter, inquiring about a child thought to be lost. Sometimes, with great pleasure, Angelique was able to reunite a family separated by war or circumstance. Those were the happiest of times.

But at this moment, the administrative tasks would have to wait. She had a matter of weeks to organize Aida's wedding. True to form, her daughter had a long list of wishes for her special day.

Angelique had hoped that Aida would want to be married at Chauvin. It was, after all, their family home, and would provide a beautiful backdrop for the ceremony, with its blooming magnolia trees and green fields. Springtime at the plantation was lovely, for sure. But Aida wanted something more stylish and elegant. Angelique suspected that she wanted to impress Michel's family and friends. New York was a world apart from New Orleans, definitely more urbane and sophisticated by comparison. Having the celebration in the city meant there would be available hotel rooms for the guests. Housing them at Chauvin would be impossible. No, Aida's decision to wed in New Orleans had ultimately been the best one.

But Angelique worried about her daughter. Aida had seemed unusually preoccupied since she arrived home, often spending time alone in her room or lost in thought at the family dinner table. She wondered if her daughter somehow worried that the guests might think her unworthy of her new husband and his fancy life. But Angelique quickly dismissed that idea as foolish. Aida never feared anything, even as a little girl, and as a grown woman, she could certainly handle the amenities of any social situation. No, her daughter would be just fine. She had simply been experiencing a bit of bridal jitters. That's all.

By the time the bell rang for the children to file into the dining hall for lunch, Angelique had arranged for the ceremony flowers and planned for the reception menu. She had received confirmation of the date for the cathedral from the Bishop, who would be officiating himself. The seamstress had sent word that Angelique's dress was ready for the last fitting. All seemed to be in order, and she knew that Aida would be pleased.

She paused to consider that soon her precious girl would be a wife, and God willing, after that, a mother. The idea of becoming a grandmother made Angelique smile. Somedays, we get a glimpse into the future, she thought, and it is quite remarkable.

CHAPTER SIX

Angelique adjusted the flowers of the centerpiece, paying careful attention to the height so that it wouldn't obstruct the view of her dinner guests. She hoped there would be lively conversation to mark the happy occasion, and she was filled with eager anticipation. The table had been set with her mother's best porcelain china, the one with the tiny blue flowers and wide gold band encircling the rim of the plates and bowls. The heavy crystal goblets glistened in the light of the late afternoon sun. Somehow, even after all these years, she still felt her mother's presence when she used these things, precious reminders of the fancy parties her parents had hosted when she herself was a child. How she had loved to peek around the corner into the candlelit dining room, listening to the sound of laughter and hushed voices. It all seemed so magical at the time, and even now, she caught her breath at the thought of the evening ahead.

Aimee had left the hospital early that day, fearful that she might be tempted to stay longer to help some sick patient who needed her. Being late for Aida's celebration would have created all kinds of drama, which she wanted to avoid. Besides, she would do nothing to disappoint her sister on the eve of her special day. She had already agreed to wear the elaborate off-the-shoulder gown to the party. It was uncharacteristically fancy, made of light green silk that Aida had brought with her from New York. When Aimee had tried it on for the seamstress to adjust one last time, she hardly recognized herself, looking more like her fashionable twin than her practical self. Secretly, she wondered what Franklin would think of her, all dolled up. He was accustomed to seeing her in the stiff nursing apron, and more often than not, covered in someone else's blood. They had worked together for years, and had grown up like family before that. He had been the one who entertained her during those dismal days as Uncle Gaston's captive. And ultimately, it was he who had been responsible for her rescue. Always her protector and confidant, Franklin was her best friend. She tried not to use the word brother, even in her own mind when she thought of him. To do so made what she felt for him feel unseemly and wrong. Still, deep in her heart, she hoped he would think that she was beautiful, even for just this one night. She smoothed her raven hair, careful not to disturb the curls, adjusted the taffeta petticoat and made her way down the stairs.

Angelique was lighting the tapers in the silver candelabras when Aimee entered the dining room.

"May I help you, Mother?" Aimee asked.

"I believe I have everything done," Angelique said. "I guess I want it to be perfect."

"It certainly looks that way. Aida will be pleased."

"I hope so. I haven't seen the Count and Countess since the night we dedicated the orphanage. So much has transpired since that time, including the impending marriage of our children."

"Nobody would have ever imagined that happening, would they? I hate to admit it, but I will miss Sissy when she leaves again."

"I know that you two are very different, but I also can see the bond that you share."

"The twin connection. It is true."

"Indeed."

A low whistle escaped from Andrew's lips as he joined them. "I am quite a lucky man. I have two of the loveliest women in New Orleans in my life, soon to be joined by a third."

"Aida has been primping for hours," Aimee said with a giggle, "I suspect that she is a little nervous."

"I'm a little nervous myself," Angelique said. "I want to make a good impression on the Count and his family."

Andrew moved to kiss Angelique on the cheek. "My darling, you make a good impression wherever you go. Simply be yourself, and the night will be a huge success."

Exactly five minutes before the guests were scheduled to arrive, Franklin threw open the front door and stood breathlessly in the entrance hall, mumbling his apologies. "Very sick patient, I'm afraid. I will be dressed and back in an instant." But as he hung his hat and coat on the rack, he turned just in time to see Aimee's reflection in the gilded mirror which hung over the fireplace in the dining room. He paused, studying her form as though he was seeing her for the first time. And then he smiled as he took the stairs two at a time.

The Count and his wife, along with Michel, a cousin, and two close family friends arrived at exactly half past seven. Aida must have been listening for the knock on the door, because at the precise moment that they were exchanging pleasantries, making formal introductions, she appeared at the top of the stairs, a vision in her white brocade gown.

"There is my beautiful bride," Michel said, extending his hand to her. She blushed as if on cue and offered her gloved hand in response.

"So happy to have you here, darling," Aida said sweetly. She then turned to kiss both cheeks of her future in laws, and greeted the other guests, whom she already knew.

Andrew stepped forward as host. "Welcome to our home. Angelique and I are so pleased to have you join us on the eve of this happy occasion. I am sure none of us imagined that when these two met at the dedication of the orphanage, we would be celebrating a wedding. Life is filled with wonderful surprises, isn't it?"

"Indeed," the Count said. "I believe that this union will be a happy one."

"I agree," Michel said, bowing low in an exaggerated gesture that seemed rather odd. Andrew cleared his throat. "My wife has prepared quite the meal. May I invite you all into the

dining room for the first course?"

The place cards had been carefully arranged that afternoon by Aida, who insisted that the secret to a good dinner party was a proper seating chart. Angelique had been particularly amused by that, having determined that her daughter would effortlessly fall into the role of the wife of a viscount.

As the guests took their seats, Aimee felt the chair being pulled for her and was surprised to see that Franklin had appeared by her side. He had changed into a dinner jacket, although only she could smell the tell-tale odor of chloroform which clung to his hair and skin, an occupational hazard, no doubt. "You look beautiful," he whispered, removing the linen napkin from the silver ring.

Aimee smiled. "Far different from surgical attire," she whispered back. He reached for her hand and squeezed it, and she blushed. Although she had touched his hand a thousand times, this felt different and exciting, which only confused her. She quickly withdrew it.

Angelique had hired help for the evening, who served the five-course meal. She had lovingly prepared most of the dishes herself, convinced that her time-honored recipes were far superior to anything that a cook might produce. And she had been right as the guests raved over the baked oysters and crawfish bisque, the bourbon-laced sweet potatoes with roast pork. Andrew had carefully selected the wine, hoping that they would approve, since he knew the Count obviously had a more sophisticated palate than he. And it felt like a victory when his guest commented favorably on the Bordeaux, swirling it in the glass to examine its color.

When the bananas cooked in rum and butter and laced with cream made an appearance to signal the end of the meal. Andrew stood, raising his glass as a toast to the happy couple.

"To Aida and Michel," he said, "May you always find love in each other's eyes, joy in each other's presence, happiness in each passing day."

"Here, here," said the Count. "I would like to add. May we soon have an heir to remind us that we are indeed immortal."

"I'll drink to that," Michel said. "I am most anxious for fatherhood."

Aida raised an eyebrow. It was clear that she would be expected to have a child sooner rather than later, something she had not considered. Law school seemed further and further out of her reach. But as she reminded herself, there would be time to think of such things, time for negotiating. This night was about their immediate future, and wedding day.

After dinner, the women retired to the parlor with cafe au lait, while the men went into the library for cognac and a cigar.

The Count and Andrew attempted to make polite conversation, but it was obvious that the two men were from two very different worlds, both socially, economically and politically. Given the state of the post-war South versus the industrial North. New Orleans and New York could have easily been on opposite continents. And when the clock struck ten, the Count looked relieved. "Goodness, it appears to be growing rather late. I suppose we should be on our way."

Andrew nodded, rising in response. "Let's go and check on the womenfolk, shall we?"

"Tomorrow I marry," Michel whispered to Franklin, "so where might I find some action tonight?"

"Action?" Franklin asked.

"As in women," Michel said, with a wink. "This is, after all, New Orleans, famous for its brothels. Point me in that direction."

Franklin cleared his throat. "I am afraid that I will be of no use to you in that regard. I spend far too much of my time in hospitals and clinics."

Michel shrugged. "Then, I suspect that I shall have to go exploring on my own."

Franklin opened his mouth to speak, but then reconsidered and simply nodded in understanding.

"Thank you for a mighty fine taste of Southern hospitality," the Count said, shaking Andrew's hand as the group prepared to leave.

"I am so pleased that we could share this evening," Andrew said. "I assume that we will be seeing more of each other in the years ahead."

"Indeed, we will," said the Count. "I look forward to the merging of our two families."

The guests departed for the hotel, eager to celebrate the wedding which was to follow. But for Franklin, there was an unsettling feeling, one which he couldn't quite describe. Perhaps Michel was just a young man wanting to sow the last of his wild oats, he thought, but he couldn't help but wonder if the prospective groom was all that he appeared to be.

CHAPTER SEVEN

Andrew stood on the wide veranda examining the post-dawn sky. It was a ritual he had performed daily since at twelve he had discovered his interest in the weather. Through the years, he had become quite adept at predicting what the day might bring in those quiet moments. But this one, more than any other, was special. On this day, he would walk his daughter, his precious girl, down the aisle and give her hand to Michel in marriage. There could be no rain, no clouds, to damper their spirits. No, this day had to be perfect. Andrew paused, watching as the sun slowly made its morning climb, and once he saw it, the crystal-blue of a cloudless sky, he was satisfied, and prepared to report to the bride and her mother that all would be well.

Inside, the house was bustling with activity. There were giggles and squeals of delight coming from the upstairs bedrooms, echoing through the hallway. He smiled. This, he thought, is what happiness must sound like.

Andrew knew it was best to stay out of the way of the womenfolk as they fussed over each other, and so, he retreated to the kitchen for another cup of coffee and perhaps a biscuit. His suit hung on the back of the pantry door. He could dress right there among the pots and pans if need be. Today, his job was to get everyone to the church on time and walk Aida down the aisle without crying. He was certain he could easily accomplish one, but wasn't so sure about the other.

At ten o'clock he lightly tapped on the bedroom door. "We leave here in ten minutes," he said.

Angelique opened the door. "Come in," she whispered. "Come and see the bride."

Aida turned to face him. Her mother moved closer to adjust the diamond tiara with its attached lace veil, tenderly tucking a lone curl behind her daughter's ear. The white silk gown was trimmed with thousands of tiny pearls and the wide brocade sash accentuated her tiny waist. Her hands clutched a nosegay of white roses. Andrew stood, unable to move. She was beautiful, and the sight of her took his breath away. He swallowed hard, trying to control his emotions.

"Well?" Aida asked.

"You are lovely. Truly lovely, Aida. It is hard for me to imagine that just a few short years ago you were a little girl, and now, a woman stands before me. And quite the vision. Michel is a fortunate man indeed."

Aida giggled. "I would like to think we are both fortunate, Poppa, but thank you."

Angelique moved to his side, squeezing his arm.

He took her hand, lightly kissing her palm. "Might I add that my bride is also beautiful."

She curtseyed. "Thank you, kind sir. This is quite the occasion for us, isn't it? Our dear girl is becoming a wife, leaving home for a place so far away."

"Most assuredly," he said, clearing his throat to fight back the tears. "Ah, but fortunately, we have a spare daughter, and here she is."

Aimee entered the room, her taffeta petticoat rustling. The light blue silk gown matched the color of her eyes, which sparkled with excitement.

"There is my bridesmaid," Aida said.

"Goodness, sissy, you have had me dressed up more in the past two days than I have in the past two years."

"You should do it more often," Aida said. "You look stunning."

"I think that word is reserved for the bride. And you are, of course."

"Two peas in a pod," Andrew said. "My amazing daughters. You make me so very proud."

"Well, you won't be very proud if we are late," Angelique said.

Andrew offered his arm to Aida as he gently guided her down the stairs. Angelique and Aimee followed. Franklin was waiting for them in the foyer.

"Wow," he said. "You are going to turn lots of heads today, Aida." He then turned to Aimee and winked. "You, too."

It took two carriages to get them to the church, and the bells began to peal to signal the arrival of the bride. Inside, the pews were packed with guests, and once Angelique had been seated among them and Aimee had taken her place, they all turned in anticipation of the bride's entrance. Andrew and Aida stood in the vestibule, poised to make the long walk to the altar, where Michel waited.

Andrew offered his arm. "Are you ready?" he whispered.

Her hand was shaking; he softly caressed it. She nodded.

The large wooden doors opened revealing the cathedral sanctuary, all aglow from hundreds of burning candles, Aida took a deep breath as they slowly made their way down the aisle.

The bishop stepped forward. "Who gives this woman in marriage?"

"I do," Andrew said as he carefully lifted Aida's veil and kissed her cheek.

Michel stepped forward to take her hand.

Andrew's eyes filled with tears as he joined Angelique in the wooden pew. She reached for his hand. "Well, at least I got us here on time," he whispered.

"Indeed, you did, my darling," she said. "Indeed, you did."

✳✳✳

Angelique bent low to light the lamp before carrying it to the walnut desk. The sun had just set, but it had done little to cool things off, the South Louisiana air so thick and humid that it hurt a little to breathe. She opened the top drawer and removed the small book bound in red velvet. She found a blank page and began to write, listing all the details of the remarkable day that her daughter married the man she loved.

When she had finished, she carefully placed the book among the others. And there were many. Searching through the stack, she located what appeared to be the oldest, a brown leather volume, secured with a brass buckle. And with reverence, she opened it. Gingerly, she turned the pages already filled with her elegant handwriting. There was a story here. Her story.

Years earlier, she had felt the need to record the details of her life in a tangible form, to leave behind bits and pieces for others to someday discover. Once she had children, it strengthened her resolve. Life is fleeting, she had thought. In the blink of an eye we pass from one stage to the next, often too busy to notice the moments, both large and small. But Angelique didn't want to forget any of it, and the books were insurance that her memories would be preserved.

"Everything vanishes," she whispered, "except that which is written."

As she skimmed the entries, she paused to read what she had been looking for, the most important remembrance of them all:

"Ours was not a fancy ceremony, with Mr. Wilson as our only guest, but it was as beautiful and meaningful as any I have ever witnessed. The priest agreed to officiate on such short notice, and we were grateful that the chapel was made available to us. Having lost all of my fancy gowns in the storm, I settled on something more practical, blue, rather than white, and I know that each time I wear it, I will be reminded of this amazing day. From this moment forward and for rest of my life, I will be Angelique Slater, and the wife of the man I love. Until I take my last breath, my heart belongs to him. Perhaps even beyond that, if love survives everything, even death. I have never known such happiness."

She removed the fragile browned flower that had been pressed between the pages and then replaced it, careful not to destroy the only remaining memento of her own wedding day.

And as she blew out the lamp, she whispered a prayer for her daughter's happiness.

CHAPTER EIGHT

Franklin tapped Francois on the shoulder. "I'm here," he whispered, careful not to startle his sleeping colleague. For several years, the exhausted physicians had taken turns in the clinic, giving up their precious days and nights off to serve the sick and poor of New Orleans. They had tried to hire a staff, but found few dedicated to their cause, especially after learning of the meager salary they were able to offer. In the end, the decision was made that the five of them would split the shifts, with occasional help from Aimee and a few of her nursing friends. As the need grew, the responsibility became even greater, and so did the work load. There was no denying that fatigue was their constant companion, but so was pride in the lives they had saved in the process.

"Anything I need to know?" Franklin asked, sliding into the threadbare chair near the desk.

"Quiet tonight," Francois said, "I am grateful for it."

Franklin nodded. "I hope it stays that way."

Franklin reviewed the list of patients. It had been Aimee's idea to keep meticulous notes in a bookkeeper's ledger. It seemed like an unusual plan and extra work for all of them, but in the end, she had been right as at each shift, it only took a moment to survey the vital signs of those who occupied the beds, and as a result, it was easier to keep an eye on the sickest of the sick.

He made his rounds quickly since there were several empty beds. Nights like these were always welcomed, and unfortunately, they were few and far between. Franklin surveyed the space. It hardly resembled the place where it began as the idealistic medical students had rolled out blankets on the floor and stole medicine from the hospital. Although the clinic was still housed behind the orphanage, which meant free rent, thanks to his mother's benevolence, walls had been erected. There was a surgical room, a quarantine area, and a large ward with real hospital beds lined in neat rows. His fancy-pants sister Aida had not only married well, but she had also used her charm to influence her husband's well-heeled friends to open their wallets and generously donate. In fact, she and Michel had even forgone the tradition of receiving household items as wedding gifts, asking instead for donations to both the clinic and the orphanage. He couldn't deny that she was more like Aimee than he had realized, instinctively kind and generous, even if she did appear to be full of herself most of the time.

Sometimes, on still nights, he thought of one of the first patients treated there. Uncle Gaston's appearance had seemed like a fluke, the kind that writers might create in a story book. That was enough to shift a person's thinking about life, for sure, but to hear the rest of the story, to learn that the man had once been married to his adopted mother, that he had broken her heart in unimaginable ways, reaffirmed his belief that none of us can change the past or predict the future, and that could be either thrilling or terrifying, based on point of view.

Franklin yawned. He wished he had a cup of coffee. It was going to be a long night.

Aimee tossed and turned. It seemed like a contradiction, but she was too tired to relax. Between the whirlwind of activity surrounding her sister's wedding and her shifts at both the hospital and the clinic, she had been operating on pure adrenalin. There was no denying that she needed the rest. Twelve uninterrupted hours of sleep, would have done her a world of good, but that was totally elusive. She adjusted her pillow, which felt lumpy, the feathers bunched into an uncomfortable ball, and then, willed herself to close her eyes. But the room felt unusually hot, the air stifling. She rose and crossed the room to open the window wider, but as she stared out into the moonlight, where all was quiet and still, she knew what she wanted to do, in fact, what she needed to do.

Quickly, she dressed and tiptoed down the stairs. She considered walking, then, thought it unwise. A lone woman wandering the deserted streets in the middle of the night was asking for trouble. The horses had been unbridled from the carriage, and certainly, she wouldn't have been able to accomplish the driving even if they were ready and waiting. She entered the stable. She had grown up on a plantation, and had been taught to saddle a horse or ride bareback, if need be. Her destination was only a few blocks away; how hard could it be, she thought. The decision made, she selected a strong mare and gracefully mounted. Within minutes, she was out the door and headed toward the clinic.

CHAPTER NINE

"What on earth are you doing here in the middle of the night?" Franklin asked.

Aimee shrugged. "Couldn't sleep."

"How did you get here?"

"Rode one of the horses."

"Seriously?"

Aimee nodded.

Franklin smiled, unable to hide the fact that he was pleased. "Well, aren't you brave? Sorry about the restless night. I am afraid that I don't have that problem. I could sleep for a week, maybe longer, but I can say that I am happy to have the company."

"I thought you might need some help."

"Well, thanks, but as you can see, it is one of our quiet nights. Thankful for that."

There was a pause, an uncomfortable silence between them.

Aimee had acted on impulse, not thinking about what she would say. Somehow, her great idea no longer seemed so great.

"You can rest if you'd like. I will stay up and wake you if you are needed."

Franklin turned to her and their eyes met. "I…." he said and then stopped as though unsure of how to continue.

"Yes?" Aimee asked, sounding more expectant than she had hoped.

"I might close my eyes for just a little while." He stretched and then rested his head against the back of the chair. Within minutes, he was snoring.

Aimee watched him, her eyes studying every inch of his face. She knew him as well as she knew herself, had seen him at his best and worst. Although she had denied it, spent years claiming that their relationship was primarily professional, and their personal connection complicated, she loved him, loved him more than she could have possibly imagined. And while she knew that a future together was improbable, she also knew that she would never give her heart to another man. Not ever. She would have to be satisfied to work by his side, live as his adopted sister, and love him from afar. That would have to be enough.

She wondered how she might feel if someday he became less driven, putting aside his medical practice to pursue a personal life. What if he became more social, and in the process, found a worthy woman to be his wife? She tried not to think of those possibilities, although they loomed large in her mind. Most surely, he deserved every bit of happiness, and that included true love.

Aimee laughed. It was no wonder that she was restless with so many unanswered questions surrounding her. Uncertainty can rob one of peace, she thought, but then, so can unrequited love. It was quite the dilemma. Perhaps it would have been more sensible to leave New Orleans, to enlist in the service of Nurse Clara Barton. There were so many ways that she could use her healing hands for the better good. But the idea of it, of not seeing him daily, was more than she could bear, and she quickly dismissed the plan.

The clock had just stuck three when she heard the noise in the courtyard. She had considered waking Franklin, but decided instead to investigate first.

Two men were half dragging a third. "Is this here the free clinic?" one of them asked.

"It is," she said. There was a strong smell of whiskey in the air, and she paused before moving forward. She had learned that a drunk man was capable of anything. "Is this man hurt?"

"He broke his leg. Happened a couple of days ago, but he insisted that it would be fine. Been drinking ever since. I don't know. It looks kind of bad to me."

"Hold on and I will get the lantern." Aimee said. She quickly returned and held the light so that she could examine the wound. "Can you roll up his pants so that I can see it?"

"No offense, ma'am, but don't you have a doctor here? Not so sure what you can do."

"I am a nurse, sir, and I can assure you that my medical knowledge is as good as most doctors you will encounter."

One of the men shrugged and turned to the other, "Show her."

The other man, knelt to handle the pants, while the injured man began to shout obscenities.

"Pay no attention to him, ma'am. He is drunk. Out of his mind with the pain. He means no offense."

Aimee sighed. She has seen more of this kind of patient that she wanted to admit, the lost and forgotten, the poor and addicted. It was why Franklin and the others did what they did. "I'm fine. Here. Hold the lamp for me." She winced when she saw the man's leg, swollen and green. A full three inches of bone had broken the skin and was sticking out at an awkward angle. She didn't blame him one bit for drinking himself into a stupor. She would have done the same in similar circumstances.

"Bring him inside," she said. As she left to wake Franklin. "The doctor will see him."

It took less than a minute for Franklin to spring into action and in less than five, the man was on the operating table, about to undergo surgery. "Will you stay and help?" he asked the men. "The leg will have to be removed, and it requires more than one assistant."

The two looked at each other, then at Franklin. "Ain't no way I can do it," one of the men said. "The sight of blood is more than I can take. I would be no use to you."

"And you?" Franklin asked, addressing the other. "I have to get home to my wife. She's gonna be wondering why I was out so long."

Franklin furrowed his brow, doubtful that the man even had a wife, much less having considered her feelings. He and Aimee would have to accomplish the gruesome task alone.

Aimee carefully washed the man's leg with lye soap and water. It was a new idea, one that Franklin had routinely adopted with all of his patients. As a result, those in his care had far fewer incidents of infection and gangrene. Others began to follow his example in both the hospital and the clinic. It was progress.

The effects of the whiskey had begun to wear off, and the man stirred, moaning in agony.

"We will have him under soon," Franklin said, setting out the bottle of chloroform. Aimee arranged the surgical instruments on the tray, a knife, clamps, needle for suturing.

Franklin reached for the saw, examining it in mid-air, poised to begin.

Amy held the rag, laced with anesthesia, waiting for his signal

As though it all happened in slow motion, the man was suddenly awake and alert, his eyes wide with fear. He looked first to Aimee and then, at the saw. "Nooooo," he screamed, grabbing the scapel from the tray and plunging it deeply into Franklin's shoulder.

"Noooo," echoed Aimee, placing the chloroform rag over the man's face, rendering him unconscious. Quickly, she moved to Franklin's side. The knife was buried deep into the flesh and bone. Franklin's eyelids fluttered as he stumbled, the blood oozing from the wound. "Pull out the knife and apply pressure," he whispered before collapsing to the ground.

Aimee moved quickly to follow his directions, pressing firmly against the injured place until the bleeding slowed and eventually, stopped. She sat, cradling his head in her lap for what felt like hours, but was really only a matter of minutes. She softly stroked his hair until he regained consciousness.

He slowly opened his eyes and winced. "Am I alive?"

She laughed, relieved. "Yes, of course. I am certainly no angel."

"You are to me," he said. "Thank goodness you were here."

"Which is why it is not wise for any of you to be alone, especially at night."

"I am convinced."

"Does it hurt?" she asked.

"Yeah. Like the devil."

"Your patient is out. Not sure what we will do with him when he wakes."

"What time is it?" Franklin asked.

"Almost six."

"Good. Then, the morning shift can deal with him. I have done my part for the cause."

"Battle wounds, Franklin."

"Yes, I know," he said, his eyes filled with pain, "but I pray that this one will have no lasting effect."

Aimee had not even considered it. The wound was deep and there would be a period of recuperation. Franklin would finally get some much-needed rest. But for a moment, the words "lasting effect" reverberated through her mind, and it scared her, scared her even more than she wanted to admit.

CHAPTER TEN

Michel kissed his bride on the cheek. In one swift move, he scooped her up in his strong arms and carried her across the threshold. Aida giggled with delight.

"I hope you won't mind staying here rather than a hotel," he said, as he gently placed her on her feet. "I thought that if we were to truly begin our life together, it would be nice to do so in our own home."

"Our home?" Aida asked. "We live in New York, Michel, not Paris."

He laughed, as he popped the cork on the bottle of champagne. "Are you sure?" he teased, handing her a glass. "You just took a vow to live with me wherever that might be."

"Oh, and I do, I mean, I will. But I am afraid that so many of the things that I absolutely cannot live without are right this moment being shipped from New Orleans to New York. That is, unless you had them all rerouted."

"You are a typical woman, my darling, worried about your ball gowns and trinkets instead of more important matters."

"To a woman, there are few matters that are more important."

He laughed. "Where is the girl with the social conscious, the one who wanted to change the world?"

"She's still here, Michel, just a little older and much better dressed."

He reached for her hand. "You do delight me in every way."

"Well, I am so glad. I had thought that perhaps you were growing tired of me. We did have quite the long ocean crossing in relatively close quarters."

"Were you afraid that I would jump ship?"

She smiled. "No, not really, but who is to say that you might not have become completely bored?"

He stroked her cheek. "You may be many things, my love, but boring is not one of them. I look forward to many interesting years together."

"You handled that very well, husband."

"Good. I had no idea that it was a test. Now, shall we talk about this apartment?"

"Oh, yes, certainly. I am sorry. I do tend to get distracted at times. Are we truly going to live here? In Paris? How? Why? What will you do with your law practice? What will your family say? What will my family say?"

"Goodness, girl, one question at a time. No, we are not moving to Paris. I thought you might want to spend your honeymoon in the home that belonged to my grandmother, especially since she is indirectly responsible for bringing us together."

Aida gasped. "Truly? Did the Countess live here? When?"

"When she and my grandfather were a young couple and the toast of Paris society, this was their city dwelling. My father inherited it, and couldn't bear to sell it, having come here on holiday as a child. It is still used occasionally by family and friends. I thought it would be the perfect place for us to spend our honeymoon."

"You were so right. It is lovely."

"If you and I can write a love story nearly as beautiful as that of my grandparents, then, we will have a happy life indeed."

Aida moved to face him. "That is all I can ever hope for, my darling. Truly."

There was a knock at the door and Michel opened it to the porter with their luggage.

"We will unpack, and then, I will take you to the finest restaurant in Paris to celebrate. But first, a surprise."

"Another one? You are far too generous, kind sir."

"I can't take credit for this one, but I hope it will delight you nevertheless."

Michel rose and offered his hand, leading Aida to the balcony. The sun was setting in the western sky. It was breathtaking. "How beautiful," she said, "and romantic."

"Just wait," he said, wrapping his arms around her.

Within minutes, men appeared from every direction, carrying long poles with a small lamp attached to the end. As though on cue, they moved from one lamppost to another, first turning the gas lever on the pole, and then, lighting the lamp. By the time darkness had set in, the city glowed, with each one burning brightly.

"Behold, the City of Lights." Michel said. "And it is all yours."

But Aida had no words, only emotion as her eyes filled with tears. It was, she determined, the happiest moment of her life.

CHAPTER ELEVEN

Michel took Aida by the hand and led her into the café. It was far less elegant than those they had frequented the preceding two weeks, and she wondered what kind of adventure he had in mind. Theirs had been a perfectly lovely, romantic honeymoon. Any misgivings that Aida might have had prior to the wedding, had vanished, although she wondered what their day-to-day life might be like when they returned to New York the following week.

The waiter appeared, but failed to greet them. He was either bored or impatient, Aida couldn't decide which, and he looked at them expectantly as though taking their order was a huge imposition. She expected Michel to leave in a huff. He was, after all, titled gentry, accustomed to a certain amount of fawning and attention. Instead, he patiently held up two fingers. The waiter nodded.

"What was that about?" Aida asked

"I ordered the green fairy, darling. This place is said to serve the best, in spite of appearances." "The what?"

"The green fairy. Absinthe."

Aida's eyes grew wide, "Really?"

He laughed, delighted with her naiveté. "Surely you tasted it in New Orleans? It is readily available everywhere there."

She could hear her mother's voice, the urgent warning about the dangers. "It is said to have made men go mad, causing them to see things that are frightening." Aida said, repeating the cautionary tale.

He thought that he saw her shudder. "Darling, that is a myth. Besides, only the foolish drink it straight."

As though on cue, the surly waiter reappeared with two small glasses half filled with pale green liquid. On the tray were two perforated spoons, each containing a cube of sugar, and a small carafe of water.

Michel suspended the spoon over the first glass and slowly poured the water over the sugar.

Aida watched with fascination as it quickly dissolved.

He repeated the process with the second glass before handing one to her. "Cheers," he whispered. "To us."

Aida hesitated. "I cannot."

Michel frowned. "My dear wife, the alcohol purifies the water. It isn't much different than what we do with wine every single day."

"But far stronger than wine. What if I faint?"

"Then, I shall carry you all the way back to the hotel and tuck you into bed."

She reached for his hand. "Sorry to be so silly. I am, after all, a grown woman."

"A married one, I might add," he said.

She winked before downing the drink in several large gulps, and then turned to him, grimacing. "It tastes awful."

"Hence the sugar. Now, close your eyes and tell me how you feel."

"Calm. Relaxed. It isn't unpleasant at all."

"Of course not, darling. I would never place you in harm's way, not ever."

"Do you promise?"

"I do."

She looked into his eyes and smiled. "Would it be terrible of me to ask for another?"

"No, it would not be terrible, but I won't let you have one."

She hung a lip and tilted her head ever so slightly. "You won't?"

"No. There is a reason why the French call it 'La Peril Vert.' There is danger if one is not careful."

But Aida was lost in her own temporary world, the euphoria etched on her beautiful face.

CHAPTER TWELVE

Aida woke on the last morning of their honeymoon to an empty bed. She wasn't sure why that was unsettling to her since sleeping with her husband still felt so new, but in a few short weeks, she had grown accustomed to his constant presence, and she missed him when he was away from her, even if that meant he was only in the next room. She reached for her silk robe and went in search of him and coffee.

He was dressed, and sat, brows furrowed, studying the newspaper. She paused to take in the sight of his handsome form, the noble features which defined his face, grateful that fate had brought him into her life.

When he glanced up and saw her, he smiled, carefully folded the paper and pointed to the spot next to him on the elaborate tapestry settee. "Good morning, sleepyhead," he said. "Come, sit with me."

"Coffee?" He asked.

She nodded as he poured from the fancy china pot into a matching cup. The fact that in spite of having grown up with servants to cater to his every whim, he didn't hesitate to take care of her, made her love him even more. Theirs was a perfect match; she was sure of it, and the marriage would be happy and strong as a result.

"Why didn't you wake me?" Aida asked, taking the first comforting sip of the coffee.

"You were sleeping so soundly that I just didn't have the heart to do it. Besides, there was no urgency to get on with the day."

"Well, this is our last one."

"Indeed, it is. And time, I suppose, to think about getting back to real life."

Aida sighed. "So do we have to? Can't we just stay here forever?"

Michel laughed. "Well, we could, but in time, this, too, would be real life. It will be up to us to maintain the magic wherever we are."

Her heart was full. "You know just what to say to reassure me."

"I hope I always will," he said.

She smiled. "I have no doubt of it. Now then, what shall we do on our last day in Paris?"

"I need a cigar, so while you are getting dressed, my dear, I will go out to get one. Then, we shall decide."

Michel kissed her on the top of the head as she sat, drinking the last of her coffee. And then, he was gone.

Aida hummed a little tune as she braided her long dark hair and then carefully wove it into a chignon, low at the nape of her neck like the fashionable women of Paris. She chose a light blue gown trimmed in lace, which was perhaps a little too fancy for day wear, but she liked the way it accented her eyes, the color of the sky on a cloudless day. They were, she thought, her best feature, and a connection to her mother and sister.

By the time she had dressed, Michel still hadn't returned, so she rang for the maid to help with the packing. An hour later, her trunk lay open, almost completely filled with her shoes and gowns. Then, she moved on to Michel's things. As the clock stuck two, she realized that she was famished, having skipped both breakfast and lunch. She sent the maid into the kitchen for tea and sandwiches and wondered what was taking Michel so long.

.By mid-afternoon, she began to worry, pacing the floor of the parlor, as she studied the intricate pattern of the Turkish rug. She sat in the gentleman's chair, the fanciest in the room, tracing the dragon's face, intricately carved into the wooden arm, with her forefinger. Absentmindedly, she thumbed through a book of poetry that had once belonged to The Countess, but unable to concentrate, she cast it aside. She counted the steps from the dining table to the front door before heading to the balcony, searching through the crowd on the street below for any sign of her husband.

At five o'clock, she was convinced that Michel had been kidnapped by pirates or was lying in some back alley bleeding to death. It was obvious by his dress and carriage that he was an aristocrat, and in a big city like Paris, there were bound to be criminals, hell bent on robbing him of his possessions, perhaps even taking his life. Aida's imagination ran wild as she became convinced that he had fallen victim to some unspeakable violence and that she would be a widow before they had even celebrated their one-month anniversary. She began to cry, inconsolable in her grief.

***

Michel closed the ornate door behind him and paused to adjust his ascot after running his fingers through his hair. He removed the gold watch from his pocket. It was almost six, and Aida would be frantic. He would need a plausible excuse, one that she would readily accept. Perhaps he could say that he had stepped into the art gallery and had become so mesmerized by the paintings that he had lost track of time. But she would protest that they had already visited most of them, so there would be no need. He could say that a man in the smoke shop had fainted and, being a Good Samaritan, stayed with the poor fella until help arrived, which took longer than expected. That might work. But in the end, he figured he would simply make up a story on the spot, confident that she would forgive him. He did his best work on the spur-of-the-moment.

He patted the inner pocket of his waistcoat. If need be, he had insurance, a backup plan. He was always preemptive, thinking one move ahead. That's what made him smart and successful.

"Flowers, sir?" the woman with the pushcart called.

He nodded and handed her ten francs for a bouquet of fragrant white violets.

"You know, they stand for innocence, sir," the woman said, wrapping the blossoms in yesterday's newspaper.

"Then, that's perfect," he said, quickening his step toward his waiting wife.

CHAPTER THIRTEEN

Franklin cried out, and Aimee rushed to his side. For the second night in a row, she had tried in vain to break his fever. The worry and fatigue were etched in her face, but she wouldn't give up on him. She couldn't. Every six hours, she changed the bandage on his shoulder. In the evenings, she applied iodine, but waited until morning for the bromine, which she knew caused him excruciating pain. She wished that there had been some other way, but infection had quickly set in, and she would use every tool in her arsenal to fight for him. She had no choice.

The head nurse had given her four days of leave for his care when she reported that his recovery had become complicated. She was grateful to be able to be by his side. They had all thought the injury would heal rapidly, and even Franklin was optimistic about his return to work fairly soon. He had spent mornings reading on the upstairs sleeping porch until noon, when Angelique would deliver his lunch on a tray. They would often spend the afternoons chatting, and both marveled at the blessing of time that his injury gave them. But suddenly, and without warning, he grew feverish, the pain unbearable, and unrelenting. Franklin, having seen far too many a patient lose a limb to gangrene, summoned Aimee to inspect the wound.

"I don't understand," she protested. "We were so careful. How could this happen?"

"How does it ever happen?" He asked. "If we knew, it never would."

Within hours, his fever had spiked, and he had been caught in the hellish place between consciousness and delirium ever since.

His colleagues, who were also his friends, came to visit with regularity, each performing an exam if for nothing more than to offer an untried suggestion for treatment. Franklin had been their unofficial leader, fearless and wise. He was a calming force, always composed and collected, even during the most difficult surgical cases. The hospital needed him and so did they.

Aimee followed through with every idea, no matter how unconventional, but felt that same pang of disappointment when nothing seemed to bring about any change. She knew they were running out of options, swallowing hard as bile collected in the back of her throat.

The clock had struck twelve just as Aimee placed another cool compress on Franklin's forehead. Angelique appeared at the door, carrying a small pot. "I've made tea," she whispered.

"Thank you, Momma. That would be wonderful."

"This isn't for you, honey. It's for Franklin."

"I don't think he is wanting any tea right now," Aimee said, wondering what her mother was thinking.

"I was in the kitchen, praying that God would spare our dear Franklin, when it came to me, and I am surprised that I hadn't thought of it before now."

"What's 'it,' Momma? I'm afraid I am much too sleep deprived to guess."

"Hannah's sure-fire potion to break a fever. She used it all the time. I have never seen it fail."

Aimee rolled her eyes. Her mother had often quoted Hannah's recipes and remedies as though they had been given to her by The Lord Himself. She was too tired to argue. "What's in it?"

"Basil mostly, followed by a chaser of turmeric and ginger."

"Sounds vile."

"Most medicine is, right? If it works, it will be worth it."

"Let's see if we can get him to drink it," Aimee offered, not convinced.

They moved Franklin into a sitting position and slowly spooned the concoctions into his mouth. He swallowed with some difficulty, but eventually, they got him to take most of it.

"One more thing," Angelique said, removing a poultice from her apron pocket. "Put this on his wound."

"What might this be? Is it another of Hannah's magic cures?"

"You can ridicule all you want, but it can't hurt. And it is honey, pure honey, straight from the hive. I had to send for it. Folks on the plantation know how to keep a queen bee happy."

Aimee tried not to laugh. It was a metaphor in so many ways. "I will use it."

"I know you will because I am not leaving this room until you do," Angelique said, her lip pressed firmly together.

Aimee sighed, but removed the bandage that covered Franklin's shoulder and placed the poultice tight against the wound before replacing it with a clean bandage.

Franklin seemed to have fallen into a deep sleep, and Angelique crossed the room to kiss her daughter on the forehead. "You need to rest, too, honey. You are exhausted, and you won't be any good to anybody if you get sick."

"I will, Momma," Aimee said, "and thanks."

Angelique turned the lamps down low before leaving the room. Aimee returned to the chair she had positioned by Franklin's bedside. Within minutes, she too, was fast asleep.

Aimee sat upright, startled by the sun, which shone through the bedroom window. She glanced at the china clock on the mantle. It was almost seven. Franklin stirred and then licked his lips. "Could I have a sip of water?" he asked, his voice weak and hoarse.

Aimee poured a glass from the pitcher and held it for him as he drank. She put her hand on his forehead. It was warm, but not hot as it had been. She then felt for his pulse, counting the cadence of its rhythm. She looked into his eyes. They were clear and bright.

"How are you feeling?" she asked.

He cleared his throat "Better, I think."

"Let me look at your shoulder," she said.

He grimaced as she removed the bandage. "Is it time for the bromine?" he asked. He winced in anticipation of what was to come.

"I am not sure," she said. "It certainly isn't healed, but honestly, Franklin, it looks much improved."

"Really?" he asked. "Bring me a mirror."

He held it up and examined the wound. "I do believe that you are right. What did you do, my little Florence Nightingale?"

"I listened to Momma, who always seems to know best."

Franklin smiled. "I don't doubt that. Whatever magic you two conjured up seems to have worked, and I am grateful." Franklin patted his stomach. "I am hungry. Do you think she will make me one of her special breakfasts?"

"I can't imagine anything that she would love more than that," Aimee said, off to share the good news with her mother.

CHAPTER FOURTEEN

The porter had deposited their trunks and they made their way up the gangway. Michel reached for Aida's hand, but she snatched it away. "Are you still angry with me?" he whispered as he held out their tickets and accepted the key to their assigned cabin.

She lifted her chin defiantly.

"I take that as an affirmative."

She sighed and then pretended to watch the other passengers as they boarded the steam ship.

"Well, like it or not, you will be stuck in close quarters with me for the next two weeks."

She didn't respond, but followed him to their stateroom, waiting impatiently as he unlocked the door.

"Après vous," he said, bowing low as he held it open for her.

"Would you like to go to the dining room for lunch, dear?" he asked. Eventually, he figured, she would acquiesce. After all, time was on his side.

She shrugged.

"Are you uncertain of your hunger for food or uncertain that you wish to share a table with me?"

"Both," she mumbled.

"Ah, she speaks," he said, pleased that he had managed to wear down her resolve a bit.

She rolled her eyes, but he could see that he had cracked her shell. It was a start.

There was a knock at the door and the maid curtsied as Michel opened it. "Your luggage is here, sir. Would you like for me to unpack it now, or come back at a later time?"

He turned to Aida. "Well?"

She nodded. "Now, I suppose."

He offered his arm. "Good. Then we are off to have lunch, where I will grovel and ask for your forgiveness for my inexcusable behavior."

"You do realize how worried I was," she said, once they had been seated and the first course had been served.

"I do."

"And that I thought you had been hurt. Or worse."

"I am afraid that it never occurred to me that you would think that something awful might have befallen me. I know that it was terribly thoughtless of me."

"Well, we certainly can agree on that."

She thought that she was hungry, but merely picked at her salad, the sight of it turning her stomach.

"Are you not hungry, dear?" he asked, noticing.

"I am afraid that yesterday took away my appetite, and I wonder if I shall ever get it back."

He laughed. "I do so love your flair for the dramatic, but I feel reasonably sure that you will want to eat again, in the fairly near future."

He was teasing her, but she would have no part of it. She had not suddenly become some poor weak damsel, willing to accept his inconsiderate behavior simply because he had slipped a ring on her finger. The opinionated woman that he had met in New Orleans and courted so passionately, the woman who believed that she had every right to happiness, was alive and well. And that woman wanted answers.

She lay down her fork and leveled her steel blue eyes on his. "I simply want to know where you were all day yesterday."

He sighed. The hours of silence between them had given him time to hone his story and practice it for good measure.

"I spent a bit of time in the smoke shop, of course. The proprietor there is a fine fellow, and since I knew I wouldn't see him again, I lingered a bit for a cigar and some conversation. After that, I am afraid that I wandered the city, completely losing track of time. Before I realized it, hours had passed, and I made my way back to you as quickly as I could."

"I might accept the first part of the story, but surely you must think me a foolish woman to believe that you simply wandered aimlessly while your wife waited for your return, especially on the last day of our lovely honeymoon."

"I didn't use the word aimlessly."

"Ah, but you did say that you wandered."

"Indeed, I did."

He was a lawyer, a very good one, and she knew that he was using his strategies on her. It was a bit of a cat-and-mouse game, she thought, one she had no intention of losing.

"And did you have a destination in mind?"

"Yes, I suppose."

"Would you care to share?"

"No, not really."

Her face flushed, and she clenched her fists as she bit her lower lip. He thought she had never been more beautiful. He smiled. "Are you angry, darling?"

She exhaled loudly. "Wouldn't you be?"

"No, I would trust that you had a perfectly good reason for being away from me and that if you didn't want to tell me why, you would have a perfectly good reason for that, too."

"Well, unfortunately, I am not as gracious."

"I think you are plenty gracious, my dear."

The waiter appeared to pour coffee from a silver pot. Michel added cream and sugar to his, while Aida simply stared into the cup.

"Please, let's not quarrel. I am sorry that I made you worry. Will you forgive me?"

"I am afraid that I cannot," she said, "and perhaps I never will."

He smirked. It was time to move his king into position and capture the queen. He reached into his waistcoat and withdrew the small velvet box.

"Perhaps this will help."

"What is it?" she asked.

"Open it and see."

She slowly lifted the lid and removed the green silk pouch. Inside, was a locket with an elaborate engraved "A" on the front, On the back were the words, "Remember Paris."

She gasped, her eyes filled with tears. "It is beautiful," she said, "and unexpected."

"It was meant to be a surprise, one that I had hoped to keep until we arrived home."

"And it is a surprise, a lovely one."

"I knew what I wanted, but it took a visit to several stores to find it, and then, I had to persuade the jeweler to engrave it while I waited. It took much longer than I had anticipated, which is why I was so late."

Aida reached for his hand. "What a silly insecure woman I have been. Now, it is my turn to ask for forgiveness. I am ever so sorry to have doubted you, Michel. Truly, I am the most fortunate woman on earth."

"I am just happy that you like it, darling. I had hoped that you would. And it is I who am fortunate. I count my blessings every single day. Now, shall we take a walk around the deck? The sun is out and it is a most beautiful afternoon."

"Indeed, it is," she said, placing the locket around her neck.

Checkmate, he thought, pleased with himself for the victory.

CHAPTER FIFTEEN

Franklin stood at the makeshift table and reached for the scalpel. He gripped it tightly and then held it midair, examining his trembling hand. He cleared his throat, and then, replaced the knife as he began again.

Aimee appeared at the doorway. It was difficult to watch him spend his days repeating the exercise over and over again, each time with the same results.

"How are you this morning?" she asked, careful not to mention his progress.

"The same, I'm afraid," he said, his voice hollow.

"This is going to take time, Franklin," Aimee said, "And patience."

"I have neither."

"You have no choice," she said, opting for honesty rather than pity.

"It has been a month. The pain has subsided, but the tremors have not. This hand is useless," he said.

"That is not true. Yes, it is not as strong as it once was, but it is far from useless."

"To a surgeon, this is of no use," he said, holding up the scalpel, which shook in his hand. "Would you let me operate on you in this condition?"

Aimee swallowed hard. She had no answers.

"I thought not," he said as he threw the instrument across the room.

"Franklin," Aimee said, "you are first and foremost a physician, a good one I might add. There are many ways to practice medicine, so many sick patients who need you. It is time for you to return to the hospital and clinic."

"To do what? Put bandages on the skinned knees of young boys and dispense colic remedies to fussy babies?"

"If need be, yes. Because that's what healers do. There is no hierarchy in medicine."

Franklin raised his eyebrows. "Is that why you have fought so hard to get into medical school? Surely you should be content to simply be a nurse if no job is more important than another."

Aimee winced. His callousness hurt, even though there was truth to his argument. She had applied to various medical colleges, desperate to continue her education. She wanted nothing more than to be a doctor, but with so few opportunities for women, all she managed to acquire was a stack of rejection letters.

He saw that he had upset her. "I'm sorry. Pay no attention to what I say out of frustration. You will get your acceptance, and I do believe that it will happen soon."

But Aimee had no desire to debate the politics. Unlike her sister, she had quietly accepted the limitations placed on her as a female, vowing to do the best job she could in her current situation. Someday, she would be a doctor. Of that, she was certain. She turned to Franklin and nodded.

"Have you had breakfast?" she asked.

"Yes," he said. "Why?"

"Because you are coming with me to the hospital. Like it or not, today is the day you return to work."

He frowned. "I cannot. I will not."

She shrugged. "You can go with me willingly or I will ask Francois and James to come here to carry you out of the house and into the carriage."

"You wouldn't dare."

"You think not? They would readily do it., too. You are needed at the hospital, Franklin. They are overworked and understaffed. I don't think you really have the luxury of sitting here feeling sorry for yourself."

"Is that what you call it?"

"Yes, because that's what it is. We leave in fifteen minutes, cooperatively or not."

Franklin shook his head, but when Aimee made her way to the carriage, Franklin was already inside, waiting for her.

"I will go today, but reserve the right to leave when I please and not return if I choose."

"Sounds fair to me," she said.

Four hours later, Aimee found him in a children's ward, listening to the chest of a child who was coughing uncontrollably. He spoke quietly to the mother and then handed her a bottle of something.

"Looks like you found a beneficial way to use your time," Aimee said.

He nodded.

"And tomorrow?" she asked.

"There is a little boy with a stomach ache," he said. "I promised him that I would check in on him."

"And so you shall," Aimee said with a wink. "So you shall."

CHAPTER SIXTEEN

Angelique read the letter and then carefully folded it.

"You look concerned," Andrew said. "Bad news from Terence?"

"Yes and no. The plantation is thriving with the latest cane crop fetching a handsome profit. We lost a bit with the cotton last season after the boll weevils did so much damage, but this year we recovered that, so I am pleased, of course."

"Terence is an asset and the men respect him. He has been able to assemble a loyal crew to work those fields, which has made all the difference."

"Agreed. So many of the neighboring plantations have suffered because they can't find willing hands. Terence knows how to treat folks."

"I think he learned that from you, Angelique. You inspire loyalty."

"You give me far too much credit. I only gave him and Jubilee what was their due after all they did for me. In those early days, I could hardly tell a cane sprout from a weed. Terence was a patient teacher. Any success we have enjoyed is because of his hard work."

"But having a stake in the harvest does make a person more prone to want it to be successful."

"That was a pretty wise investment, if you ask me."

Andrew stoked the fire. "It is cold in here."

"Really? I hadn't noticed."

"So what's the bad news?"

"Nothing yet. Let's just say that there is a concern. Jubilee wrote that there has been some unrest nearby, and she is a little troubled."

"What kind of unrest?"

"The racial kind. There are still a few fools who want to pick a fight because they still can't accept the fact that slavery was abolished during the Civil War."

"But it has been over ten years."

"Those who can't move on want to claim a victory by intimidation, so they try to force what they couldn't win on the battlefield. They cover their faces like cowards, ride through the night, and make threats. In some places, there is real violence."

"Really? That sounds bad."

"Some of the acts they commit are unspeakable."

"But I thought such things had been outlawed."

"Yes, there is a federal law to prohibit it, but there are a few diehards, rebels who don't think the laws apply to them."

"I hate hearing that, but I can't say that I am surprised. It is pretty hard to talk sense into the ignorant. Is Jubilee afraid? Has something happened at Chauvin?"

"Not yet. She wrote that she had gone into town with Terence and a few of the men were making comments about the school close enough for her to hear."

"What kind of comments?"

"Jubilee has done very well with her little school house. She has taught the children of the field workers how to read and write, along with basic math. A few of them have gone on to study a trade. She hopes that some will even go on to college; Jacob, especially."

"Their son is a mighty fine young man. I sure do hope that happens for him."

"So now you understand the problem. When the children of former slaves are smarter and more educated than some of their white neighbors, there is a need to destroy that if they can."

"I am sure that you have already considered what to do about it."

Angelique laughed. "You know me far too well. I need to know that everyone is safe. I think it is time that I paid a visit to my plantation, protect my interests, so to speak. Want to come along?"

"If it's a quick trip, then, sure. Besides, I don't feel very comfortable letting you fight this potential battle alone. You tend to go charging in without thinking of the consequences."

"I knew I could count on you."

"Is this what you had planned all along?" "Perhaps. But I'll never tell. Shall we leave day after tomorrow? We can surprise Terrence and Jubilee."

"Day after tomorrow it is."

CHAPTER SEVENTEEN

Angelique closed her eyes and took a deep breath. The country air was like an invisible welcoming party, the scent of grass and flowers a familiar perfume. Although she loved New Orleans, and the professional opportunities the city provided for herself and her children, her heart belonged along the river road with its wide levees and graceful plantation homes. This is where she had grown up, learned to be a young woman, and although this is where she had learned the meaning of grief, regaining her family home had taught her to fight for what was important. How she missed it.

The carriage ride from the city seemed interminable, which is one reason why she visited so infrequently. Of course the demands of the orphanage took up much of her time, and Andrew's work obligations meant that he was rarely able to accompany her. Aimee and Franklin, were far too busy, while Aida lived thousands of miles away, so except for an occasional Christmas celebration, Chauvin Plantation was less like the family home and more like a business venture. That realization was unsettling for Angelique, who loved the place, the way the floorboards in the parlor creaked, the kitchen where Hannah had listened to her prattle on and on as a child, giving her sweet tea cakes in order to hush her for a moment. She loved the rich black dirt that nurtured the crops and picnics under the grove of pear trees. It would always be the place that nurtured her soul and recharged her spirits.

Terence was plowing one of the fields when they passed, and she enthusiastically waved. Within minutes, he had set down the plow and ran to meet them.

"Welcome back, Miss Angelique. Why didn't you tell us that you were coming?"

"Because I know that you and Jubilee would have made a fuss. Andrew and I are only here for a few days."

"Well, we could have at least opened up the house for you. Jubilee will be pleased to see you, though."

"I am pleased to be here. It has been far too long."

By the time Terence had unhitched the horses, and Andrew had carried their satchels inside, Jubilee was in the front hall.

"When Jacob told me that you were here, I didn't believe him. What a wonderful surprise this is," Jubilee said.

"I brought you two boxes of books for the school. I wish I could have brought more, but we decided to come at the last minute, so I didn't have as much time as I would have liked. I did bring all of the ink and pens and paper we had at home. I can replenish our supply later."

"Mighty grateful for that, Miss Angelique."

"How are things going? I am ever so proud of the work you are doing here."

"It is going well, considering."

"Considering?"

"I think I wrote you about the grumbling among some of the men over this school. Not sure why it never bothered them before. Maybe they didn't realize that the field hands were learning how to read while they themselves couldn't."

"The field hands?"

"Well, I figured that I could work with the children during the day, but I got the idea that at night, I could have class for the adults. It has been really great, Miss Angelique. Almost everybody comes after supper. The children help their parents, so it reinforces their instruction."

"That's remarkable. May I come and see for myself tonight?"

"Why certainly. It would be a pleasure if you and Mr. Andrew would come. Maybe he could teach us all one of those star lessons."

"If the sky is clear, I know he would love to do it."

After a dinner of fried eggs and cornbread, Andrew and Angelique followed Jubilee down the dirt path into the worker's village, which at one time had been the quarters for the slaves. It had changed over the years. The tiny shacks had been painted various colors. Several had wide porches and flower gardens.

"My goodness," Angelique said. "It looks like Rainbow Row in Charleston."

"This happened by accident. Every time Terrence would go into town to buy supplies, he would ask about paint. Somehow, in his mind, a man had truly moved up in the world if he lived in a painted house."

"I agree," Andrew said.

"Anyway, he would buy whatever was the cheapest, regardless of the color, and that's how we ended up with this patchwork."

"I think it is beautiful."

"Thanks. Look there," Jubilee said, pointing to the biggest house. "That's ours."

"It is beautiful," Angelique said. "And pink," with a laugh.

"We had just enough white and just enough red. Mixed the two and got this. But when we started the painting, I thought of those little girls, and I was thrilled. Remember how we taught them that they lived in the pink house?"

"What a wonderful memory."

"I assume this is the school?" Angelique asked.

Jubilee nodded. "We have added onto it several times. Every time one of those big trees falls, we make use of it and mill the lumber. The school has cost little to nothing."

"Thanks to your ingenuity."

"Well, and Terence's hard work. He is pretty good about making my dreams come true."

"Mine, too. Jubilee," Angelique said. "This plantation couldn't run without him."

Jubilee nodded. "Let's go in and start the lesson."

"Andrew and I will stand in the back and watch."

Jubilee instructed the adults on new vocabulary as the children passed out the faded books. One man read a passage; another explained what it meant. When the group applauded, the men beamed with pride.

"And now," Jubilee said, "I am happy to introduce Miss Angelique. She owns this plantation. Mr. Andrew is a scientist who has written about the weather. We are going to go outside, so that he can tell us a little about the sky."

Andrew nodded. The night was dark with the wide arch of the Milky Way traversing the heavens. "Do you know why it is called that?" Andrew asked.

"Looks like spilled milk," one man said.

"To the ancient people it did. If you look here, you see the big dipper, which pours into the little dipper."

"Follow the drinking gourd," a man said. "My momma used to say that if we ever escaped from the master, we would follow those stars to go North to freedom."

"That's a very good point," Andrew said. "It remains in a northern position, even though the earth moves from night to day."

Terence pointed to a group of men on horseback at the edge of the property. "There they are."

"There who are?" Andrew asked.

"The men. The night riders. They have been coming every night just as we end these classes. I think it is intended to scare us."

"The men wearing white sheets over their faces?" Andrew asked. "They look like ghosts, but I suppose that coward is a better word to describe them."

One of the men heard the term and moved his horse forward. "Who you calling a coward?" he shouted.

"Come closer, and I will tell you," Andrew said.

The four men approached the crowd. Andrew felt for the pistol he had shoved in his back pocket as they left the main house.

"You over here educating the colored people?" one of the men asked.

"I certainly am," Andrew said.

"What's wrong with you?" another asked, inching his horse toward the group.

"Not a damned thing," Andrew said.

Angelique could feel the blood rising to her cheeks, the anger churning deep within her belly. She had heard enough. "This is my property. The way I see it you four are trespassing," she said. "I could easily have you shot and be completely justified."

"I don't think you want to do that, ma'am."

"Then leave before I do."

One of the men was laughing under the disguise. Angelique leveled her eyes. "I see no humor in trying to create fear nor in cruelty toward other human beings. Perhaps you might want to share what you find so funny as you hide underneath your ridiculous costume."

"I just think that the whole idea of teaching the coloreds how to read is a bit of a joke."

"Is that because you aren't able to read yourself?" Angelique asked.

"I take offense to that," the man said.

"I meant it to be offensive," Angelique said. "For whatever reason, you men have had your minds poisoned; I simply ask that you examine your conscience. But I also would hope that you could see that this country has changed, especially the South."

"Don't have to like that change, do we? We got the right to do as we please."

"Only on a parcel that you own. This is mine." She paused and narrowed her eyes. "Wait. Billy Belanger is that you?"

There was silence.

"I asked you a question. Is that you?"

Silence again.

Angelique laughed out loud. "If you want to intimidate somebody, you might want to make sure that they don't know you, watched you grow up. I know your voice. In fact, I sold your daddy that horse five years ago, and I gave him the bridle, too. See that red braiding around the top? I wove that myself. You are a fool, Billy Belanger. But you are also a lawbreaker. I am going to stop by your parents' house tomorrow on the way to see the sheriff. They should know about your nighttime activities before it gets you into some big trouble. I pay taxes in this parish, and I expect that my property will be protected. But I also expect that the people who work for me won't feel threatened on my land. You can best be believing that if you and your friends show up here again, you will be arrested or shot. And you can count on it."

The four men said nothing, but turned and rode away into the darkness.

Andrew exhaled as he pulled out the gun. "I had come prepared, Angelique. I wasn't going to let anything happen here tonight."

"I know. I saw it in your back pocket. That's why I knew I was safe, although I am sure that it has been a while since you have pulled a trigger."

"Doesn't matter," Andrew said. "Sometimes just looking down the barrel of one is enough persuasion."

"Lawd, Miss Angelique. I forgot what a force you are when you get mad," Terence said.

"I won't be bullied, not by fools wearing their mother's bed linens. I will see the sheriff tomorrow. You won't be bothered by these men anymore," She said.

"Thanks, Miss Angelique," Jubilee said. "There was a school in the next parish that was burned to the ground. I was pretty worried."

"We are here for two more days. I want to enjoy the visit."

"You can always help with the plowing, if that strikes your fancy," Terence said, tipping his hat.

"I just might do that," Angelique said.

"That's my wife. And with that, we will bid you all a goodnight," Andrew said as he reached for Angelique's hand.

CHAPTER EIGHTEEN

FALL, 1876

Aida stifled a yawn as she rummaged through her dresses, searching for something to wear to dinner. She was tired, although she had no real reason to be, and she wondered if boredom was the cause. Somehow, she had imagined that her life in New York would be quite different. She had fully intended to embrace the excitement, to seize the opportunities. Instead, she spent her days in mind-numbing idle chatter with her mother-in-law. Needlework and afternoon tea held little appeal to her. She longed for more. Much more.

Evenings involved long four-course meals, fancy dress-up affairs, with a varying array of table guests. Aida didn't mind these so much since there was often stimulating conversation, although she was occasionally given a reproaching look from her mother-in-law when she joined in, especially when she voiced her opinion. More often than not, she listened and mentally argued, smiling to herself, when she had made a valid point.

"Ah," Michel said, as she entered the drawing room, "there is my lovely wife."

"Indeed she is," one of the men commented, rising to greet her.

"Thank you, kind sir," she said, raising her eyes to meet his.

"Johnson Walker, may I present my wife Aida."

"It is lovely to meet, you, Mr. Walker," Aida said, offering her hand. "My mother-in-law will be down shortly, but in her absence, let me welcome you to their home."

Aida was keenly aware that she and Michel were guests of her in-laws. He had insisted that they live there for at least the first few months of their marriage, giving them the time to search for a suitable residence. And she suspected that he had thought it wise for his mother to school his bride during that time, to mold her into a proper obedient wife. But they had been there far too long, in Aida's mind. The only arguments between them, except for his mysterious disappearance in Paris, were about her outspokenness and candor. She protested that the characteristics that had delighted him during their courting days caused him great dismay during their marriage. And she wasn't entirely wrong.

Johnson Walker bowed. "I hope that you will do me the honor of sitting next to me at dinner."

"I would love nothing more," she said, tilting her head.

She was young and attractive, and she knew it. Politically, she may have had no voice, but beauty is power, she reminded herself, and she would use it if need be. She adjusted the skirt of her black velvet gown so that it fanned out when she sat. Absentmindedly, she fiddled with the diamond and emerald necklace that ended where her exposed bosom began.

When they had taken their seats at the table, Aida turned to her dinner companion. "If I may be so bold as to ask, Mr. Walker, what is your line of work?"

"I am in the service of the law, my dear, formerly a barrister, but now, a magistrate with the circuit court. I intend to run for the Senate next year. I have the backing of a few in power positions, your husband among them."

Aida smiled, revealing her dimples. "My husband is a very good judge of character, so I may only assume that he deems you infinitely qualified to serve in such a capacity."

"You flatter me, but I rather like it."

"May I ask you something else?"

"Of course. Anything."

"What is your opinion on women's suffrage?"

He laughed, a little louder than necessary. "Are you one of those progressive females, hoping to be able to vote someday?"

"Well, I do more than hope, sir. I truly believe it is an idea whose time has come."

"Do you?"

"Indeed, I do. If you win in your bid for the Senate, then you will actually have the opportunity to make that happen."

"You have my attention, although I think you may be a little premature in visualizing me as drafting legislation."

Aida took that as a cue to continue, "I'm afraid that the recent Supreme Court decision that recognized women as citizens, but in a special category, and therefore not allowed to cast a ballot on issues that affect them, was disheartening."

"Perhaps, but I would think that the recognition itself would be quite an achievement. Progress, if you will. It certainly acknowledges some rights. Most states have allowed women to own property, for example."

"Which is my point, Mr. Walker. My mother owns a plantation, yet is unable to vote for the legislators who determine such things as taxation on her property. It seems rather unfair. You can't be half a citizen. Either you are entitled to the benefits and liable for the obligations, or not."

He raised an eyebrow. "Ah, yes, but the Constitution doesn't confer the right of suffrage on anyone. In other words, we have not yet defined citizenship."

Aida was silent. She was thinking. He used the opportunity to continue. "Not one state in the union has automatically given its citizens the right to vote, and I dare say, it won't happen without a specific Constitutional amendment."

"Even among men?"

"As crazy as it sounds, yes. That is inferred, not specified."

"Seems convoluted. But I have read that some of the territories have allowed women to vote. Wyoming comes to mind."

"Indeed, but they are not states."

She bit her lower lip. Clearly, she had been outwitted, but it softened the blow to think that his was one of the most powerful legal minds in the country. At the very least, she had been able to follow his argument, and she would carefully consider her refutation in the days ahead.

He reached for her hand. "My dear, as much as I appreciate your position, we can only interpret the law as it is, not as we wish it to be."

She nodded. "I thank you for an attentive ear."

"It was my pleasure. I don't think I have ever engaged in a debate with such a delightful and worthy opponent."

Aida blushed, secretly pleased. He had called her "worthy," not pretty or gracious or sweet, but worthy. She had always prided herself on being intelligent, strong-willed, opinionated. Marriage had somehow caused her to nearly lose sight of that.

"Michel," Jackson Walker teased, as the evening drew to a close. "You should send your wife to law school. I think she would be a good addition to your firm."

Michel laughed. "My dear Aida will be far too busy as a wife and mother, I'm afraid. We intend to have ten children." He turned to her. "Don't we, darling?"

But she refused to answer, standing straight and tall, defiant if only in her posture.

CHAPTER NINETEEN

Aida settled into a chair by the fire. She had been restless for days, fatigued, but unable to sleep, with a gnawing queasiness in the pit of her stomach that never subsided. Closing her eyes, she did the mental math. It was too soon to be sure, but she had missed her time of the month twice, and she was reasonably certain that given her symptoms, she was expecting. It was her secret, one she kept close to her heart. When she was sure, she would share it with Michel, who would be overjoyed. He had made it abundantly clear that he wished to be a father eventually and that since the responsibility of carrying on the family name and title rested squarely on his shoulders, he intended for them to have a large family. To Aida, that meant altering her life, rethinking her future. She could no longer ponder the delayed dreams, since it was clearly understood that those dreams would be impossible. Even with household help, with nannies and cooks and maids, she had no intention of relegating the job of parent to anyone else. If anything, she had grown up with the perfect role model of a loving mother, and she hoped to be half as nurturing to her own children. No, if indeed she was with child, everything was about to change for her, a thought that while unsettling, wasn't altogether disagreeable either. If she wanted a career, she couldn't imagine one more challenging or important.

"My dear, you seem quite lost in thought," the Countess said, taking her place on the settee opposite to where Aida sat.

"Hmmmmm. Not really. I am just enjoying the fire."

"It is rather cool this afternoon. I suppose that we shall have a rather cold winter. I am afraid that I dread the snow. At my age, my bones seem to respond to it rather unpleasantly."

Aida nodded, preoccupied. She counted the months. If she had figured correctly, the baby would be born in the late spring just as she and Aimee had been. Pregnancy and childbirth seemed such a mystery to her, one that would soon be revealed. Nevertheless, she had so many questions. Her heart clenched and for a moment she longed for the comfort of her mother's kitchen.

She thought of her mother in this same uncertain place so many decades earlier. How had she felt as she awaited the birth of her first child, Aida's half-sister, Josephina? How devastating her untimely death must have been. Aida considered the complicated nature of the life story we write with each passing day. Heartbreak arrives, often taking us by surprise. Surely, there are angels stained with our suffering. But her courageous mother had certainly triumphed, even if the early chapters of her tale were filled with adversity and sorrow. Aida wondered what hers would be like years from now when her own children paused to consider their mother's existence. She hoped that they would think of her fondly, that the memories would be happy ones.

"My dear," her mother-in-law said, clearing her throat. "I have come to speak to you."

"Of course," Aida said, suddenly jolted from her reverie. "About what?"

The Countess took a deep breath and Aida sighed. She was about to receive a lecture.

"I understand that you are a progressive woman, a smart one as well. I can see that is what attracted my son to you. Well, that and your beauty."

Aida smiled. The older woman had been instructed in diplomacy, having been part of a noble family for the thirty-two years that she had been with the Count. Flattery before criticism was her way of softening the blow. Aida braced herself for what was to come.

"Thank you, Countess. I would think that my husband had been searching for a wife who could challenge him intellectually when he met me. I am proud of my education and fully aware of how few women are given one."

"Well certainly. Michel has a brilliant mind, as you well know."

"Indeed," Aida said, pleased that she had managed to steer the conversation away from her and whatever transgression she had committed.

"That's perhaps where the conflict lies," the Countess said, redirecting the subject. "You see, it is our view that perhaps you are a little too opinionated at times, and that it might be beneficial if you became a more attentive listener when we have dinner guests."

"'Our view?' Who might that include?" Aida asked. She was not going to let her mother-in-law off so easily.

"Well, the Count and I, for sure. I am reasonably sure that Michel shares our concerns."

"Has he told you as much?"

"No, not directly, dear, but I could see the pained expression on his face the other night. I know my son. Someday, when you are a mother, you will understand the bond, the manner in which you are in tune with your child."

Aida bristled at that remark, uncertain if it was meant to sound as hurtful as she had taken it. "Well, Countess, I would hardly call Michel a child, but I must insist that if he has not mentioned his distress over my behavior to me, then, it is a non-issue. I would expect that my husband would tell me if I had displeased him, don't you?"

The Countess squirmed in her seat. She was obviously uncomfortable.

Aida rather enjoyed it. She had so few opportunities to use her analytical mind, and even if it was over something so petty, it was fun to mentally spar. Besides, her mother had told her so much about Michel's grandmother, Countess Maria. She was rather progressive herself, an independent lady of means, who had little time or patience for frivolous, shallow women. Aida couldn't help but wonder what their relationship had been like. Had she been impatient with the pompous attitude of her daughter-in-law, who was obviously concerned with decorum and public opinion? The thought of it was most satisfying.

"Aida," The Countess said, "I am going to be perfectly honest with you here. You are a guest in our home. My husband and I invite some of the most influential people in New York to dine with us. Politically and socially, it is important for his career, and for that of your husband. We wanted for to you stay with us as you settled into married life so that Michel could continue to make the proper connections and…"

"So that I can learn to be a proper wife," Aida said, finishing the sentence.

"Well, I wasn't going to put it so bluntly, but yes, I suppose so."

"I think that calling me a guest in your home was blunt enough." The statement only reinforced Aida's resolve that they should move into a place of their own sooner.

The Countess blushed. "I didn't mean that to be as harsh as it sounded."

"I understand."

"Do you?"

"I think so. But I would like for you to be specific about the topics of conversation I am to avoid. Am I, for example, allowed to speak of the weather? May I complain about the availability of good domestic help? Should I comment on the meal and speak of the foods which appeal best to me? Or perhaps, I can talk of travel and the places I would like to see. All of these seem safe and fall into the parameters of what is expected of me."

"Each of those subjects are worthy of discussion. I am glad that you are able to see it."

Aida had to fight hard not to laugh out loud. She was being sarcastic and the poor women thought her to be compliant. "Would you like for me to also speculate over which matters I am to avoid? I would assume that suffrage tops the list."

"Aida, dear, I understand your passion, but those to whom you express your very strong opinion don't necessary share it."

"Do you?"

"Do I what?"

"Share my opinion. Do you believe that women should be given the right to vote?"

"It doesn't matter what I think."

Aida sighed. There was the problem. Her poor mother-in-law was afraid to think for herself, and that was not only pathetic, but dangerous as well. "It matters to me, Countess."

The Countess paused as though she had never considered that possibility. Finally, she leaned over and whispered, "Yes, I do. Certainly, voting is a right that accompanies liberty. Didn't we fight the British because we wanted the freedom to self-govern? And so, who is given that independence? Under what circumstances is it right to assume that a woman is less entitled to it than a man?"

"It seems that you have given this some thought," Aida said, hoping to hear what else the older woman had to say.

"I have. We know that women are far stronger in many ways. Perhaps men know it, too, which is why they fear giving us voting power. I dare say if men were charged with the responsibility of bringing a child into the world, we would have far fewer in our current population."

Aida smiled and moved to the settee. She took her mother-in-law's hand in hers. "This pleases me so much to hear. But why, may I ask, haven't you spoken of it, ever?"

"Peace, my dear. I have learned which battles to court and which will only be an exercise in futility. Suffrage polarizes men and women. And I am expected to be a gracious hostess for those who visit. Besides, demands and outbursts rarely bring about the desired results. I know the art of subtlety, which may seem like subservience to you, but in reality gets me exactly what I want."

It seemed like such a contradiction to Aida, who rarely held back on something she felt. But more often than not, voicing her views did little to persuade others. "Do you feel that you must make yourself smaller in order for your husband to feel bigger? It seems that way to me."

"Oh course it does, Aida. I allow him to save face in all things, which sometimes is difficult, but watch closely, and you will see how often he defers to me. It is an art that has taken me years to prefect. Men are predictable, simple creatures."

Aida raised an eyebrow. Perhaps she had misjudged the woman. "That also sounds like power."

"It is. That's exactly what it is."

She lightly touched her belly. It was not the time to share her news, but when it was, she would do so proudly. The Countess, she thought, would be a wonderful grandmother.

CHAPTER TWENTY

"Are you sure?"

Aida nodded.

"When?"

"Spring."

"I can't believe it. It is an answer to prayer, my darling. You have made me so happy."

"I suppose that I have had a few more weeks than you have to become accustomed to the idea, but yes, it is quite remarkable."

"Because we are a perfect match."

Aida laughed. "Biologically, it seems."

"Let's tell my parents straight away," Michel said, scooping Aida into his arms and spinning her around. "They will be as overjoyed as I am."

Aida smiled. "I am so very anxious to share the news with them as well, Michel, but if you don't mind, I'd like to talk to you about something else first."

"Of course," he said, leading her to the edge of the bed. "What's on your mind?"

"Our living arrangements."

He furrowed his brow. "What about them?"

She was going to have a bit of a fight on her hands, she feared, but she had a trump card, one that she was willing to play, if necessary. "Don't you think it is time that we leave?"

"No. I had not even considered that. In fact, I thought it utterly convenient for us to be living here. We will have as much help as we need.

"That's all the more reason for us to move. We are expanding our family, Michel. It is time for us to have a home of our own. I am ever so grateful to your mother for her hospitality, but I want to raise my child, our child. I want to be a proper wife, which won't happen as long as I am the second most important woman in the house."

He kissed her on the forehead. "My dear Aida is quite the little lady."

She shifted to face him. "I am not your child, Michel, nor will I allow you to treat me like one."

"I know, darling, I was trying to make light of your sullenness."

"I don't want to make light of it. I am serious. We have five months, maybe six, before the baby is born. I want it to happen in my bed, under my roof. Is that too much to ask?" She looked at him and smiled sweetly. "I know that you will want to make sure that we are cared for, and that you have a place for your friends to call once he or she arrives. You are, after all, an excellent provider. I have come to depend on that."

He paused as though mulling over the possibilities. "Let me think on it. We still have time."

Aida opened her mouth to continue and then, reconsidered. She had won the small battle, best to not offer another challenge.

Throughout dinner, Aida waited for Michel to make the announcement, but instead they chatted on about one mundane subject after another. With each long pause, she expected for him to seize the moment, but he simply sat in silence. She wanted to scream, to blurt out their news, but had reasoned that deferring to her husband was in her best interest, and so instead, she pushed the peas around her plate, hoping the ordeal would soon end.

"No appetite, dear?" her mother-in-law asked after noticing that Aida had hardly eaten a bite of the first three courses.

"I am afraid not," Aida said, offering no further explanation.

"Are you having something between meals? I certainly don't mean to offend you, but for someone with such little interest in food, you do seem to have put on a few pounds of late."

Aida rolled her eyes and looked to Michel. He popped a bite of chicken into his mouth and winked at her." Pass the potatoes, Mother," he said.

When the butler asked if they would take dessert and coffee in the drawing room, Michel answered for the group. "Yes, we will."

It wasn't until they had all taken their place on the velvet furniture, amid the ancestral portraits and cut crystal lamps that Michel cleared his throat and began to speak. "We have some news for you, Mother and Father."

The Count looked up from his plate of apple pie. "And what might that be?"

"We are expecting a child."

His mother gasped and rose to hug Aida, while the Count shook his son's hand.

"So we are to be grandparents," the Count said. "What a mighty fine day this is for all of us."

"He pointed to the portrait of the Countess Maria. "My mother would have been delighted, Aida. I am sure that she would have never imagined that her grandson and the daughter of her dear friend Angelique would be responsible for the next generation of the de la Martinque family."

Aida smiled. It really was quite remarkable, so much so that her mother had often hinted that she thought the

Countess to have been a guardian angel, responsible for every bit of good fortune that had come her way after her friend's tragic death during the Last Island storm.

"I do believe that a toast is in order," the Count said, moving to retrieve the bottle of sherry from the silver tray.

"My dear," he said, handing it to the Countess, who poured four small glasses.

"Here is to my grandson," he said.

"Or granddaughter," Aida added.

"To our growing lineage," he said, raising his glass.

"Here, here," Michel said, beaming with pride. "There is one more announcement."

"What's that, son?" The Count asked. "I am not sure that I can handle anything more."

"We are moving soon. Within the next month, I hope. It is time that I carry my bride over the threshold of her own home."

CHAPTER TWENTY-ONE

Aida studied her reflection in the full-length mirror. The tiny crimson drop on her white linen nightgown sent a wave of fear through her so powerful that she thought she might faint. The first few months of her pregnancy had been uneventful, and except for the morning sickness, she had never felt better. But as she began her second trimester and the fluttering in her belly reassured her of the presence of the growing life inside, she had become concerned. There had been some aching, deep and low where the baby resided. Although it quickly subsided, it was enough to place her on high alert to anything, which might have indicated that everything wasn't as it should be.

Aida examined her porcelain skin for the source of the blood, a scratch perhaps, or an insect bite. And when she located the spot on her thigh, a simple blemish, she breathed a sigh of relief and took a seat at her dressing table.

She removed the combs from her chignon and reached for the ivory handled brush. Her hair, black as coal, fell in soft ringlets around her shoulders. As a child, she had loved to watch her mother perform the evening ritual, which she referred to as her "toilette," carefully undoing the intricate braids before turning to her daughters.

"Shall we count?" she would ask, as they nodded in unison.

Aida would try to raise her voice above Aimee's as they squealed with delight, responding with a number each time the brush slowly guided through her mother's raven locks. When they reached one hundred, they would cheer loudly and then beg to stay up a little longer, before reluctantly going off to bed.

It was a sweet memory, and Aida marveled at how incredibly sentimental she had suddenly become, brought about, no doubt, by her own impending motherhood. As she tenderly touched her swollen belly, she secretly hoped that she was carrying a girl, a sweet daughter with the same dark hair and steel blue eyes. Michel would someday have his son, she thought, but this baby that had come to live under her heart and make her a mother was hers. This baby had changed everything.

Michel quietly entered the room and removed his coat and tie, draping them over the velvet chair. He crossed to where Aida sat, wrapping his arms around her.

"My beautiful wife," he said, kissing her neck.

"You flatter me, sir."

"No, my dear. I simply speak the truth."

He took her hand in his and kissed her palm. "So soft."

She giggled.

As he reached for her other hand, he lifted her from the bench and carefully guided her to the bed. "I want you," he whispered.

Her body responded with equal desire, but her heart beat rapidly, the concern rising. "I don't think it is a good idea," she said softly. "The baby."

"The baby is just fine," he said, pulling back the covers.

"No. I mean. I am just not sure."

"I am sure enough for both of us," he said, drawing closer.

She smiled. "I am already an overprotective mother."

"Shall I make you an absinthe?" he asked. "It might calm your nerves."

She closed her eyes, remembering the peaceful calm that came from the drink on their honeymoon. It was tempting to feel that again. "No, I really shouldn't."

"It would help you sleep."

"Then, perhaps a small one."

He moved to the cart in the adjacent sitting room where he poured two glasses, one for himself and a half portion for her. He dropped a sugar cube in each

"Here," he said, handing her a glass. He pointed to the spot on her gown. "What's this?"

"Nothing. A scratch. But it scared me, too."

"You are carrying this baby so well."

"I am trying, but everything worries me," she said, taking a sip of the green liquid.

He shrugged and downed his drink. "I suppose that you are allowed to be overly cautious where my son is concerned."

Aida smiled as she slipped into the bed, leaving the rest of the absinthe untouched. "Or your daughter."

"Perhaps. Is it going to be like this between us until the child is born? You know what I mean," he asked. "It has been weeks."

"I am not sure," she said, trying to be honest. "I will ask the doctor. But.."

"You should do that, Aida," he said, the obvious disappointment in his voice. "I have a right, you know. It's coverture."

What the law might have allowed could also be thought of as morally reprehensible and terribly unfair, she thought. The child was her primary concern, and it should have been his as well. She opened her mouth to speak, but reconsidered. It seemed futile. Besides, as she was well aware, arguing before bedtime was never good for a marriage.

Michel turned the lamps down low and then extinguished each light. Neither spoke as he joined her. She was restless, listening to their synchronized breathing, its rhythm, annoying. He cleared his throat, sighed, then turned over. Her lids grew heavy, the wooziness brought on by the single sip of liquor and within minutes, she was asleep.

She was dreaming, struggling against some faceless monster who held her tight. She tried to scream, but there was no sound as she fought against the hands on her body. And then, as she opened her eyes, trying to process what was happening, she recognized the shadows in the darkness, his smell, the warmth of his breath on her neck. It was Michel. She exhaled, although she hadn't realized that she had been holding her breath. Was he dreaming, too, she wondered? He eagerly kissed her lips and pulled at her hair as he yanked at her gown. "No," she said, pushing against him.

"Yes," he pleaded, "you are my wife."

"And the mother of your unborn child. One I am trying to protect."

"I will not hurt you or the baby," he whispered. "Please?" he begged. "I need you."

Her heart softened, which was in stark contrast to the fear rising, the bitter taste of bile in the back of her throat.

"No," she said. "We must not."

But her words fell on deaf ears. "I love you," he mumbled into her hair, as he entered her. "I do so love you."

Aida simply lay in the darkness, praying that her unborn child was strong enough, that her fears were unfounded and foolish, and that the man she married wasn't the awful beast that, at that moment, she thought him to be.

CHAPTER TWENTY-TWO

The pain came suddenly and without warning at daybreak. Aida lay very still willing it to go away, concentrating on every breath. She recited a prayer, one she had learned as a young girl, which always managed to calm her fears.

"Michel," she whispered, and then tentatively, reached over to his side of the bed, which was empty.

She sat upright, surveying the room. He was gone, awake and dressed far too early to avoid her, no doubt. She replayed the events of the previous night in her mind. He knew that she was afraid. He had jeopardized the welfare of their unborn child for his own pleasure. How could he, she wondered?

The cramping continued and Aida placed her hand protectively over her belly. She tried not to consider the worst, the consequences of his selfish behavior, but her mind could not be calmed and with each contraction, the panic rose.

Aida carefully considered her options. She could lie in the bed and wait or get up and move around a bit, which might ease the discomfort. Neither seemed like a good choice. Ultimately, she rationalized the need for help as the discomfort grew worse, and so, donned in her dressing gown, she slowly made her way down the stairs.

By the time Aida had reached the reception hall, warm blood was trickling down her leg, forming a crimson pool at her bare feet. She stood, watching the stain grow larger with a strange detachment, the emotions too raw to express. As her uterus tightened, she cried out and then, unable to contain the horror, began to scream louder and louder until the sound of her own voice echoed in her head and the dizziness swirled around her like a windstorm. A cloak of darkness enveloped her as she crumbled to the floor.

A chambermaid was the first to reach her, and stood rooted to the spot, unsure of what to do. Within minutes, the Countess appeared, along with the rest of the staff. The doctor was quickly summoned, and Aida was carefully carried to her bed.

By the time Michel had returned home two hours later, it was all over.

"What happened, Mother?" he asked, hastily hanging his coat on the walnut hall tree.

The floor, still wet from having been scrubbed clean, glistened in the noonday sun.

"She has lost the baby, I'm afraid," the Countess said, her face etched with worry. "It all happened so suddenly."

Michel nodded. "And Aida?"

"Sleeping. You must understand that she has been through quite an ordeal."

"Of course, she has. Did she say anything?"

"What would she say, son? This is a great burden for any woman to bear."

"Certainly." He cleared his throat. "I mean; did she say why?"

"I don't think that she knows why, although she was quite delirious, calling for you over and over."

His face reddened. "Did she?"

"Indeed," the Countess said, "Poor girl. The doctor said that it couldn't have been avoided, that such things are nature's way."

"Did the doctor also say that it would hinder her ability to have children in the future?"

The Countess raised an eyebrow. "That's a rather indelicate question to ask at this time, don't you think?"

"Yes, of course. I don't know what I was thinking."

"You weren't."

"I should go up to her," he said.

"Of course. But do not wake her."

"I won't," he said taking the stairs two at a time.

She was asleep, the early afternoon sun casting shadows on the flowered wallpaper. How beautiful she was, he thought, and yet how pale and fragile. He crossed to where she lay and sat on the edge of the bed, kissing her lightly on the forehead. Her eyelids fluttered before she opened them.

He smiled. "Hello, my darling. How are you feeling?"

She turned her head, unable to look at him.

He reached for her hand, but she pulled it away. "Please," he whispered.

"Please what?" she asked, her voice hoarse and raspy.

"Please forgive me."

"Give you dispensation for abusing your wife and killing your unborn child, you mean?"

"I think that might be a little dramatic, even for you, Aida. My intention was to do neither."

"Dramatic? You have no idea how dramatic I can be, Michel. Perhaps your mother and father might want to hear of how their first grandchild was lost. That might alter their high and mighty opinion of you."

"Aida, I beg you not to be irrational. The doctor said that such things happen, that it isn't unusual with a first pregnancy."

"One that I was trying to sustain."

"I know. I wasn't thinking. I honestly thought there would be no risk. But this is our loss. I do share it with you."

She turned her cold gaze on him. "Really? You don't know what it is like to feel life in your womb one minute and have it gone in the blink of an eye. To believe in a future that will never be." She began to cry.

"I am so sorry, my darling. Truly, I am."

But her tears flowed and her body shook, barely able to contain the grief that she was asked to bear.

"What can I do? How can I make it better?"

"Do you really want to know?"

"Yes. Ask anything of me."

"Move out of my bedroom." She said, between sobs.

"Certainly, you don't mean that? What will my parents think?"

"I do mean it. And quite frankly, I don't care what anyone thinks."

"For how long? Until you have recovered, I assume."

"Perhaps forever," she said. "I can't stand the sight of you right now, much less the idea of sharing a bed with you. Now, please leave."

He sat quietly for a long while, the sounds of her weeping filling the air. Then, he took a deep breath.

"As you wish," he said, pausing at the door. "I will not subject you to my presence if that is what you truly want."

"It is," she said flatly.

For three days, Aida remained in bed, unwashed and indifferent. Her mother-in-law brought her meals, which she was either unwilling or unable to eat.

"I fear that she is of a fragile state of mind," the Countess whispered to her son.

"I can see that. She has removed me from the bedroom. Now, she won't even speak to me."

"It is a painful thing for a woman to endure, Michel. She needs time."

"I think I know what she needs, Mother, and I will see to it that she gets it."

Hours later, a butler delivered two envelopes on a silver tray. Aida stared at them as though she was unable to determine what to do next. Finally, she sighed and opened the first one.

My Dear Aida,

At your request, I have avoided you for the past few days. I understand your need for time. Certainly, there is nothing I can do or say to erase what has happened, nor to express the depths of my sadness over the loss of our child. I am filled with regret over my actions. I want nothing more than to remain in your affection, which at this point seems impossible. I am trying to understand, to be patient and kind, but I seem to be failing miserably. I thought that perhaps a change of scenery would do you some good that it might soften your heart towards me, given some distance between us. Can absence make the heart grow fonder? I certainly hope so. I suggest you return to those who can truly help you to heal and return to me when you are able to find a way to forgive me. I pray that will be soon. I do so love you.

Michel

Aida reached for the other envelope. Inside was a first class ticket aboard the steamer bound for New Orleans. Her eyes filled with tears. Never in her life had she needed her mother more.

She rang the bell for the maid. "Come and help me pack," she said, her voice barely audible. "I'm going home."

CHAPTER TWENTY-THREE

Aimee entered the darkened room and pulled back the heavy curtains, filling the room with sunlight. "Sissy, you are not going to spend another day in this bed," she said. "Get up and get dressed."

"Maybe tomorrow," Aida mumbled, pulling the covers over her face.

Aimee furrowed her brow. "Not tomorrow. Today. I understand that you have been through an ordeal, that what happened was infinitely unfair, but life isn't always going to be fair. I learned that lesson when I was five years old, and I think it is time for you to learn it as well."

Aida leveled her eyes on her sister. "That was cruel, Aimee. You have no idea what it is like to lose a child."

"No, I don't. I am not a mother. But you have one. Goodness knows, you have the most sympathetic ear on earth right downstairs. She is worried sick. You need to stop shutting us out and concentrate on getting better."

"I will never be better," Aida moaned.

"Yes, you will. And the process starts now."

Aimee moved to the washstand and poured water from the porcelain pitcher into the matching bowl. "Let's start by washing your face." She reached for Aida's hand, moving her to the edge of the bed.

"Talk to me, Sissy," Aimee said, gently wiping her sister's cheek before moving to her arms. "There is more to this, isn't there?"

Aida nodded, tears forming in her eyes.

"What is it? Being so far away from home?"

"I don't want to talk about it."

"You have to talk about it. Here, you are free to do so. You know that."

Aida shrugged. "I suppose being away is part of it. New York is exciting, although I am little more than a china doll who is dressed up for dinner, and paraded around. I am constantly reminded of my place."

Aimee laughed. "I can't even begin to imagine you as anyone's little doll."

"My big mouth gets me into trouble daily. I am far too opinionated,"

"That's nothing new. What else?"

"It's Michel. I'm afraid he isn't what I thought him to be."

Aimee undid Aida's braid and began to brush her hair. "Most men aren't," she said, "but what specifically makes you say that?"

"He is gone from home for long periods of time."

"Well, he does work, right? I thought that his law career was appealing to you."

"It was, especially when I idealistically thought that I might learn from him, that someday I would be a lawyer, too."

"There is still the possibility of that happening."

"Not for me. Not if I am to be a proper wife to a titled man."

"Perhaps that is true for now, but who knows what the future may bring? Besides, it isn't like you didn't know what kind of family you were joining when you agreed to marry him."

"I know. I was blinded by love."

"And now?"

"Now, I think I am just blinded."

Aimee smiled. "We all are Sissy, by one thing or another."

"I can't help but think that there is something more to the man I married than I know. He can be kind one minute and harsh, the next. Losing the baby was his fault."

"His fault? In what way?"

Aida blushed. "It is a little indelicate to discuss."

"Gee, Sissy, I am a nurse. Do you think I don't know the facts of life?"

"Let's just say that he insisted on having relations in spite of my delicate condition."

Aimee nodded. "You do know that married couples don't stop being together just because a baby is on the way, right? I think the timing may have been coincidental."

Aida wiped away a tear. "I am not convinced of that. Besides, he can be a contradiction, which is probably why he was a bachelor for so long. There is a side of him that remains a mystery. He has secrets, of that I am certain."

"Secrets?"

"Yes, which I am slowly discovering."

Aimee lay the brush on the table and looked into her sister's eyes, which were so much like her own. "What specifically? You are being far too vague."

Aida blushed. "Well, for one thing, he has six toes."

Aimee paused allowing the image to settle into her brain, and then, she began to laugh. "Seriously? Six toes?"

Aida nodded and then giggled. "It was quite the discovery on our wedding night."

"Must be one of those aristocratic things, handed down from the original Count."

"Or Countess," Aida added. "I never did ask the question, although my curiosity was piqued, for sure. Do you think our children will be so afflicted?" She paused, swallowing hard. The mention of babies made Aida cry.

"You can't worry about that. Besides, I am thinking that your side of the family with their normal feet will prevail." She began to laugh again.

"Aimee, you must stop. I am sorry that I ever told you."

"No don't be. We have always shared such confidences," Aimee said. "It is just that I will never be able to look at him with a straight face again,"

"Oh, no, you mustn't breathe a word of it to anyone, not even Mother or Franklin."

Aimee smiled. "I won't, but this is one secret that will be hard to keep."

She handed Aida a blue cotton housedress. "Here. Put this on. We may need to burn that nightgown. You have worn it for a full week."

Aida quickly dressed and examined her face in the hand mirror. "I look so pale," she said.

"You have been through an ordeal. But time is a great healer. We are here for you, Sissy. Always."

"I am grateful for that."

"Now, let's continue our chat. I have much to share about Franklin. And Mother waits for us in the kitchen, where she has made biscuits. I was told not to return without you."

Aida nodded. "You are most persuasive, but that's something we share, I suppose."

"Indeed, it is," Aimee said, offering her hand.

CHAPTER TWENTY-FOUR

"Here is your other daughter, Mother," Aimee said. "I have delivered her to you as promised. But now, I have to get dressed for work."

Angelique wiped her hands on her apron before crossing the kitchen to embrace Aida.

"I am so glad that you have decided to rejoin the human race," she said. "You have been missed."

"Not so sure that I am ready, Mother. I can't shake this feeling of overwhelming sadness."

Angelique nodded as she placed a cup of steaming coffee on the kitchen table and pointed to the empty chair. "Here. Sit and let's talk."

Aida shrugged, but did as she was told.

"I'm so sorry, ma chere," Angelique said, handing her a biscuit on a pink porcelain saucer. "But the melancholy won't last forever. That is what is so remarkable about the human heart. It is soft. It may bruise, but it won't break."

"I wish I could believe that. My heart certainly feels shattered."

"Of course, it does. I understand. Truly, I do."

Aida sighed as she broke the biscuit, and laid the pieces back on the saucer. "Please don't say that. I don't see how you can know what I am feeling."

Moving to her daughter's side, Angelique took Aida's hand in hers. "Shall I tell you about the baby I once carried and loved, one that I lost in the sugar cane fields of Chauvin Plantation?"

Aida's eyes grew wide. "Really?"

Angelique nodded.

"When did it happen?"

"When you and Aimee were around ten."

"Why didn't you ever tell us?"

"Aida, a miscarriage is a very personal thing for a woman. I told no one besides your poppa. Certainly it was not an appropriate discussion to have with my children, for many reasons."

"For fear that we might think that someday it could happen to us as well, you mean?"

"Well, yes, I suppose so. But grown up issues are best kept between the grown-ups, don't you think? Besides, grief is a peculiar thing. Sometimes, when it is shared, it is halved, but it takes a while to feel comfortable doing so. I kept it very close to my heart."

"That is true. I am processing the sorrow in my own way. I am so grateful to be able to do that here."

"This is your home, Aida. It forever will be. I hope that you will remember that you are always safe and protected here. I adore you, my daughter."

Aida smiled for the first time in weeks. "Yes, I know. It is comforting."

"You have always assumed that you had to be strong, a confident woman of the world." Angelique said. "And you are! But sometimes, that strength is tested. That's when we learn who we are. Unfortunately, tragedy knocks on our doors. Life is going to bring you sorrow, but often, it brings you joy. That's a universal truth. But the bad times don't last forever. There will be happy moments to come. Remember that."

"Had I heard this from anybody else, I might have simply assumed they were trying to make me feel better, but throughout my life you have shown me what that means."

"Goodness knows, I have had my share of trials, but who hasn't? The point is, I never gave up, and you shouldn't either."

Aida sat in silence, processing her mother's words. She nodded.

"Experience changes us, for better or worse." Angelique said. "Sometimes, I think that the orphanage was born from the grief of that loss and my empty womb."

"And sissy's spent time in that awful one."

"Yes, that certainly was a dark period for all of us, the most frightening experience of my life. Use this time of healing to discover the important work that you were called to do."

"But isn't motherhood important work?" Aida asked.

"It is the most important work of all," Angelique said. "Rest assured, your time will come. There will be many babies in your future."

"Do you think so?"

"I know it. But currently, there is one big consideration."

"What's that?"

"You will have to return to your husband to make it happen."

Aida's face grew somber. "I just don't know if I can. He has hurt me so deeply."

"I will not pry into the intimate details of your relationship, Aida, but don't forget that you are newlyweds with a bright future. This is a tragedy you must bear together. Love will see you through whatever troubles you may have as a couple. I truly believe that."

"It isn't that easy. Quite frankly, I don't know if I can ever trust him again."

"Certainly that is a choice that only you can make. But never underestimate the power of love. Do give it some careful consideration before you make a decision that you might later regret. Sometimes, there is no turning back."

"But sometimes that is the best road to travel."

Angelique sighed. "Forgiveness is something reserved for the strong. You do it for yourself, so that you can let go of the hurt and move forward. It is the only way that you are able to experience peace. Trust me, I know. Anger and resentment will only consume you until you no longer resemble the person you once were. Bitterness is the ultimate path to self-destruction."

Aida nodded. "But why is it so difficult?"

"Because for most of us, it isn't easy to live in the present. We keep looking back, holding onto the hurts of the past with a firm, tight grip, simply unable to let them go. But life always moves forward, and if we drag the pain along with us, eventually we are worn out from the heaviness of the load."

"How did you get so wise, Momma?"

"I have lived, honey, and I have learned. So will you."

"But why do the lessons have to be so hard?" Aida asked.

"Because that's the only way we remember them."

Aimee entered the kitchen, waving an envelope in the air. Her starched uniform and petticoat rustled as she walked. "Letter for you just came, Sissy. I do believe it is from that wayward husband of yours."

Aida took a deep breath.

"Remember what I told you," Angelique said. "You get to decide how to proceed with your life, always. I pray that God will guide you to make a wise choice. And now, I will let you read your mail in private."

She kissed Aida on the top of the head. "You are dearly loved. Never forget that."

CHAPTER TWENTY-FIVE

Aimee and Franklin could hear the screams from inside the clinic and rushed to the doorway to investigate. A young woman, covered in blood, clutched a lifeless child to her bosom. "Please," she cried, "help my baby. He is hurt, and it's pretty bad."

Aimee moved quickly, taking the boy from her arms and carefully placing him on the nearest examination table. Franklin searched for the source of the bleeding, while she felt for his pulse.

"It's weak and irregular," she whispered.

He nodded, and after locating the deep gash on the child's inner forearm began applying direct pressure, quickly replacing one blood soaked bandage with another.

Franklin addressed the mother. "Can you tell us what happened?"

"I was in the back yard cutting up a chicken for supper. I turned my back for just a minute, no longer than that, and Freddie, he had picked up the cleaver. It all happened so fast." She began to sob uncontrollably. "There was so much blood. I remembered you folks had this clinic. It was the closest place, and I am ever so grateful to find you here."

"I think that he has severed an artery," Franklin said, "He needs surgery to repair it right away, but there is no one here to do it. We will need to take him to the hospital."

Aimee looked to Franklin. "Do you think there is time?"

"I don't know. I can apply a tourniquet to stop the bleeding, but that could result in the loss of his arm."

The mother, who had overheard the exchange, began to wail more loudly. "Oh, Lord, please don't let my baby lose his arm. It will change his life forever. I beg you to save him. Do what you can."

Worry etched Franklin's face. "We have no choice," he said to Aimee. I'll get the buggy ready, and we will take him in."

"We do have a choice. We have everything here to do it. Time is of the essence, Franklin."

He narrowed his eyes, fixing his gaze on her. Then he held up his trembling hands. "How?"

"Let's prep him for surgery, and I will show you."

The mother was instructed to sit and wait. Franklin and Aimee carried the boy into the clinic's operating room. He began to stir, softly whimpering as they calmly spoke to him.

"Freddie, you are going to be just fine. Try not to move if you can."

The boy's eyes fluttered as he grew weaker.

"I can't perform this procedure and you know it," Franklin said. "Are you trying to make a fool out of me while costing this child his life?"

"Is that really what you think?"

"I don't know what to think," Franklin said.

Aimee turned to face him. "I have seen you do this dozens of times. It isn't complicated."

"Not with these useless hands."

"That's why I am going to be your hands, Franklin. You will talk me through each step. We can do it. We can save this child."

Franklin shook his head. "That's insane."

"Well, call me crazy, but unless we do something, this boy is going to die. We can argue about it, or we can try. If I get in over my head, we will apply the tourniquet and stop the bleeding long enough to get him to Charity. But this is our best shot. Let's see if he we can make sure he has an arm to throw a ball or hug his momma. Agreed?"

Franklin swallowed hard and nodded. Aimee carefully laid out the surgical instruments while Franklin prepared the chloroform. Within minutes, the boy was in a deep sleep.

"You are going to need to try to control the bleeding as much as you can so that I can see how badly it has been severed. I need to make certain that there are no other injuries, tendons, muscles. If there is more involved, we won't even attempt it. Agreed?"

Aimee nodded. "I will follow your lead."

"Apply the clamp, the smallest one you have. Then, swab it with a bandage. Use the dropper to remove any blood that obscures your sight and then, step back so that I can take a look."

Aimee worked swiftly and with precision as Franklin inspected each step.

"Looks pretty clean. I think it is a small tear in the artery. Use the fine suture to make tiny stitches to repair the gap."

"Looks like the bleeding has stopped," Aimee said, exhaling.

"Now, use heavier sutures to close the wound."

Aimee slowly and methodically did as she was instructed.

"Goodness! How did you learn to do that?" Franklin asked.

"I have been practicing just in case I get into medical school someday. Southern ladies do needlepoint; I
do surgical stitching."

"Impressive," he said as he wrapped the child's arm with a clean bandage. "I'm afraid that it looked
far worse than it was. You made the right call."

"I'll admit that I was scared to death."

"Calm under pressure. That's the mark of a good surgeon."

"Well, that, of course, and unfortunately, also being a male," Aimee said.

"That won't be the case forever."

"I hope that you are right, but those opportunities are limited."

"Let's move him to a bed and tell the mother that she can stay with him through the night. We will watch for fever, of course. The next two days will be crucial to his recovery."

"Of course," Aimee said, "but Franklin?"

"Yes?"

"Don't tell anybody what happened in there. Promise me, will you?"

"Why not? You were brilliant."

"So were you. And that's what I want you to remember."

Franklin felt his heart open. Sometimes he forgot what an amazing woman Aimee truly was.

CHAPTER TWENTY-SIX

It took a few minutes for Aimee's eyes to adjust to the dim light of the university library. She glanced at the clock. She had exactly thirty-five minutes before closing time and could only hope that would be long enough. She approached the circulation desk to speak to the librarian.

"I am looking for medical journals."

The woman peered over the thick glasses which rested on the bridge of her nose and pointed. "Third row to your left."

Aimee stood riveted to the spot. "I am afraid that I wasn't finished with my request," she said. "I am specifically looking for recent material on rehabilitation following an injury, perhaps something written by an army doctor, familiar with gunshot or knife wounds to the shoulder."

"That's pretty specific."

"Yes, it is, which is why I have asked for your help." She had already gone to the Parish Library and had come up with nothing. This woman was her only hope of finding help for Franklin's ongoing tremors.

"Near closing time, too." Aimee detected the sarcasm in the woman's voice, but she was undeterred.

"I understand that it is. But this is rather urgent. You see, I am a nurse. I appeal to you as one professional woman to another."

The woman sighed, but appeared to be secretly pleased that the title of professional had been bestowed upon her. She came out from behind the counter and adjusted her skirt. "Let's see what we can find."

Aimee followed her into the dark cavernous row of books.

"I think what I am looking for is in this area," the woman mumbled, mouthing the names of random titles as she searched. "Ah yes, here it is. I catalogued this one myself, which is why I happened to remember it. You are in luck."

"Indeed, I am," Aimee said, taking the book into her hands. *Restoring Function to the Extremities Following Injury.* She opened the cover to reveal pages and pages of exercises, each designed to aid in recovery. Franklin's recovery.

"I do believe that the author discovered these techniques following the Franco-Prussian War. He is a French physician, I think. His biography should be on the last page if you want to read about his research."

Aimee read through Doctor Emile Lenoir's impressive credentials. She smiled. "This will do quite well," she said. "May I borrow it for a time?"

"Do you have a card? Are you a student at the university?"

"Well, no, but I was at one time."

"Then, it is not possible."

Aimee swallowed hard. "Please. I am on the staff at the hospital. Could you possibly use that to qualify me?

The librarian glanced at the clock. "We close in five minutes," she said, as though that fact might make Aimee less resolute.

"Which is all the more reason why I need you to make this decision now."

The librarian pressed her lips together. Suddenly, this had become a battle of wills, and she intended to win. "I am sorry. I cannot."

Aimee opened her purse and removed a $20 gold piece. She had just been paid and this was a month's wages. "Then, perhaps you will sell the book to me," she said firmly. "You can reorder one for your collection; in fact, you should be able to purchase several copies for the price I am willing to pay."

The librarian stared at the shiny coin for several seconds, mesmerized by its potential worth. "It is highly unorthodox, you understand. We are not a bookstore. Perhaps you should try the one on Canal Street?"

"It is unlikely that they will have such a specialized title and you know it. I beg of you. This is a matter of great importance for someone. May I be so bold as to say it could mean the restoration of a life?"

"A patient of yours?"

"In a way, yes. Someone whose existence has been forever changed by a grave injury. The information in this book could help him regain the use of his hand. At least, I am hopeful that it can. Could you, out of the kindness in your heart, make this possible? Would you?"

The clock struck five as the custodian moved in to close the windows and lock the doors. Other workers stacked books to be sorted later. The librarian leaned in and whispered. "Take the book," she said as she palmed the coin, "but tell no one how you got it."

"I promise," Aimee said, with a wink. "Bless you."

"I just hope that it works for you and your patient."

"Me, too. You have no idea how much."

CHAPTER TWENTY-SEVEN

Aimee handed the cloth bag to Franklin. She had stitched it herself out of remnants from her mother's sewing box. and then, carefully filled it with dried beans. "What's this?" he asked.

"Your new toy," she said, stifling a giggle.

"I am afraid that I outgrew children's games a long time ago," he said.

"Not this one."

"You are being rather mysterious, Aimee. What is this?"

"Something to help you regain the use of your hands," she said.

He frowned, and then tossed the bag to the floor. "That's not funny."

"It wasn't meant to be. Just humor me, will you?" She knelt before him and handed him the bag once again. "Place it in your palm and squeeze it."

"I don't see what good that is going to do," Franklin said. "Nothing is going to make a difference."

"Then, will you at least agree that it couldn't hurt to try?"

He narrowed his eyes. "Aimee, you can sometimes be the most exasperating woman I have ever known."

Aimee smiled. "Blame it on my mother. Tenacity is a strong trait among the females in my family. But then, you already know that, don't you?"

He nodded. "I guess that tenacity is what saved me from the life of a poor miserable orphan. If it pleases you, I will squeeze your silly bag. What is inside of it, by the way?"

"Dried beans."

"Ok, then, I will squeeze your silly bean bag, and if we get hungry in a little while, we can open it and cook the contents."

"Make all the jokes you want, Franklin, just keep squeezing."

"How many times?"

"Forty. And then raise your hand above your head and hold it there for thirty seconds."

"Are you trying to prove that you can get me to look foolish without much effort?"

"No, I am trying to get you back into the operating room."

"We seem to be doing quite well with our current arrangement. You are becoming quite the surgeon."

Her face grew serious. "If we are discovered, we will both be fired. I am not a physician and you have no business allowing me to operate on patients, even under your guidance."

"Seems to me it was your idea, Nurse."

"Yes, to save a child's life. I didn't expect that it would become a common practice, especially not at the hospital."

"Well, you have been my right hand for so long, I guess this seemed like a natural progression. We are being careful, and we won't get caught. Besides, most of our procedures are done at the clinic, where we make the rules. Our patients are in desperate need of care. It is a good thing, Aimee. I can continue to use my skill and training, and you are learning. This has done more than anything to improve my state of mind."

"Of course, I am happy to hear it, but still, it would please me if we could get you back into the role of surgeon. I want to be a doctor more than anything, but not like this."

"It will happen for you; I just know it. Those doors can't be closed to women forever. The need for doctors is far too great."

"I hope you are right. I have waited a very long time already. I hope when I am allowed to cross the threshold, I won't be too old to walk on my own. Now squeeze."

He laughed. "Yes, ma'am. My, but you are bossy."

"Yes, I am. Now, raise your hand over your head. I'm timing you now."

"I still don't see what good this will do."

She held up her hand. "I want for you to push your palm against mine as hard as you can."

"Are you sure that you aren't just using this as an excuse to hold my hand?" he teased.

She rolled her eyes. "And no, we are not going to reenact the "hands pray" scene from *Romeo and Juliet*, either. Now, do it again."

He laughed. "Where do you get these crazy ideas?"

"From Shakespeare."

"No, the exercises."

"I'll show you." She crossed the room to retrieve the book from the library table where she had been studying it. "Here."

"What's this?"

"Look at the title and then, start at the beginning."

"Honestly, Aimee. This is a bunch of hogwash. People enjoy peddling hope to the hopeless."

"Read his credentials. He started this therapy working with injured solders during the Franco-Prussian War. He has had great success."

"Or so he says."

"We live in hope every day, Franklin. That's the premise of medicine, isn't it? Hope is the belief in possibilities. And I believe in you. When we are deprived of the ordinary days, we find joy in those that are less than ideal. There was a time when I feared that you might die."

"But I didn't, did I?"

"No. Once you regain the use of your hand, you will appreciate everything in ways you never did before."

"It may be a shot in the dark, but if you believe, then, so can I. Hand me that bag, will you?"

Aimee smiled. "Forty times. OK?"

CHAPTER TWENTY-EIGHT

"It is so good to have you home, my dear," Michel said, lightly kissing her cheek as he handed her a glass of sherry. "My worst fear was that you would never return to me and my life would be empty without your shining light."

Aida tried not to cringe. Since she had left New Orleans, she had worked hard on her attitude, reminding herself of her mother's wise advice. But she had also come to understand that forgiveness is often easier said than done. It would take time for her heart to soften toward her husband. However difficult it might be, she knew she had to try.

He had done his best to please her, ceremoniously presenting her with a key to a new house the day she had stepped off the ship. She feigned excitement, knowing full well that it was his peace offering, an expensive one at that. If for no other reason than it meant that she no longer had to live under the same roof as her in-laws, she was pleased to see that he had made the effort.

In some ways, it was like they were courting again. He had graciously moved into the guest room, whispering, "until you are ready," when the maid delivered her bags to her room and began to unpack. She had breathed a sigh of relief, knowing full well that she was both unable and unwilling to share a marital bed with him yet. Time, she reminded herself, was a great healer. She hoped that adage would prove to be true.

Her duties as the wife of a viscount remained, and so, she spent more time in the presence of her husband's family than she would have liked. A footman would often knock at her door midafternoon with a note in her mother-in-law's elaborate handwriting requesting that she be available for some kind of command performance or another. Dinner. A tea for charity. It was all tedious to her. She would have preferred to stay at home, read from her husband's legal library or sew the baby layette she was secretly making. In spite of all that had transpired, the loss and heartbreak, she firmly held onto her two life goals, to become a lawyer and a mother. Deep in her heart, she believed herself to be destined for both roles. Once she had made up her mind about such matters, she was determined.

"You have become quite the toast of New York society," the Countess said one afternoon on one of those rare visits when she had come to call. "I can't tell you how much it pleases me."

Aida shrugged. "I am not so sure that I would attach that label to myself. It seems a bit self-indulgent."

"On the contrary, my dear. You have earned your place as a fine representation of this family. Your genteel upbringing is evident in social situations." Aida tried not to laugh as she recalled her youth spent running through the cane fields of Chauvin Plantation or chasing chickens with Aimee and Franklin.

"My mother would be delighted to hear it, Countess."

The Countess surveyed the parlor, elaborately furnished with matching brocade chairs and tasseled curtains. Porcelain figurines adorned the marble mantle, while cut glass lamps illuminated the room. "You have made my son a fine home as well."

Aida focused her gaze on her mother-in-law. She knew her far too well. She was leveling compliments because she wanted something, something she knew Aida might not want to give. But it was far too much fun to play along, and so, Aida encouraged the conversation to continue.

"You are very kind. It has been my pleasure to serve both you and my husband." As soon as she had said it, regret washed over her. She had been outwitted.

"I am so happy to hear you say that, my dear, because I have a request of you, one I hope you won't refuse."

Aida took a deep breath. "Really?"

"Indeed. The Women's Auxiliary of New York has taken on a very worthy charity, one which has been passed over by so many other organizations because of its delicate nature."

Suddenly, she had Aida's interest. "What kind of 'delicate nature' might you be referring to, if I might ask?"

Her voice grew low, almost to a whisper. "There is a clinic in Harlem that caters to women who have found themselves in unfortunate circumstances." She cleared her throat. "Many of them might be called 'fallen.' It was started a few years ago, but with little to no financial support, medical care has fallen by the wayside. There are a few diehard volunteers, but not many. It faces imminent closure if someone doesn't step in to help."

"Your group of privileged women has chosen to offer that help? It seems a little unusual to me. Most of the well-heeled I have met are only worried about elaborate parties and fancy gowns."

The Countess blushed. "Oh, well, none of us are planning to go there. I mean, it isn't like we intend to mingle with them. We just want to have something to raise money, you know, perhaps a dinner dance. I have been asked to enlist you as the chairwoman of the event."

"In other words, you want me to plan a gala for whores?"

"Oh my," the Countess said, her face turning crimson, "must you use that word in my presence?"

"It is certainly more appropriate than 'fallen,' Countess, which makes them sound like a group of clumsy women who trip and skin their knees."

"Perhaps. But I do believe that the Bible teaches that all are worthy of redemption, even the morally deficient. I think it is wonderful that this organization wants to help."

"If that's the motivation, then, I agree, but if this is simply about drinking champagne and dancing the night away, then count me out. I have had to endure far too many of those evenings with women who live in their husbands' shadows and have never had an original thought in their entire lives."

"My dear, must you be so blunt? I can assure you that the intentions here are good. We need your young blood and innovative ideas to make this a success."

Aida sighed. She had been caught, much like a wild animal in a trap. She had desperately tried to pick her battles with her mother-in-law. And this, unfortunately, was one she could not win.

"How long to do I have to plan this?"

"Two months. And you will have help. There is a Junior Auxiliary who stand ready to assist in whatever capacity you may need."

Aida resisted the urge to make a snide remark. "I look forward to meeting with them," she said. But in reality, nothing was further from the truth.

CHAPTER TWENTY-NINE

"Your mother paid me a visit today," Aida said over dinner that night.

"Good. I know that she is happy that you are home once again. She worried during your absence."

"About me or about what people might think of her runaway daughter-in-law who left her precious son so abruptly? I am quite certain that we were the topic of many gossip sessions among the silly superficial women whom she considers her friends."

Michel chuckled. "You shouldn't concern yourself with what people think, my dear. There will always be speculation about what happens in other people's marriages. I suppose our position makes us fodder for idle chatter."

"And what is 'our position?' "

He reached for her hand. "Whether you embrace it or not, Aida, we are a titled family. People view us differently."

"It is your title, not mine, Michel. I would be perfectly content being a part of mainstream society. Maybe then, I could live my life as I wish, not in this goldfish bowl."

"I beg to differ. Rank has its privileges. I would think that more doors are opened for you because of who you are. That should mean more opportunities to do important work."

"Like hosting a charity ball so that your mother's group and their daughters can dress to impress each other? I can't help but think that if they just stayed home, donated the money spent on an evening's finery, they could really make a real difference with some of the causes that they claim to support."

"I am afraid that's the way it works. It's all a game. The peacocks pay to show off their feathers and the barnyard chickens benefit."

Aida laughed. "That's an interesting way to look at it, but you are absolutely right."

"May I ask what has sent you on this tangent? Was it my mother's visit?"

"Yes. I hate to admit that I reluctantly agreed to host a gala for one of her club's new charities."

"Who will be the recipient this time?"

"The Women's Center of Hope in Harlem. It is, I believe, a place for the downtrodden Jezebels of New York, 'fallen women' as your mother called them. I thought it was an unusual beneficiary for her benevolence, given her high and mighty moral view of the world, but I continue to be surprised by what people do."

Michel paused. "Ah yes, I know the place. There are a few poor barristers with a limited clientele who give their talent and education away. I have heard that some of them take on the cases of these women pro bono. Prostitutes and the criminal justice system often collide, you know. It is rather seedy, of course, but I suppose that even whores deserve legal representation, as long as I don't have to provide it."

"That's rather elitist of you, don't you think?"

"Not at all. I am a damn good lawyer, and I expect people to pay for my services."

Aida sighed. "Perhaps that's why we need female lawyers. Women tend to have softer hearts; therefore, they don't mind working for the common good, especially if it means helping another woman."

"Perhaps. But it will be a long time before we admit women to the bar. At least not here in New York. Of that I am certain."

"Do you mean that there are no female lawyers in this, the largest city in the country?"

"Not true barristers. Perhaps there are a few who dabble in it without full license or expertise, but most I have encountered are really more like clerks."

Aida could feel the quickening of her pulse, her blood pressure rising. "That's rather unfortunate, don't you think? Are men so afraid of our collective power that they must limit us? I certainly have not given up my dream of practicing the law or casting a vote."

Michel laughed a little louder than Aida thought necessary. "That will not be possible, my dear. You are an upper-class woman. Working outside of the home in any capacity is completely inappropriate. As far as voting is concerned, women are simply not ready to make an informed decision in such matters."

"I hope you don't believe that," Aida said, wondering if she should enter into this familiar debate once again. "What you claim may be true today, but I have high hopes for tomorrow. Things change, Michel. I am counting on that."

"And I am counting on the fact that motherhood will keep you so fulfilled and busy that you won't have a moment to long for any other way to spend your days."

Aida tilted her head, locking her eyes on her husband. "It seems that I must invite you back into my bedroom in order for that to happen."

"Indeed it does. Like you, I have my own high hopes for tomorrow. As you said, 'things change.' I, too, am counting on that."

He offered his hand. "Shall we have a glass of sherry in the library?"

She nodded, placing her hand in his. Her heart softened a bit. If she couldn't be a lawyer, she would most certainly be a mother. She longed for a baby of her own. If she was smart, she would never let him know just how much.

CHAPTER THIRTY

SPRING, 1877

The young woman cried out in pain. Like so many of the penniless, lost, and forgotten, who had found their way to the clinic behind the orphanage, she had waited far too long to seek help.

Aimee replaced the compress on her forehead with another. "Her fever has risen," she said to Andrew, "and so has her discomfort."

"Let me examine her again," he said.

"Here," Aimee said, as she pulled back the sheet to expose the woman's belly, "let me help." She was incredibly thin with ribs protruding on either side. "You can count the bones, can't you?"

"She is awfully malnourished," Franklin said, gently pressing on her distended abdomen. The woman moaned as she stared at the ceiling, her eyes hollow and lifeless.

"Do you think that's the problem with her? Lack of food? Perhaps she has been poisoned? It is obvious that she has been living on the streets for quite a long time."

"I thought so when she first arrived, but now her symptoms confirm it is her appendix. We will need to remove it before it ruptures."

"Are you sure?"

"Doctors are never sure, Aimee. We make an educated guess based on the information we have and hope for the best."

Aimee nodded. "But I have never done an appendectomy before."

"I dare say that every surgery you have done has been a first for you."

"Yes, of course. It's just that most have been simple procedures. This is beyond my scope of knowledge."

"Fortunately, it is within mine. I have performed this many times. And I will be there to guide you. You are, after all, my hands."

"Only until you are able to use your own again. That will happen soon. I just know it."

Franklin shrugged. "I miss being able to do surgery, but I am practicing medicine again. That's something. Who knows, maybe those wacky exercises that you insist I do will work someday."

"You are still doing them, right?"

"Twice a day, as promised. Now, let's see if we can save this young woman."

Like a couple accustomed to dancing together, they began the choreography of surgical preparation, readying the patient and laying the instruments in proper order. Once the young woman had been sedated, Aimee took her place on the side of the table. She took a deep breath.

"Make an incision about four inches long on the patient's right lower abdomen. Cut through the muscle wall and into the peritoneum."

She placed the scalpel against the woman's pale flesh. "Proceed."

Aimee slowly made the incision "Done."

"Now, visually, examine the intestines until you reach the appendix. In her case, it should be red or inflamed. There may be other signs of increased infection."

"There is a lot of bleeding, Franklin. I can't seem to find it."

"Just take your time. Use the bandages to remove as much of the blood as you can. Gently feel along the bowel."

"I don't feel anything. I don't know where to look."

"Remain calm, Aimee. It is there. You will need to free it from the surrounding tissue."

"I can't."

"Yes, you can. Move over and let me see if I can locate it."

Aimee stepped aside as Franklin took her place. He carefully placed his hands into the woman's abdomen. "Ah, yes, there it is. Hand me the scalpel."

She reached onto the tray and firmly gripped the surgical instrument. "Here," she said.

"Can you see if you can swab some of the blood?"

"Yes, of course."

"Good. That helps. Now, bring the tray closer so that I can place it in there. I fear the infection could poison her."

"It's right here."

"I have it." In one skillful move, he had the appendix grasped firmly between his fingers and dropped onto the enamel tray."

"That's it!" Aimee whispered.

"And now to close the incision, or would you like to do the honors?"

"Your surgery, your privilege."

Franklin carefully stitched the wound closed, then covered it with a clean swath of white cloth. He exhaled loudly.

For a few minutes they simply watched the rhythmical rise and fall of the young woman's chest as she remained in the deep sleep of the anesthesia. Later, she was wheeled into the recovery area, where a volunteer nurse waited for her. By that afternoon, she would be in a hospital bed on the ward.

"You do know what you did, don't you, Franklin?"

He nodded.

"It's remarkable. Truly."

"Let's go outside," he said. "I think we could both use some fresh air."

Aimee followed him into the courtyard and watched as he quietly moved to sit under the shade of the massive oak. She sat beside him. Somehow, words seemed to fail both of them, and they remained silent, each processing the enormity of the day's events.

Franklin wiped away a tear with the back of his band. Aimee pretended not to notice.

"We did it," he finally said.

"No, you did it. I couldn't be more proud."

"Forgive me for making fun of you for those silly exercises."

"You are forgiven. When did you realize that they had worked, that your tremors were gone?"

"A few days ago. I wasn't sure, which is why I didn't say anything, but I have seen consistent improvement. It really is a miracle."

"Or perhaps it is what was meant to be. We often concentrate on what we expect to happen instead of what we want to happen. Sometimes, it then becomes self-fulfilling."

"As much as I hate to admit it, you may be right. When I saw a little progress, I started to believe that healing was possible."

"Perhaps we can help others who have suffered a similar injury."

"Ah yes, a new technique to add to my medical repertoire."

"You can't mock it now. I don't think your success is a fluke," Aimee said. "Goodness gracious, Momma will be overjoyed, not to mention the folks at the hospital. It means that you can return to surgery full time."

He nodded. "I hope that you are pleased."

"Me? Why, of course, I am. You are a gifted doctor. Your patients need you."

"Do you need me?"

She smiled. "I have needed you since I was five years old. You took care of me then. I am glad that this time, I could return the favor."

"That isn't exactly what I meant, Aimee."

She bit her lower lip and furrowed her brow. "I don't understand, Franklin."

"I think you do," he said, reaching for her hand. "I think you have understood for a very long time."

Her heart beat so wildly that she was certain that he could hear it. She could not speak.

"It is you, Aimee. It has always been you. I love you. Nothing in the world would make me happier than if you would agree to be my wife."

Aimee took a deep breath, the bitter taste of bile rising in her throat. How could the happiest moment of her life also be the most terrifying, she wondered? It was a question that hung in the air until the words softly floated away, taken by the wind into a place where dreams go to die.

CHAPTER THIRTY-ONE

"Well?" Franklin said. "A man likes to think that his proposal is received with joy rather than silence."

Aimee's eyes filled with tears and she swallowed hard, willing herself to keep the dam that held back her emotions from breaking. She had much to say. The many reasons why a marriage between them was not possible, swirled through her mind. But she knew that she would need to choose her words carefully. She hoped that she could.

"I don't know, Franklin. I must admit that I never thought it was a question you would ask of me."

"But truly you have known for some time how I feel about you."

She nodded.

"Do you love me in return?"

She nodded.

"Then that's all either of us need to know. Many happy marriages have been built on far less than that."

"But you are missing the obvious, are you not?"

"Unless you are secretly married to another, I don't think so."

Aimee tried not to laugh. She wished it had been that simple. "Franklin, you are practically my brother."

"But I am not, am I? No shared blood flows between us."

"We grew up together, lived in the same house for most of our lives."

"Which is why I am so certain. I know you, Aimee, and you know me. There are no secrets between us, no terrible habits to be discovered a few months from now. Ours is the most open and honest relationship that two people could possibly have."

"But you are my best friend."

"Which is all the more reason for me to also become your husband. You have changed my life, altered my path in ways I could have never imagined. And every day, you change it a little bit more. You make it better. You make me better. If you say 'no,' there will be no other. Not now, not ever."

Aimee carefully considered his words. She could have said the same about him. There had never been anyone else. But the nagging doubts remained. "What will people think, Franklin? Our colleagues, friends? I don't want to be fodder for the gossip mill at the hospital or anywhere else."

"If they truly know us, they will probably think that it is about time for us to have recognized what must be obvious."

"Do you really think they will be happy for us?"

"I am certain of it. Quite frankly, I don't care what the rest of the world thinks. This is our life, and we are entitled to live it as we please."

Aimee gasped. "But what will Momma think? Poppa? Aida? If they object, I couldn't possibly consider it."

"There is only one way to find out, isn't there?"

"We should ask them?"

"Indeed. And Aimee?"

"Yes?"

"I have a real advantage. My future in-laws already love me. Now let's go get their blessing."

CHAPTER THIRTY-TWO

Angelique was in the kitchen rolling out the dough for a pie when Aimee and Franklin entered.

"Well, hello there, you two. I didn't expect to see you in the middle of the morning."

"We have been at the clinic. Had a serious case very early. Neither of us have to be at the hospital for a few more hours. Besides, we have news."

"Good news, I hope," Angelique said.

"Very good news," Franklin said.

"Is Poppa home?" Aimee asked. "We were hoping that he would be."

"Yes, as a matter of fact, he is working on a lecture in the library. Shall we go talk to him?"

Aimee nodded.

"We have come to disturb you, Andrew," Angelique said, leading the way.

"When it is you, it is always welcomed, my love."

"I have the children with me, too."

Franklin laughed. "We are hardly children, Mother."

"Yes, of course, Franklin, but you always will be to me."

Aimee blushed. Her mother's comments only confirmed her uneasiness.

Franklin held up his hands for inspection. "Notice anything?"

Angelique gasped. "You are no longer shaking. When did that happen? Oh my goodness. I have prayed for this moment. How wonderful!"

"It most certainly is. Aimee's book of exercises really was a godsend."

"I must admit that I had my doubts, Aimee, but it appears that there was something to your theory. I suppose that is true of most medical breakthroughs," Andrew said.

"I actually performed a surgery this morning," Franklin said.

"He saved a woman's life," Aimee added.

"I know that they will be pleased for your return in full capacity at the hospital, Franklin. Your skill is desperately needed," Andrew said.

"I am looking forward to it," Franklin said.

"Well then, this is turning out to be a very good day, a very good day indeed," Andrew said.

"There is more to share. We hope that you will find this equally as exciting."

Angelique smiled. "Do tell!"

"I have asked Aimee to be my wife," Franklin announced.

No one spoke. Aimee held her breath.

Finally, Andrew rose from behind the intricately carved walnut desk and walked over to where the three stood. He cleared his throat. "Are you serious? You and Aimee? It is a bit unconventional, don't you think?"

"Yes," Franklin said, "I am sure that it seems that way."

"Forgive me if I am taken aback, but I am quite stunned," Andrew said. "So have you come to ask for our daughter's hand in marriage?"

Aimee chuckled. "I am certainly well above the age of consent, Poppa."

"That's true, Aimee, but I suppose I am a bit old fashioned in that regard, although what you are asking is certainly unorthodox."

"Perhaps, but it is what we want."

Andrew nodded.

"If you would like, then, yes, I am asking for Aimee's hand. But more importantly, I am asking for your blessing."

Andrew looked to Angelique. "What are your thoughts?"

Angelique sighed. "Anyone would have to be blind not to have recognized the devotion you two have for each other. I think that I truly understood how Franklin felt on the evening before Aida's wedding, when I saw how he looked at you, Aimee. After he was injured, all of those nights when you sat by his bed, trying to break his unrelenting fever. It was then I knew that you loved him, too. I wish I could say that I am surprised that this would be the outcome of the long standing commitment between you two, but I suppose I am not."

"Do you agree that they should marry?" Andrew asked.

"It is not our decision to make. They are grown now, no longer subject to the rules that we might impose as parents, regardless of how we might feel."

"But do you give your blessing?" Franklin asked.

Angelique turned to her daughter. "Aimee, what will make you happiest in this world?"

"Becoming Franklin's wife. I love him, Momma. I think I have loved him since I was a little girl. He has always made me feel safe and protected, especially when times were difficult. But more than that, we are a team, Franklin and I. It is as though we share one soul."

Franklin moved to Aimee's side, lightly kissing the palm of her hand. "You do honor me."

Angelique smiled. "There will be naysayers. People won't understand. You must be prepared for what is to come."

"We have considered that. But we also hope that there will be an equal number of people who are happy for us."

"It is an optimistic thought," Angelique said. "But I can see that you are resolved. I would prefer to be a part of your lives than not. Families support each other, regardless. So yes, you have my blessing."

"And Poppa?" Aimee asked.

Andrew sighed. "I have my reservations, which will fall on deaf ears, I am afraid. The heart wants what the heart wants. You have my blessing as well."

"It is far too early in the day for us to toast with champagne, but I will prepare a special dinner tonight."

"Thanks, Momma," Aimee and Franklin said in unison.

They looked at each other. At that moment, all anyone could do was laugh at the irony of it all.

CHAPTER THIRTY-THREE

Unlike her sister, Aimee had no need for pomp and circumstance, and so, the small intimate wedding, which consisted of the couple and five of their closest friends, took place in the courtyard of their family home.

Aimee chose the light green silk gown that she had worn to Aida's wedding dinner for the occasion. It seemed like a perfectly sensible decision since it had been an extravagance at the time and was practically brand new. Franklin was pleased when he saw her just as he had been that night when he knew that his love for her was true. She was beautiful, whether in her nurse's uniform or in an elaborate dress, he thought, but more than that, she was strong, honest, and loyal, everything that he wanted in a wife.

Aimee had pronounced it the most important day of her life, while Franklin said that for him, it was the happiest. When they had exchanged their vows, pledging a lifelong commitment, there wasn't a dry eye among those in attendance. Although it was an unconventional match, those who knew them understood the depth of their affection for each other.

Franklin had managed to find a small apartment halfway between the hospital and the clinic within weeks of his proposal. Aimee thought it was a sign that the universe approved of their union since housing was in short supply in the city. "Even if we have to pitch a tent behind the clinic," she had said to Franklin, "we will not live with my parents once were are legally wed." He had readily agreed. Just the thought of it was so unseemly that she had made herself ill until he had announced that he had secured a home for them.

There was no honeymoon. The demands of the hospital and clinic were far too great for either of them to consider being away for any length of time, but on those rare moments when they were unencumbered by job responsibilities, they dreamed of the places they might go and the sites they wanted to see.

"It's a great big world," Franklin had said. "Perhaps we could take a Nile River cruise."

"I could pretend to be Cleopatra," Aimee responded, laughing at her own joke.

"Well, there's a thought."

"We could go visit Aida and Michel," Aimee said, "I wouldn't mind seeing Niagara Falls. We could go there from New York City."

"Are you honestly considering a visit to your sister as a suitable honeymoon?"

"Never mind. How about Italy? I would love to see Venice."

"I do believe that is perfectly romantic."

Aimee held up her pinky. "So we promise that Venice it will be."

Franklin linked his finger with hers. "Venice. Before we are old and grey."

"I hope it will be sooner than that. I want to celebrate our marriage, not our retirement," Aimee said.

"We will have a lifetime together," Franklin said, lightly kissing her on the lips. "So many milestones yet to celebrate."

"And I am looking forward to each and every one," Aimee said.

CHAPTER THIRTY-FOUR

"My sister is married," Aida said to Michel over breakfast. "I wish I could have been there. It makes me sad that I was unable to share in this important time for her. We have never missed those pivotal moments in each other's lives."

"I know you do, my dear, but given the short notice and long distance, such a trip was impossible."

"True. I am not surprised that Aimee had a small wedding. She never was into fancy gowns or elaborate parties. Besides, under the circumstances, I understand her desire to have a small private ceremony."

Michel smiled. "Ah yes. It does seem rather incestuous to the casual observer."

Aida narrowed her steel-blue eyes and leveled her gaze at her husband. "What a vulgar thing to say about my sister's marriage. Incidentally, you are not, by any means, a casual observer. You are family."

"I meant no offense. It just seems that with so many women in this world, why Franklin would feel the need to wed his adopted sister is beyond my understanding."

"It sounds like some ancient Greek tragedy when you put it that way, but I can assure you that both Aida and Franklin are of both sound mind and strong character. Love has a strange way of showing up in the most unconventional ways. If they are happy together, then I wish them well."

"Of course, of course."

"Don't worry about me describing my complicated family dynamics at the next dinner party you host. I would hate for your genteel friends to think that your wife comes from a clan of morally deficient people."

"I must admit that it crossed my mind."

"Then, let it be a fleeting thought. I will protect my sister's reputation at all costs. You just happen to benefit from that loyalty."

The clock on the mantle began to chime. "Goodness. Look at the time. I must get to the office, my dear. I am afraid that I will be late this evening. A very important client has requested a dinner meeting. Those are tedious, but necessary."

"It seems that you have quite a litany of excuses to recite for your absence from home lately."

"No excuses, Aida, reasons. I have commitments to the firm and those we serve. I must honor them."

"What about your commitment to me?"

He laughed, and she immediately detected the sarcasm. "Perhaps when I am allowed back into your bed, we will discuss the meaning of commitment."

It was a convenient argument for him, one he used each time she criticized his behavior. But theirs had become a battle of wills, and they had reached an impasse. "That door is more easily opened with time and attention," she said.

"Ah, Aida, how I would love to sit and spar with you, but I must go. What are your plans for the day? Shopping? Tea with the ladies?"

"I have received the proceeds for the gala from the bank. It is a rather sizeable amount, and I think rather than sending it, I will deliver it myself."

"You will do no such thing. That part of the city is quite unsafe, filled with unsavory types. I would never allow you to go there, especially alone. Don't invite trouble, Aida."

"Allow me?"

"I do believe that is what I said. Now, give me the bank draft, and I will send someone from my office with it."

"Thank you, Michel, but that won't be necessary. I will place it in the mail, special delivery. It is a nice day. A walk to the post office will do me good. That little store I love so much is on the same block. I can spend a bit of time there when I am done."

"As you wish. But promise that you will stay safe."

"Certainly."

As soon as the front door closed, Aida retreated to her bedroom to dress for the day. "Hmmmm," she said to herself, "I wonder what is fashionable in Harlem? What does one wear to meet a group of reformed ladies-of-the-evening? Something red, I think." She reached for a crimson bonnet to complete her ensemble.

CHAPTER THIRTY-FIVE

Aida walked the two blocks from her house and then summoned a carriage. She knew too well that their regular driver reported her comings and goings to her husband on a daily basis. He who controls the money, has the power, she thought, a fact that always irritated her. If she was going to be defiant, she certainly didn't want to get caught.

"West 137th Street," she told the driver.

"You going to Harlem, madam?" he asked.

"Is that not the address I gave you?" she asked, her voice firm.

"Yes, of course, just checking to make sure."

The carriage wound its way through the crowded streets of New York, and for a moment, Aida sat back and enjoyed the view. When she was a child, she used to like to observe people in their hectic daily lives and make up stories about where they were going and why. Sometimes, she would share them with Aimee, who would clap her hands, begging for more. She missed those days, when life was simple, before adulthood complicated things. She wondered if that was the case for most people.

It hadn't come as a surprise that her sister had chosen to marry Franklin. They had been a couple since the day Aimee was rescued from the orphanage. The two were completely dedicated to each other. But as much as she hated to admit it,

Michel was right: others might view it as improper. People rarely held back their judgments when discussing choices that they viewed as inappropriate, although certainly, it was none of their business. Even in a progressive city like New York, there was lots of idle chatter about perceived respectability. Aida's sense of fair play kept her from joining in such discussions, for the most part, and then, she smiled, reminding herself not to make any assumptions about the place she was about to visit either.

The driver guided the horses to the curb and within minutes was opening the door for her. The streets were busy and as unfamiliar to her as if she had been dropped off in China. She considered the return trip, unsure of how long she would even remain there. Perhaps she would simply walk in, look around a bit, and hand off the check. That would satisfy her curiosity, if nothing else. It might even make her feel better about having spent so many tedious hours with the superficial women assigned to help her organize the gala. By the night of the event, she had been so exhausted from listening to idle chatter from the dimwitted socialites that she thought she might fall asleep for months, like some fairy princess under a spell. Nevertheless, she vowed never to be placed in such a position again, regardless of how insistent her mother-in-law was or how worthy the cause might be. She would focus her energies on fund raising for her mother's orphanage, which would give her a plausible excuse for turning down any future requests from her in-laws.

"Can you be back to get me in half an hour?" Aida asked.

"I am sorry madam. I have another fare, one who is waiting for me now."

"Oh," she said, concern rising in her voice, "then, how shall I get back home?"

He raised an eyebrow. "You can ask someone in there," he said, pointing to the dilapidated building that housed the Women's Center of Hope.

She blushed. "I am here on a benevolent mission, sir," she said, angered by his assumption.

"Look, madam, there are carriages for hire all over. Simply ask if one will take you to Manhattan. It's only a few blocks, after all."

She nodded, then paid the fare. As she stood on the sidewalk, she paused to reconsider. Under most circumstances, she would have felt confident, armed with a smile and the perfect words to say. But this was different. This was uncharted territory, far away from where she felt comfortable. She wondered how her mother might have conducted herself at such a moment. Certainly, she was always gracious and kind, even among orphans and field hands. That was the secret. Aida took a deep breath and opened the door.

Inside, there was one large dimly lit room, meant to serve as a reception area. Cobwebs clouded the ceiling and the room smelled of old smoke. There were a few threadbare chairs, a pink brocade sofa with a missing arm. A dead plant in a cracked green pot occupied the corner. To the right, a heavy library table, laden with cups and random dirty dishes, held the only lamp. Aida strained to see as she surveyed the area.

"Can I help you?' a voice called through the darkness.

"You lost?" asked another.

"Oh," Aida said, "I'm sorry. I didn't see you there."

"We are used to being invisible," the first one cackled.

"Yup," the other confirmed. "How'd you stumble in here? You lost?" she repeated.

"No, not exactly. Is there someone in charge?"

"Yeah. She's here. But we are her welcoming committee. You want her, you go through us."

Aida could see that three other women had entered the room. She tried to retain her composure, smiling nervously as she shifted her weight from one foot to another. But she was outnumbered and more than a little apprehensive.

"State your business," a new voice said.

"I am here to help. I have the best of intentions," Aida said.

"Of course you do. Wanted to visit the seedy side of town out of curiosity?"

"No," Aida blushed. The woman's comment was close to the truth. "That isn't the case at all. I represent an organization that would like to make a donation."

Several of the women laughed.

"Well, you can just hand that over to me," one of the women said.

"Don't you dare. She will just spend it on the devil."

"Shut up, Maisie, what do you know?"

"I know enough," the woman said before turning back to Aida. "Now, you were offering us some money?"

"Yes," Aida said, "which is why I would like to speak to whomever is in charge."

"You know, we aren't some kind of pitiful charity. Sure, we may be down on our luck, but we are human beings, and we have some pride."

"Agreed," another said.

The women who seemed to be the leader of the group stepped forward to face Aida. "We have seen your kind before, and don't think we don't know exactly what your motives are. You come here with your frilly pocketbook and throw us a few bucks to ease your conscious about your big fat fancy life so that you can sleep at night, thinking you have done your part to save the world. The worst of you are the ones who come to help. You want to get your hands dirty, but not really. We get to know you and we think you really care, but then you disappear, and we are left wondering what the hell we did. So which are you?"

"I don't know."

"Well, at least that's honest."

Aida took a deep breath. "Listen, I understand that from your point of view, I live in a completely different world. You are right. I do. I have never had to face the same kinds of obstacles that most of you have, but it doesn't mean that I haven't had hardship in my life, that I haven't had to fight for something I thought was important. We all have trials. They matter to us because they are ours.

My mother raised me with an awareness of others, especially those who want help, whose survival depends on it. She founded an orphanage, not for fame or glory, but because she saw a need and then, figured out a way to meet it. My twin sister is a nurse in a hospital, but on her days off runs a free clinic that she helped to start. You are right: when I compare my privileged life to theirs of service, I feel that I have come up short. But for all of you to assume that I am here to gawk or pry makes you as judgmental as the women you claim to resent.

I don't know how I may be of service to any of you. But I have a bank draft in my pocketbook that I would like to give to whomever is in charge. It may not be the help you are looking for, but it will keep a roof over your heads and your bellies full. At least for a few months."

A tall woman with broad shoulders and curly black hair appeared from the shadows and began to applaud. "Very nice. Most of our visitors don't have two words to say. That was pretty impressive."

Aida blushed.

"I am Gretchen McMahon. I suppose you are looking for me since I am the house mother here."

She offered her hand.

Aida thought that her eyes were kind, yet filled with fire. She was obviously a woman who had lived. "Nice to meet you, Mrs. McMahon."

The woman laughed. "Call me Gretchen."

"I'm Aida. Aida Slater." She thought it more prudent to use her maiden name than the fancy de la Martinique that her husband had bestowed upon her. And she certainly didn't want to reveal that she was the wife of a viscount.

"Well, Mrs. Slater. Come into my office and let's talk a bit."

Aida nodded and followed her into a small space which barely contained the wooden desk.

"Sit," she said, pointing to a chair. "And now, how can I help you? As you can see, we don't get many visitors. The girls tend to be a little suspect when we do. I hope they didn't intimidate you."

"No," Aida lied. "I wanted to deliver this myself. It seemed more personal to do so." She reached into her pocketbook and removed the envelope. "I hope that you will be satisfied with the amount of the donation. Truth be told, my mother-in-law enlisted me to do the fund raising. Under most circumstances, I have little patience for the women who run the charity circuit for the very reasons that those women out there expressed. It is all very shallow, and I can't help but wonder about their intentions. It's rather ironic for me to say that, isn't it?"

"Hmmm. Well, now, that's unusual."

"What is?"

"An honest, down-to-earth rich woman. I didn't think it was possible."

"I hope that is what I am."

"Unless you are play acting, that is what I see. That's pretty refreshing," Gretchen said. "I like you, Mrs. Slater."

"Please, call me Aida."

Gretchen nodded. "Our home exists for women who have found themselves down on their luck for various reasons. Sure, lots of them were prostitutes, but not all. Many have been abused or became alcoholics. We give them a bed and a meal, but we also work to help them enter mainstream society once more. Several of them have jobs during the day, doing laundry or dishwashing. It is hard to convince them that honest work is better than selling yourself, especially since a hooker can make a lot more than a chambermaid. But some of our biggest success stories have gone on to become secretaries, nurses. Nobody would ever suspect their past. And that's what keeps me doing this, Aida."

"It sounds like noble work."

"I'd like to think so. We are supposed to do what we can to help each other, right?"

"Indeed we are." It was her mother's philosophy, one she lived by as well. "I was wondering if maybe there was something I could do. You know, besides this." She pointed to the check resting on the desk.

"If you are serious, and willing to make a commitment, then, yes, of course. Most of our girls can't read and write. They don't know basic math. I am assuming that you are an educated woman?"

Aida nodded.

"Then, how would you like to teach a class. Once a week, maybe?"

For most of her life, Aida had felt impassioned about the rights of women. Certainly literacy was a right. If the time ever comes where we are able to vote, she thought, that knowledge would ensure that we are informed as well. This seemed like an ideal first step toward advocacy. She smiled.

"Yes. Absolutely. I think it would be a perfect arrangement for both of us."

"Good. Then, we will expect you next Tuesday, let's say around 2?"

Aida did the calculations in her head. Michel was rarely home on time, but if he was, she could still be there to greet him. "Perfect."

"Just one stipulation."

"Yes?"

"This can't be a one-time shot. I need your word. You heard those women. They have had their hearts broken many times by people they thought had their interests in mind, but ultimately, were self-serving."

"I will do my very best. You have my promise. And now, I have a favor to ask of you in return."

"Certainly."

"Can you help me get a carriage back home? I am afraid that I wouldn't know how to begin."

Gretchen laughed. "Guess, you are still a bit of a pampered lady after all. In a few weeks, you will be adept at arranging transportation. Trust me, Harlem will feel like your own neighborhood. Things are changing here. Apartments and business are being built, which means growth. We are invested in this community. Soon you will be, too."

"I think you may be right, Gretchen." Aida said. "It will be interesting to see what the future holds. For both of us."

CHAPTER THIRTY-SIX

Gretchen was right: after a month of regular visits to the Women's Center of Hope, Aida had developed a routine for getting to and from Harlem without a hitch. Her new driver appeared like clockwork on Tuesday afternoons at half past one, and when she left the center at four, he was there, curbside, waiting for her. She paid him handsomely for his dedication and his discretion, but she considered it a worthwhile investment and the arrangement, mutually beneficial.

On her first visit to the center, she brought supplies, books she had culled from her own personal library, a few extra pens with two ink wells and a package of paper she had procured from the stationary shop around the corner from her house. The women, unaccustomed to having such items around, poked fun as she unpacked each one and placed them on the table.

"What do you expect us to do with this?" Maisie asked, holding up a leather bound poetry journal.

"We shall read them," Aida said.

"Well, maybe you will," one of the women added, "but most of us can't read nor write our own names, not even if our lives depended on it."

Many nodded in agreement.

"I am here to rectify that," Aida said, as though teaching was the most natural thing in the world to her.

"Are you going to show us how to hold our pinkies up as well?" Maisie asked, and the other women burst into laughter.

"If that's what it takes to turn you into educated ladies, then, yes."

That brought about even more laughter. "Well, you got part of it right. Some of us have been called 'ladies of the evening.' "

Aida chose to ignore the comment. "Well, then, ladies, have a seat; I want to share something with you."

She opened the book and began to read:

> *"Shall I compare thee to a summer's day?*
> *Thou art more lovely and more temperate.*
> *Rough winds do shake the darling buds of May*
> *And summer's lease has all too short a date:*
> *Sometimes too hot the eye of heaven shines*
> *And often is his gold complexion dimmed,*
> *And every fair from fair sometimes declines,*
> *By chance, or nature's changing course untrimmed:*
> *But thy eternal summer shall not fade.*
> *Nor lose possession of the fair thou ow'st,*
> *Nor shall death brag though wander'st in his shade.*
> *When in eternal lines to time thou grow'st.*
> *So as long as men can breathe, or eyes can see,*
> *So long lives this, and this gives life to thee."*

"Sonnet number 18, by Mr. William Shakespeare," Aida said.

There was silence among the women. "Wow," Maisie finally said, "that's beautiful."

"It certainly is," Aida said. "The words are pretty, for sure. But what do you think it means?"

"He must have truly loved her, whoever she was. So romantic."

"I am sure that he did," Aida said. "He compares her to everything important that we might possibly imagine, right?"

"Yup. And then some," one of the women said. "Wish I could find me a man like that."

The other women laughed and then, nodded in agreement.

"But consider this," Aida said. "The poem was written 175 years ago. So how do we even know that this woman lived?"

"You just read it to us."

"Ah. So if Shakespeare had not used his considerable talent to celebrate this woman by writing about her, we might never have understood the power of what he felt, right?"

They nodded.

"So to write about her, goes beyond all of those things he claims is beautiful. It makes her immortal"

"What does that mean? Maisie asked.

"She can never die," one of the other women said.

"That's right," Aida said, "Why is that so?"

"Because we are still reading his words."

"Yes," Aida said, clapping her hands. "Do you not see why it is so important to learn to read and write? These things have withstood the test of time."

"Like the *Bible*. We still read that."

"You need to," Maisie said. The others laughed.

"The *Bible* is a perfect example. Can you name anything else?"

"The Declaration of Independence? Somebody once told me about it, although I can't quite recollect who it is. Anyway, I saw it once when I ducked into the court building one day, looking for a place to keep warm. I couldn't read it, but it sure looked impressive."

"That's a perfect example, although I am sure what you saw was a copy," Aida said. "Want to know my favorite line from that document?"

"Do you know it by heart, Aida?" one of the women asked.

"I do. 'We hold these truths to be self-evident, that all men are created equal, that they are endowed by their Creator to have certain unalienable rights, that among these are life, liberty and the pursuit of happiness.' "

"Wow. That's pretty good. Do you believe that, Aida?" a woman named Rose asked.

"I do. We all have the right to live in freedom, to be happy and successful. All of us."

"Even women?"

"Especially women. We are in charge of training the children. We need to be educated. And learning how to read is the first step toward that for each of you. Now who's ready to start?"

"Me," Maisie said.

One by one, the women raised their hands. Aida was quite satisfied with her first day of school.

CHAPTER THIRTY-SEVEN

Angelique entered the dining room at half past seven. It was a routine she had followed almost daily since opening the doors to the orphanage five years previously. Having breakfast with the children was important to them, but it was also important to her, and often, it was the best part of her day.

"Good morning, Momma," the children said in unison.

"Good morning." She smiled. Sometimes, she felt like the little old lady who lived in the shoe from the nursery rhyme, but the title brought her great joy. The need was ever-present, and most of the time, the orphanage was filled to capacity. Nevertheless, she had given strict orders to the staff that they were never to turn a child away. As a result, there was often overcrowding, with some children sleeping on floor pallets rather than in a real bed. That bothered her, but she rationalized it by imagining the alternative for those with no family and no place to live.

Thanks to Aida's ongoing fundraising and a few local benefactors, she managed to keep a roof over everybody's head and food in their bellies. Aimee and Franklin tended to their medical needs. The clinic building behind the orphanage had been a godsend on more than one occasion. She had carefully selected the staff, especially the teachers. That, she had come to understand, was the secret to happy children. But she also had to worry about their monthly salaries as well.

It was a delicate dance, for sure, but Angelique knew the steps by heart, and how she loved the children she served.

"What are we having this morning?" Angelique asked.

"What we always have," a boy about eight years old said, "oatmeal and bread with jam."

"Do you know why?" Angelique asked the boy.

He shook his head.

"Because it is my favorite!"

The children began to laugh. Angelique was sure that they would have loved eggs, perhaps with sausages on the side, but such an extravagance was not possible, especially with a three meal a day requirement to fulfill. The menu varied, based upon what the head cook could find in quantity and at a good price when she went to market, but there was food always, a fact that gave her a great sense of pride. No child went to sleep hungry. Not ever.

"Whose turn is it to offer the blessing this morning?" Angelique asked.

A little girl with dark hair and blue eyes shyly raised her hand. She smiled brightly, revealing a missing front tooth. Angelique thought of how much she resembled Aida and Aimee at that age. How she missed those days when her own children were so young. "You are Suzanna, are you not?"

The child giggled, "Yes, ma'am."

"Well, then, Suzanna, you may begin."

"God is great. God is good. And we thank him for this food. Amen."

"That was perfect," Angelique said. "Now everyone, eat before it gets cold. School begins in just fifteen minutes."

There was the clanging of spoons and high pitched laughter as the children ate. Angelique spoke to those who sat close to her, a privilege earned for good behavior. The teachers had figured out an elaborate reward system, which was overwhelmingly successful. The children loved being first in line or carrying the flag for the morning salute, and they worked hard to be recognized among so many.

Angelique smiled. She was filled with joy as she surveyed the room. The Countess would have been pleased too, she thought. This was a wise investment of the inheritance from her dear friend. She had never doubted that.

One by one, the children brought their bowls into the kitchen and hurried down the hall into the classroom, the echoes of their laughter filling the air. Angelique retired to her office for an hour or so of paperwork before returning to her home and the duties which awaited her there.

She had just settled in behind her desk when the secretary appeared. "You have a visitor, Miss Angelique."

"Really? Who?" There were people who occasionally came to call, vendors keen on selling whatever product they thought they could get her to buy or someone eagerly looking for a job. She welcomed the new volunteers, although those were few and far between. But the best visits were from those looking for a child to adopt, although she had learned to carefully screen them. More than once, she had managed to discover motives that were less than pure. She was not in the business of providing children to work in the family's kitchen or fields, she would announce, adding that she would insist on follow up visits that she would personally make. That often deterred those folks. And she had become quite adept at sizing people up while learning of their true intentions. And so, she trusted the adoption process to no one but herself.

"A young couple. They have the Bishop with them!"

"Show them in."

"My dear Mrs. Slater," the Bishop said, offering his hand.

"Bishop. What a pleasure to see you. It has been a very long time since you paid us a visit."

"Far too long, I'm afraid. The duties of the Diocese keep me busy. But I have it on good authority that you are doing quite well here and that the children are thriving. I can't tell you how much it pleases me."

"Well, I know that you took a chance on us, on me really, so long ago. There have been challenging days, of course, but most of the time, things run rather smoothly."

"So many orphaned babies who have come through the church have made this their home. It is comforting to me to know that you stand ready to welcome them, bless their tiny souls."

"I love all of the children who live here, Bishop, but I must admit that I have a soft place in my heart for the infants. Being born into this world and then losing one's parents so soon afterwards is, I believe, one of the greatest tragedies to befall a human being. It breaks my heart."

"Fortunately you stand ready to remedy that situation. We are most grateful to you."

"It has been my privilege to serve," Angelique said. "I hope to be able to carry on until my days on this earth are done."

"That certainly is my prayer as well, Mrs. Slater." He turned to the couple he had brought along. "Please forgive me for not making proper introductions. May I present Mr. and Mrs. Dupont? I have known their respective families for years. When they asked me to come along for moral support, I happily obliged."

Angelique smiled. "Nice to meet you. Welcome." She pointed to the settee and chair. "Please sit. May I offer you some coffee?"

"No, thanks. We had some earlier," the Bishop said.

"Very well, then," Angelique said. "May I ask the nature of your visit?"

"Of course," the Bishop replied. "I suppose I should have made that clear from the start. The Duponts would like to adopt a child."

"Oh my, that's wonderful. I am happy to help you with the process. There are so many here who deserve a home with loving parents. I hope that this visit will prove to be successful. May I ask you a few questions? I am afraid that I am quite protective." So far, neither had said a word, and she certainly had no intention of allowing the Bishop to speak for them. Without skipping a beat, she continued. "Why are you considering adoption?"

The woman immediately began to cry, pulling a lace handkerchief from her purse to wipe away the tears.

"I am afraid that it is far too painful for my wife to discuss," Mr. Dupont said. "We have tried to have a child for many years now, to no avail. The doctor recently confirmed that she is barren."

Angelique winced, and then hoped that no one had noticed. It was a word that she found offensive, a label placed on women that somehow diminished their value. Motherhood was a role most aspired to and when, through no fault of their own, that possibility had been taken from them, it was heartbreaking. She thought of Aida who had already lost one baby. She wondered if someday she, too, would be unable to bear a child. She turned her focus to the couple. "I am so sorry. It happens, unfortunately." She had no other words of condolence to offer without sounding condescending. "I will do my best to place you with the right child to complete your family."

"We surely would be so grateful," Mr. Dupont said.

"How long have you been married?" Angelique asked.

"Four years, ma'am. We are ready to expand our family."

"Your home?"

"In town. It is modest, but comfortable. And we have a little yard."

"That's nice. Perfect for a child. Shall we take a walk, then? The children are in school. We can visit the classroom. There is also a nursery for the babies and little ones. Have you a preference? Boy or girl? A certain age?"

"My wife has her heart set on a baby, I think."

Angelique turned to the woman. "Is that so?"

The woman nodded.

They began in the nursery. The couple walked along the rows of cribs, peering into the faces of swaddled infants. The wife stopped to gently rub the head of a baby boy, before moving on to the toddlers. The husband picked up a ball and gently tossed it to a little boy about three, who giggled with glee as he chased it across the hardwood floor. "Again," he said, handing it back. Their game lasted for a few moments until both seemed to grow tired of it.

This part was always unnerving for Angelique. She hated having the children on display like wares in a store. Certainly, these people weren't choosing a puppy to bring home. These were human beings, precious souls who simply wanted to be loved. "Shall we visit the classroom now?"

The teacher was in the midst of a reading lesson. The older children were in the back of the room, reading from a primer, while the younger ones were up front, reciting the alphabet as the teacher pointed to each letter. "Children, we have a visitor," she announced, curtseying in deference to the Bishop. "Can you say, 'good morning?' "

"Good morning," the children responded in unison.

"This is Mr. and Mrs. Dupont, children," Angelique said. "Aren't we fortunate to have them come to see us today? Please, carry on with your studies. We are just here to observe for a bit. I have told them how smart you all are."

"Who knows what letter this is?" the teacher asked.

Several of the children raised their hands. "Frederick?"

"It is an F," Frederick said. "My name begins with that letter."

"Excellent," the teacher said, "You are right. Can you all make the 'F' sound?"

They all complied.

"Now can any of you give me a word that begins with 'F?' "

"Fox," a little boy called out.

"That is correct," the teacher said, "but please raise your hand. Now, can someone make a sentence with the word fox?"

"Gerald?"

"The fox was in the barnyard and chased the chickens."

"Very good. Does someone have another word that begins with an 'F'?"

A little girl raised her hand, "Yes, Suzanna?"

"Family. Someday I will have a family."

The other children laughed. "You wish," one of the boys teased.

"Stop it," Suzanna said. "It could happen."

The teacher frowned. "That's enough, children. I am ready for you to identify another letter. Who knows this one?"

Angelique turned to the Bishop and the Duponts. "Shall we go out into the hall?" she whispered

"Now then," she said, once they had left the classroom. "At this point, I would suggest that you spend some additional time with the children whom you think might be a good addition to your family. We can return to my office, and I will have them brought to you one at a time."

"That won't be necessary," Mrs. Dupont said.

Everyone turned to face her. "What do you mean, dear?" her husband asked.

"I have already decided."

"So quickly?" Angelique said. "I urge you to make sure. We have had a few unfortunate situations where people have chosen a son or daughter without truly weighing the seriousness of their decision, only to change their minds a few days later. As you can imagine, such a situation can be heartbreaking for a child. I do my best not to let that happen."

"I can assure you that it will not," the woman said.

Angelique was struck by the fact that Mrs. Dupont had already spoken more in the past minute than she had all morning. "So will you share your thoughts with us?" she asked.

"Yes," said Mr. Dupont. "I am curious as well. Is there one baby in particular?"

"No baby," said Mrs. Dupont. "I want the little girl in the classroom, the one with dark hair and blue eyes. She wanted a family as much as I do."

"Suzanna?" Angelique asked.

"Yes. Suzanna is about to become my daughter."

"Are you sure you don't want an infant? I thought you had your heart set on a little one?" Mr. Dupont said.

"There is something about her. I can't explain it. It was as though a voice whispered in my ear 'pick me.' "

"Then, I will send for her straight away."

Minutes later, the secretary returned, holding the little girl by the hand.

"Come here, Suzanna," Angelique said. "I thought you might want to talk to Mr. and Mrs. Dupont for a while. They were very anxious to meet you."

Mrs. Dupont moved to the settee and patted the seat beside her. "Please, Suzanna, sit with me for a moment."

The girl did as she was told.

"So may I ask you what your favorite color is?"

"Blue" Suzanna, said, "the color of the sky."

"And your eyes," Mrs. Dupont added.

Suzanna nodded. "Where do you live?" she asked.

Angelique smiled. Somehow the tables were being turned on the interview.

"Not very far from here."

"Do you have any little boys or girls?"

"No, but I hope to very soon."

"Really? Do you have a baby in your tummy?"

Mrs. Dupont sighed, but kept her composure. "No, but I think one has come to live in my heart."

Suzanna giggled. "That's not where babies come from, you know."

"You are right," Mrs. Dupont said, "But it is where love grows."

"In here?" Suzanna asked, pointing to her own chest.

"Yes. Do you know who is in mine at this very instant?"

"No, who?"

"You are, Suzanna. Mr. Dupont and I would be honored if you would agree to have us as your parents. What do you say? Would you like to come and live with us?"

Suzanna smiled. "Truly? Do you want me to be your little girl?

"We do," Mr. Dupont said.

Suzanna turned to Angelique. "What do you think, Momma?'

"I think it is a fine idea," Angelique said.

"Then, yes," Suzanna said.

"God is good," the Bishop pronounced. "I feel like I have witnessed something quite sacred."

"Sir," Suzanna said.

"Yes?" answered the Bishop, bending on one knee to face the child.

"God is everywhere, you know. I have talked to Him every night after bedtime prayers, asking for a family of my own. Momma always told us that God listens, especially to little children. Now, I know that is the truth."

Angelique smiled. "He certainly does, my dear. I am so pleased that your prayers were answered. Now, let's get you packed for your new home."

The secretary offered her hand to Suzanne, who waved goodbye to everyone. "Don't leave until I get back," she said.

"We won't," Mr. Dupont said.

"Mrs. Slater," the Bishop said, "you are doing God's work here. I have no doubt about that. I have a proposal I would like to make to you. Perhaps you can come to my office in a few days so that we can discuss it."

"Certainly, Bishop."

Angelique turned to Mr. and Mrs. Dupont. "It has been a pleasure to meet you both. Suzanna is a special little girl. I know that she will be a wonderful addition to your family. Certainly, I am going to miss seeing her sweet face. I have some papers for you to sign, of course, so let me get those prepared for you. Then, you all can celebrate."

"Thank you, Mrs. Slater. I never thought that this day would come, but yes, we have much to celebrate. Today, I became a mother."

"You will be an excellent one," Angelique said, offering the woman a hug. "I have no doubt in my mind."

CHAPTER THIRTY-EIGHT

SUMMER, 1878

Aimee wiped away a tear with the back of her hand. She hadn't told Franklin about her application to medical school, hoping that she could surprise him with the news of her acceptance. So when the rejection letter came in the mail, she was disappointed. Actually, it was much more than that. The possibility of never being able to practice medicine beyond her limited role as a nurse was heartbreaking. She had all of the qualifications necessary to be a good doctor. Her references were stellar. Apparently, the only obstacle was her gender. Society had changed in so many ways, she thought, except when it came to the rights of women. It was unfair, pure and simple. In that moment, as she tore up the letter and tossed it into the trash, she understood why her sister had been so passionate about equality. And she prepared to join the fight.

She had been at work at the hospital for an hour when the first group of victims from the warehouse fire had arrived. The staff sprang into action, assessing the most critical first, assigning them to a treatment area based on the severity of the injuries. Some, had suffered from smoke inhalation and were placed in front of open windows in order to clear their lungs. Others had minor burns. Franklin and the other surgical staff moved in to help those who were most seriously hurt.

"Aimee," Franklin called. "Get as many clean bandages as you can find, along with clear water and sponges. I believe that there may be some additional morphine in the cabinet in the operating room on this floor. "Round up the nurses who are not with patients to help. We need all available hands."

Aimee had gathered what she could find and she, along with three other nurses, distributed the supplies to the doctors, who began the treatment process. The sound of screams pierced the air as the staff worked to clean the burns as gently as they could.

"It is one of the most painful things imaginable," Franklin said as she appeared at his side with a jar of salve. "I dread seeing this kind of patient more than anything."

"Please," the man on the table begged, "help me."

"We will do what we can," Franklin said.

"What if we used the chloroform?" Aimee asked. "Just in small amounts, but enough to put these men out of their misery while we treat the wounds."

"Of course," Franklin said. "It is a compassionate thing to do. How much do we have here?"

"On this floor? Half of what would be sufficient."

"Then bring that to me and search the hospital. Bring any surplus here beyond what is needed in the surgical suites."

"Will do."

Aimee had removed half of the second floor supply of chloroform and a few extra bandages before returning to Franklin. "This is all I could find. It will have to be sufficient. The quantity of morphine stock is very low."

"I think that there is a stock room on the third floor. You might check there."

"The third floor? I didn't think there was such a place."

"Well, I do believe that it is more or less attic space. I know that John has managed to find supplies up there when there were none to be had. He said that there were old beds and tables, waiting to be pressed into service if need be. Maybe that's a secret storage space to keep us from hoarding things. Who knows? Take the stairs next to ward three. I think that is the only way to access it."

Aimee nodded. "I'll go and have a look."

"Aimee?"

"Yes?"

"Bring a lamp. I assume that it is pretty dark up there."

"Will do."

"And one more thing?"

"Yes?"

"Be careful."

"Always," she said with a wink.

Aimee stopped at the nurse's desk. "I am taking the extra lamp for a little while," she said to her friend Miranda.

"What are you up to?"

"Trying to find a clandestine storage closet."

"Sounds rather intriguing," Miranda said. "Let me know what you discover. Who knows? Could contain hidden treasure."

"I doubt it," Aimee said, "but if there is, we will split it."

"Deal."

Aimee lit the lamp and made her way up the darkened stairway. The third floor was exactly like the two below, although it looked like a graveyard, a repository for every broken piece of furniture and equipment that had been cast aside in the past few years. She held up the lamp, trying not to trip, as she searched for a possible supply closet. There were two doors, one nearby and the other at the end of the long hall. Both were securely shut, and Aimee hesitated for a moment, wondering which she should try first. The closer one made more sense, and when she twisted the knob, it easily opened. She exhaled loudly and then laughed, unaware that she had been holding her breath. The shelves in the room held a few boxes, enameled bedpans, and several beakers. One of the boxes, she discovered, held the bandages she needed, along with chloroform and a lone vial of morphine. Satisfied that she had obtained what she was looking for, she closed the door behind her and made her way to the stairwell.

"Ohhhhh." The noise of a low groan, echoed through the darkened hall.

She stopped, and listened for it again, wondering if her imagination was playing tricks on her in the stillness of the eerie space.

"No, no, no." There was desperation in the voice, which was most certainly that of a female.

Could it possibly be spirits, Aimee wondered as she felt herself shiver? Surely, many people had died in the rooms below where she stood. If their souls were not at rest, perhaps they wandered the halls of this very floor. She had heard tales of such places.

She turned on her heels, resolved to leave as quickly as she could.

"My baby," another called, as clearly as if it was nearby. The sound came from the end of the hall. Of that Aimee was certain.

She lifted the lamp to illuminate the space. Slowly, she made her way to the second door and placed her hand on the knob. It was locked. She tried again. But it still refused to budge, even as she pushed with all of her might. She placed her ear to the door and listened. The low, hollow hums of high pitched wails resonated in the distance.

Something or someone was in there, she thought. And the sound of their cries haunted her just as surely as if they were ghosts. Some situations are impossible to walk away from, and Aimee knew that this was one of those. Reluctantly, she made her way to the stairs and the hospital below.

"I'll be back," she whispered. "I will help you." She didn't know when or how, but she knew that it was a promise she fully intended to keep.

CHAPTER THIRTY-NINE

"Well?" Miranda asked, as Aimee returned the lamp. "Did you discover a vault filled with gold coins? I get half, remember?"

"No," Aimee said, still shaken by the experience, "but I did discover a rather unnerving mystery."

"Really? Do tell."

"I will in a bit. Have to get these supplies to Franklin and his team. But I am going to need your help to figure it out."

"Now you have me all curious, Aimee," Miranda said, "hurry back."

"Soon as I can," Aimee said.

"Goodness, you look like you have seen a ghost," Franklin said, searching her face. "I wondered what took you so long. I was about to send a search party after you."

Aimee forced a smile. Franklin knew her so well that it was hard to hide her emotions from him. But he was busy, running from one patient to another. This was not the time to discuss the phantom voices in the hospital attic. She wasn't so sure if she ever would, at least not until she had done a bit of investigating on her own.

"Here," Aimee said, "you were right about the supplies hidden away, although not the great surplus you might have imagined. Fortunately, there were bandages and chloroform and a bit of morphine."

"Great. I was afraid that you might have found it empty. You never know if somebody had beat us to it and wiped out what was there."

"That's true, but fortunately for our patients it didn't happen," Aimee said. "Not sure how many people even know that the place exists. How many times have I been in ward 3 and yet, I have never noticed the stairwell? It is rather well concealed by screens. Not sure if that is accidental or on purpose."

"I am sure it is on purpose, to keep folks from exploring on their own. Makes sense to me."

Aimee nodded. Or was it to keep people from discovering what was truly being hidden, she wondered?

"Come. I need your help. The patient in bed five requires surgery. His hand has been burned beyond any hope of saving. I rarely suggest amputation as a course of action, but this time it is my only option. Will you assist me?"

Those kinds of surgeries were the most difficult for her emotionally, and she was always relieved when her help wasn't required. But she and Franklin worked so well as a team, often reading each other's minds while in the operating room. When she was by his side, it was as though he had four hands instead of two, which made a positive outcome more likely. She put her personal feelings aside on such occasions. She sometimes had to remind herself that it was the professional thing to do.

"Of course," she said. "Shall I prepare for the procedure?"

"Yes. Operating room two should be available. Check there first. I will inform the patient."

An hour later they wheeled the young man into the recovery ward. Mercifully, he was still unconscious, oblivious to the pain and his altered physical condition. It was the patient's initial discovery of the missing limb that always tore at Aimee's heart, the tears of sadness shed by stout-hearted men who wondered if they would ever experience life in the same way as they once had. She breathed a sigh of relief after delivering the patient to the charge nurse and apprising her of his after-surgery care.

"I need a break," she whispered to Franklin. "It has been a long day, and it appears that it won't get any easier. Can I have thirty minutes or so?"

"Of course, my darling," Franklin said. "I tend to overwork you sometimes, and I am truly sorry for that. Take the time you need."

Aimee nodded and then returned to the nurse's station in search of Miranda.

She was completing a patient's chart. "I never get used to having to write down every single thing," Miranda said.

"None of us do," Aimee said, "but at least it gives you a chance to sit."

"True," Miranda said. She placed the paper and inkwell on the counter and leaned on her elbow. "Now, do tell me what you found upstairs."

"Honestly, I don't know. But there is something strange happening up there."

"Strange? Define strange."

"I heard voices, high pitched like they belong to women."

"Are you sure you weren't hallucinating from fatigue? You do work very long hours trying to keep up with that husband of yours."

"I realize that it sounds irrational. At first, I thought I was hearing things, too, but then, I followed the sounds."

"And?"

"They came from the end of the hall. There is a locked door behind which I do believe there is some kind of ward, hidden away."

"A ward?"

"Yes, I put my ear to the door. I am certain that there are women sealed away in there."

"That makes no sense, Aimee. Who could it be? There are sanitariums for the insane. De Paul's just opened a new facility a month ago. The Sisters of Charity used to have a ward on the first floor, but that has long been closed, converted to a maternity ward."

"I know what I heard, Miranda."

Miranda looked at the clock in the hall. "How long would it take for you and I to investigate? I mean a quick trip up there and back?'

Aimee shrugged. "Five minutes? Maybe a little longer. You won't be missed, will you?"

"I don't think so. Most of the patients are asleep. Let's do it. This seems to bother you, Aimee, and I must admit, I am more than a little curious. Do we need the lamp?"

"Yes, there are windows at the landing, but otherwise, the hall is quite dark."

Miranda lifted the lamp and nodded. "Quickly, then."

The two women walked down the hall to ward 3, then around the screen to the stairwell.

At the top of the stairs, Miranda lifted the lamp. "So this is where they bring every broken piece of furniture and equipment."

"Yes," Aimee said. "Not sure why they keep these things, since they will never press them into service again. But be careful. It is definitely a trip hazard."

"Down there," Aimee said, pointing to the end of the hall.

"Ohhhhhhh," a voice echoed through the still space.

"Did you hear that?" Aimee asked.

"Loud and clear," Miranda said. "Try the door. Let's see if it is locked."

"I did earlier. I don't think that's changed." Aimee placed her hand on the knob and turned. It refused to budge. She tried again. "No, it is not going to open."

"Listen," Miranda whispered. "I hear crying."

"So now you know that I haven't lost my mind, right?"

"I never doubted you, Aimee, but let's get out of here. Maybe we can figure this out downstairs."

Once back at the nurse's station, Miranda looked at the clock. "Five minutes exactly. And it appears no one even noticed my absence."

"I've got a bit longer before Franklin expects me back. What do you think it is, Miranda?"

"I have no idea, a mystery, for sure."

"How do we gain access?"

Miranda's eye grew wide. "Are you really thinking of breaking in?"

"No," Aimee said, "but I am wondering how to find the key to that door."

"That might not be possible," Miranda said. "But certainly someone makes regular visits up there. Those people have to be fed, right?"

"Unless they are ghosts."

"Sounds like real people to me. I say if we are able to see when that happens during the day, we might be

able to figure out how to get in," Aimee said.

"Follow that person in, you mean?"

"Well, that could prove tricky, unless you can figure out how to become invisible. But you might see where they keep the key."

"Makes sense," Miranda said.

"When do you work on ward 3 again?" Aimee asked. "Franklin keeps me in the surgical area, so it might prove difficult for me to keep an eye out."

"I am there next Tuesday and Wednesday. Honestly, Aimee, I can't help but wonder how many times someone passed me on their way up there, and I simply didn't notice."

"Might not have been as often as you might think."

"Really, what makes you say that?" Miranda asked.

"I would assume that they visit the women in the wee hours of the morning or perhaps late at night. It is the only way to escape detection. You can't exactly carry a tray of food through the hall and then disappear with it and not have someone wonder where you are going."

"That's true."

"I work the night shift week after next, and I will be in ward 3 Thursday evening. If they are making visits up there, I will know about it."

"That's what I like about you, Miranda. You are always up for a challenge."

"Look, Aimee, I am as concerned about those women as you are. If something sinister is going on, then, I think we owe it to them to help. We have to try."

"I certainly hope so," Aimee said. "Lives could be hanging in the balance."

"We make a good team," Miranda said.

"If nursing doesn't work out, we can become private investigators," Aimee said.

"Well, let's hope we don't uncover something that can get us fired," Miranda said. "I am not so keen on starting a new career."

Aimee nodded. She hadn't considered the possible implications. But she knew that it was a chance she was willing to take.

CHAPTER FORTY

Miranda passed Aimee in the hall and whispered, "I have information to share."

Aimee's eyes widened. "Have you seen something?"

Miranda nodded. "I think I know the pattern. I'll tell you all about it when we can chat."

"How about lunch? I can sweet talk Franklin into giving me a break whenever I need it. He can't replace me, and he knows it."

"Well, it helps when you sleep with the boss."

Aimee blushed. "I suppose that is true, but I would hope that he also gives me a bit of credit for how hard I work."

"I am just teasing. I should be able to get away in an hour. How about if you meet me in front of the hospital? We can take a walk. I don't think it is a good idea to talk about this where others might hear."

"Really? Certainly people know we are friends," Aimee said. "Do you think we have aroused suspicion?"

"I don't think so, but I am not sure. Let's face it: if what we think is true, there is something mighty secretive going on around here."

"You are right, of course. We can't be too careful."

"At noon, then?" Miranda asked.

"Yes. I'll be waiting on the steps." Aimee said.

The nearby church bell tower rang out, indicating it was the middle of the day. Miranda appeared exactly on time.

"So do tell what you have uncovered," Aimee said, anxious to learn what she could.

"Let's walk a bit, shall we?" Miranda suggested.

Aimee nodded.

"Just as we suspected, I saw nobody enter or leave the stairwell entrance on the days I worked in ward 3," Miranda said. "But out of my own curiosity, I stayed a little later, and sure enough, a maid appeared with a full food tray at half past six and disappeared behind the screen. I think the timing was interesting since it is when the day shift leaves and the next one comes in to replace them. Most people are too busy to notice a maid when they are busy, right?"

"Yes, of course," Aimee said. "Anything else?"

"This is where I made my biggest discovery," Miranda said. "I pretended to be busy with a patient, but I watched where the maid went afterwards. She returned to the pantry that services the ward."

"What did she do in there?"

"At first, I wasn't sure. It took me a while to figure it out, but after a careful inspection of every inch of that place, I found it."

"What, Miranda? Goodness, the suspense is killing me."

"A key, Aimee. I found a key, hanging on a peg inside the cabinet used to store the brooms. Evidently, she had returned it to its hiding spot."

Aimee exhaled, the possibilities whirling through her mind. "Makes sense. So now we have access."

"If my hunch is correct, then, yes. I assume that it will open the locked door. But there is more."

"More?"

"Yes. I traded my shift so that I could be in ward 3 the next night. I knew that they weren't just sending a tray of food up there and leaving it at that."

"Goodness Miranda, you are amazing. What did you uncover?"

"There was a nurse who appeared later in the evening."

"A nurse?"

"Yes. I don't know who she is, so she must not be a part of the hospital staff, although I am sure that I don't know everybody who works here," Miranda said. "She uses an outside entrance that I thought was only to be accessed in case of emergency, like if we needed to evacuate the hospital."

"That's strange."

"I thought so, too. I suppose like everything else surrounding this mystery, the reason was to keep her comings and goings as secret as possible."

"Late at night, the hospital operates with a smaller workforce. Anything else?" Aimee asked.

"Did she use the hidden key?"

"No, so I assume that she has her own."

"That would make sense."

"Yes. I think this is the most significant bit of information," Miranda said.

Aimee stopped and turned to her friend. "Most significant? What is it?"

"A nun came to visit very early in the morning, around daybreak. She was carrying a sack, which I assumed was food."

"How bizarre."

"The whole thing is bizarre, Aimee."

"Which is why I am more determined than ever to see what or who lies beyond the locked door," Aimee said.

"Listen, I think that you should discuss this with Franklin. He has been a part of this hospital for a long time and is well respected. If there is something menacing going on, you want him to do the investigating."

Aimee sighed. "I suppose you are right. But he is so busy, working long days that would exhaust anyone. I have witnessed him fall asleep at the dinner table in the middle of a meal."

Miranda laughed. "How romantic."

"I knew of his dedication when I married him, and I usually don't mind being second. I know how important his work is to him and the patients he serves," Aimee said, "but that is also why I don't want to lay some new burden on him. Couldn't you and I investigate and include him once we have a little more information to share?"

"I guess we could. If you think that is the wisest course of action."

"I do."

"But promise me that once we have a better idea of what is happening, we will involve Franklin and anybody else in a position to do something."

"Of course. I am not foolish enough to think that you and I can handle something with this kind of potential implication."

"Good," Miranda said. "We agree on that."

"But what if it is a harmless situation, one we have misconstrued? What if it is simply an overflow ward placed there because there is no available space in the hospital?" Aimee asked.

"Do you really believe that?" Miranda asked.

"No. But anything is possible."

"That's true. But not plausible. And Aimee?"

"Yes?"

"Don't go off investigating this on your own. Who knows what the situation might be. It could be dangerous. Doors are usually locked for protection."

"Or because there is something to hide."

"Or both."

"I promise. If I decide to go up there, you will know about it. You would be my safety factor, my surefire escape, right? I mean just in case there are monsters, ready to swallow me up whole. I'd depend on you to rescue me."

"Don't even joke about that, Aimee. It would be foolish to attempt such a thing by yourself."

"I have been known to do some foolish things on occasion."

"Promise me that your curiosity won't get the best of you. We are in this together."

"Together. That much I can promise," Aimee said as she reached into the pocket of her apron. "Here," she said, handing an apple to Miranda. "I brought you some lunch."

"Great," Miranda said. "I was starving."

CHAPTER FORTY-ONE

The moonlight streamed through the tall window. Mother Nature had provided the earth with a nightlight, Aimee thought, and then smiled at the absurdity of it. The rhythm of Franklin's breathing was both comforting and unnerving, and for a moment, she was envious of his ability to sleep so soundly, leaving behind the worries of the day. She wondered what time it was, and based on how long she had lain there, figured that it was probably close to 2.a.m. She willed herself to close her eyes, knowing full well that she would be exhausted the next day without the much needed rest. And yet, her mind raced with possibilities. The meeting with Miranda had only fueled her desire to discover what secrets existed in the hospital attic. But there was more to it than that. She wanted to help. It was hard to erase the haunting sounds of the women crying, their desperation apparent through the locked door. This was no overflow ward, of that she was certain, but what it was, still remained a mystery. She turned over and whispered a prayer. Usually, those quiet moments with God calmed her, but even that was unable to stop the flow of thoughts, which like a raging river, seemed to have no end.

She was finally sleeping soundly when Franklin kissed her goodbye at daybreak. "I am off to the hospital, my love," he whispered. "Why don't you stay in bed for a while? You have been working so hard. I sense how tired you are."

Aimee wiped her eyes. "No, I'll get up. It won't take me long to dress."

"It isn't necessary. I only see patients in the morning today, and then, I am off to the University for a meeting. I suspect that it will last well into the evening, so don't worry if I am late."

"A meeting? You hadn't mentioned it."

"Sorry. I guess it slipped my mind. The collaboration is part of it. There will be training from a team visiting from Chicago. Some new surgical technique that we are all anxious to learn."

Aimee nodded.

"Get some rest. It is still early. The hospital will survive without the both of us today."

Aimee smiled as Franklin kissed her on the forehead. Within minutes, she was fast asleep.

She roused with a start sometime mid-morning. Her head pounded, and her arms felt heavy. She had been dreaming, she recalled, a vivid picture story, slowly unfolding in her mind. In it, she was climbing the hospital stairs until she reached the darkened hall. The door, once inaccessible, easily opened, and inside there were children of various ages, all dressed in the same white nightgown that she had worn before her mother had rescued her from the orphanage. For a fleeting moment, she was once again that scared five-year-old girl, staring out of the window, praying that she would be found. The images of that time, she realized, had stayed with her, as did the fear, buried deep in her mind and imprinted on her soul.

When she awoke, she was more resolved than ever. Whoever is trapped in that room on the third floor of the hospital is experiencing that very same terror, she thought. And it was time to stop thinking about it and do something.

It didn't take Aimee long to get up and dressed, but instead of donning her nursing uniform and apron, she wore street clothes. If she was to be nondescript, she needed to dress the part. And by the time she had arrived at the hospital forty-five minutes later, she had formulated a plan.

She appeared at the ward where Miranda usually worked, hoping that the two of them could finally explore the secrets of the locked room together.

"Miranda won't be here until six," the charge nurse said. "She is on night duty."

Aimee sighed. She hadn't planned on that. "Can I leave her a note?"

"Certainly."

Aimee remembered that she had called her friend her "safe escape," although it seemed like an unnecessary precaution since she had every intention to find out what she needed to know and be out by the time Miranda was back on duty. She hoped that she would be able to talk to Franklin later that night, too, getting his advice, based on what she would have uncovered.

"Can I have paper and a pen?"

The charge nurse slid both across the oak desk toward Aimee. She tried to be cryptic just in case someone was to read it. She knew that Miranda would understand.

Opportunity calls. I am off to investigate the situation, to answer our questions once and for all. Thanks for looking out for me. I will see you tomorrow. Aimee.

Aimee folded the note and handed it to the nurse. "Will you see to it that she gets it?"

"Not to worry. I will leave it here for her."

Aimee nodded and then headed toward the pantry in ward 3. There were a number of storage cabinets in the ample space, and she had opened more than half of them before finding the one that contained the brooms. And just as Miranda had said, there was a key on the peg inside. Actually, there were two, which Aimee hadn't been expecting. She removed them and held them in her hands. They looked alike, with slight variations on the way they had been cut. She wondered if she should take them both since certainly one might not open the door, and then, decided to chance it with the first one on top. If someone came looking in that cabinet, the fact that a key remained, wouldn't raise suspicion. Besides, if she was wrong, she could always come back to retrieve the other one. It wouldn't be efficient, but if necessary, it would work.

She was grateful when she also found an unused candle and pressed it into service. Even in the middle of the day, the long corridor which led to the room could be dark. She wondered how the maid had navigated the space while carrying a tray and assumed that she, too, must have had a candle, which was far less cumbersome than a lamp.

Pausing at the foot of the stairs, she took a deep breath. By the time she had circumvented the broken furniture and stood in front of the locked door, beads of sweat were forming on her forehead. She stood frozen, key in hand, as the sound of her rapidly beating heart echoed in her ears. She swallowed hard and placed it in the lock. For a moment, she considered turning back, returning to the safety below. But then, she heard the low sobs. Someone in there needed her. Deliberately, she turned the key until she heard a click and then, cautiously turned the knob.

She gently opened the door and closed it behind her. It took a few minutes for her eyes to adjust to the darkness, for although it was midday, the shutters had been bolted, with only tiny slivers of light allowed to enter the room. She held up the candle to get a better view.

There were eight iron beds, each occupied by a woman. They stared blankly at her as though her presence was that of a ghost.

"My name is Aimee," she said, her voice calm and soothing. "And I am here to help."

CHAPTER FORTY-TWO

Aimee stood riveted to the spot, not sure of what to do next. "Can you tell me who you are?" she asked.

They looked at her with hollow eyes, unresponsive, as though the question had fallen on deaf ears. She approached the closest bed and tried again. "What is your name?"

The woman shrugged.

"And you?" Aimee asked, moving on to the next. There was no answer.

Four of the women had obviously been bleeding heavily at one time, although they seemed oblivious to it, their gowns and bedding stained a deep rusty crimson. Aimee was alarmed by the sight and wondered if they would allow her to examine them. "Are you in pain?" she asked.

In spite of her years of experience as a nurse, she was not prepared for this, her confidence shaken. She took a deep breath, but immediately began to gag in response. The stench of unwashed bodies was overpowering. An unemptied chamber pot stood in the corner, and Aimee wished she had brought some lime, if for nothing more than to control the odor. It struck her as odd that all she might have needed for their hygiene was only a short distance away, and yet, these women lived in another world, locked away from everything that made them human.

She struggled to breath. "We need some fresh air," she whispered as she walked to the first of two windows, yanking on the shutter with a strength she didn't know that she had. After some effort, she was able to loosen the bolt and suddenly, the room was flooded with light.

The women shielded their eyes, squinting in the brightness. Two of them moaned loudly.

"Just give yourself a minute to adjust," Aimee said, blowing out the candle.

Opening the window proved equally challenging, and for a moment, she considered taking off her shoe, using it to break the panes. But being unsure of the patients' mental state and assessing the potential for danger, she thought better of it. She pulled at the frame with all her might, to no avail, and was ready to give up when she was joined by one of the women, who placed her hands next to Aimee's and pulled with her. In one swift move, the window gave way as the room was filled with a warm breeze. Aimee inhaled deeply, the air filling her lungs and calming her mind.

She turned to the woman. "Thank you for your help. What is your name?"

"Molly," the woman said.

"Well, then, Molly, I am Aimee. It is nice to meet you."

The woman nodded before returning to her bed prison.

Aimee continued to walk along the rows. Most of the women, it seemed, had recently given birth, the milk leaking from their engorged breasts as they sat, lost in the reverie of their own thoughts. Occasionally, one of them began to cry. She found this commonality between them odd, and difficult to explain.

"Molly," she said, "can you help me understand why you are all here in this place?"

"Babies," Molly said, and then, covered her face with her hands.

As though on cue, most of the women began to wail, the trigger word starting an avalanche of emotion that Aimee didn't know how to contain.

"Where are your babies?" Aimee asked. "Molly, do you know?"

Molly shook her head.

"Please help me to understand." Aimee said, "It is the only way I can help you."

Molly nodded. "I had a baby boy. I heard him cry. I held him in my arms." The tears rolled down her cheeks.

"What happened to him?"

"Lost. He is lost."

"How did he become lost, Molly?" Aimee asked.

"I don't know. I was just so very sad. I couldn't stop crying. And so they took him away."

"Who is 'they?' " Aimee asked.

"The Sister. The one who comes and makes us pray."

Aimee was confused, but then remembered Miranda's mention of the nun with her visits at dawn. "Is that who brought you here?"

Molly nodded.

"Some days I think I am better. We all do."

"Is that true?" Aimee asked, addressing the other women in the room. Molly's confession had made a few of them bold.

"I'm Libby. They took my baby girl on the third day of her life. Sister said that she was afraid I would harm her, but I wouldn't do such a thing, ever. I just thought I would be so happy after she was born, not filled with tears."

"Did you have no family who could step in to help care for your daughter, just until you were better, I mean?"

"No. They all live up North. They have kids of their own. It wasn't possible."

"But why would they lock you away in this room, away from your husband?"

"It is treatment. That's what the nurse called it," Libby said. "If we take our pills and don't cause trouble, we will be out soon, and able to go home. They even said that they would bring our babies back."

"Pills?"

"The medicine we get. It is supposed to make us better."

"But it's a lie," one of the women said. "It's all a lie."

Aimee walked over and sat at the foot of her bed. This woman had her attention. "And you are?"

"Serena."

"Well, then, Serena, why would you say that it is a lie?"

"The pills only make us sleep. At least then we can forget all that has happened."

Aimee considered what the women might have been given, opium perhaps, which would create a new set of problems for them. "Tell me your story," she said.

"I was among the first ones here. I couldn't tell you how long it has been. I tried to keep track, to make a mark for each sunrise, but I gave that up. Time has no meaning when this is your existence, but I do know that it was soon after the twins were born. I had an overwhelming feeling of sorrow as I held them. I tried to nurse them, but my milk was inadequate, which only made me more melancholy. I feared that they would starve to death. One day, as I looked at them sleeping in their cribs, I thought that they would be better off without me, and I left the house, just to clear my head. I walked as far as I could. When I had returned, Sister had come and taken my babies with her. Just to keep them safe, I was told. Then, I had what you might call a breakdown, cried and screamed for days. My husband had no idea what to do with me. I think I scared him, and so he called Sister back. That's how I ended up in this dismal place. I am better, but the sadness remains, but it is for all that I have lost, all that was robbed from me."

"But weren't you later cleared to return to your home and reunited with your children?"

Serena laughed. "Didn't I just tell you that those kinds of promises are just a lie? I am quite mad. Sister has told me so on many occasions."

Aimee shook her head. "That's not true. You seem perfectly sane to me. All of you do."

"They don't think so, and they are in charge."

It was unfathomable to Aimee. She thought of Aida, who stayed in bed crying for a full two weeks after losing a baby. Childbirth exacted an emotional toll on some women. She had seen many such situations, but it wasn't insanity, and they didn't deserve to be locked away, their infants snatched from their arms. It was cruel and callous. Inhumane. She was more resolved than ever to assist.

"If I leave, do you believe me when I say I will return as soon as tonight, or tomorrow morning at the latest, and I will have people with me who can help?"

"Will you?"

"Promise?"

"I will. You have my word on it. In the meantime, stay strong. Don't take whatever medicine the nurse gives you tonight. Pretend that you are swallowing it, but place it under the mattress instead. Can you do that?"

"But why?" Molly asked. "It is supposed to make us better."

"I fear that it is only making you all worse," Aimee said. "Let's try tonight and see if your mind is clearer in the morning."

Aimee stood and made her way to the door. "I will be back," she said. She turned the knob, but it wouldn't budge. Pulling the key from her pocket, she placed it into the lock. It didn't fit.

"What on earth?" Aimee said. "Why would the door lock from both sides?"

"Do you not have the other key?" Serena asked. "It is part of the precautions they take to keep us here. Like I said, I have been here the longest. I pretend not to notice, but I see and hear everything. Welcome to our prison, Aimee."

Aimee tried not to panic. In just a few hours, Miranda would find her note and alert the hospital staff. She could sit tight for a little while longer, and use the time to get to know the women." She took a deep breath. Everything would be just fine.

And one floor below, a custodian emptied the trash can near the nurse's station, taking Aimee's note along with him.

CHAPTER FORTY-THREE

As the light began to fade, turning day into night, Aimee regretted that she had extinguished the flame of the candle. Had she worn her nursing apron, she might have had a random match tucked away in the pocket, but the day dress held nothing which might be useful.

"What do you do when it gets dark?" Aimee asked. It was a general question, posed to the group rather than any one individual.

Molly laughed. "We sit, and we wait."

Aimee remembered that the maid was scheduled to appear with the food tray in the early part of the evening. That would be her chance to escape. But moments later, the muffled sounds of someone outside the door lasted for only short while before growing silent once more.

"Was that our dinner?" Libby asked.

"I think so."

"Then, why didn't she bring it in as she normally does? I am so very hungry."

Aimee cleared her throat. The answer to that question was the key she held firmly in her hand. Her intention was to return it to the peg inside the broom closet, well before the maid delivered the evening meal. The consequence of her decision not to take both keys weighed heavily on her mind. "I am afraid that I know why."

"What, Aimee?" Libby asked.

"I used the maid's key to unlock the door. She is unable to get in."

Libby began to cry.

"Stop it," Serena said. "Aimee was just trying to help, and she is the first person who has made such an effort. Everyone else is perfectly content to keep us prisoner. Don't you ever wonder why our families have not asked of our whereabouts? I do. I truly believed that my husband would have come for me by now. Instead, I am left here to wonder if he has taken on a new wife, created a new family. That possibility hurts more than missing a meal."

Aimee thought of Franklin. He would be returning home soon, and finding the house empty, would begin to search for her. Of that she was certain. She swallowed hard, thinking back to those moments when, as a lonely and scared five-year-old, he had entertained her, and ultimately helped to release her from her own confinement. He had been her hero then, and he would be again. She just knew it.

"My husband will come," Aimee said. "He is the most constant man I have ever met."

"They all are until things go bad," Serena said.

"We have had more than our share of challenges, and he has never shown himself to be less than that. I have faith in him," Aimee said.

"I hope you are right." Molly said. "In the meantime, the nurse will feed us when she comes to bring us our medicine."

"Which you have all agreed not to take, right?" Aimee confirmed.

"We agree," Libby said, "although I wonder if I will be able to sleep at all without the pill. I know that it keeps me calm for a very long time."

"But it also keeps you from thinking clearly." Aimee said. "That's how they are able to control you, all of you. If you hide it, you won't have lost the opportunity to take it later if need be."

"Right." Libby said. "I hadn't thought of that."

"What's the nurse's name?" Aimee asked, wondering if she knew her. The medical community was pretty small, and Charity was the largest hospital in the city. It was possible that they had once worked together. If so, she might be able to leave without a fight. But if there was something more ominous at work here, it wouldn't be that easy.

"None of us know," Serena said. "She never has introduced herself."

While Aimee thought it odd, she realized that to the nurse, these women had no identity as real human beings. They were little more than caged animals, forced to live in captivity for the remainder of their days. It strengthened her resolve to help them.

"What does she say when she comes in the evening?" Aimee asked, anxious to learn what she might expect from the woman.

"Nothing, really. She gives each of us a pill and a sip of water to wash it down. We share the same cup, so sometimes, the last person in line has none."

"But she seems to have softened a bit," Serena said, "When I first arrived here, she would beat me if I cried."

"Beat you?" Aimee asked.

"Almost every night."

"She tied my hands to the bedpost one whole night." Libby said, "Fortunately Sister set me free in the morning."

"So what is Sister like? I assume that you don't know her name either."

"We just call her by her title. I think that there is a kind side to her, or at least there once was, but I do believe that we have become a burden to her," Serena said.

Aimee considered that for a moment. "But she designed this prison, didn't she? What on earth did she think the outcome would be?"

"I think she thought we would all die."

Libby began to cry, "Like my baby."

"What do you mean, Libby?"

"One day, when I asked about my baby, Sister told me that my daughter had died. I don't think that anything will ever stop the pain of that kind of loss. It is probably best for me to stay in here rather than face a world without her in it."

"She said that my baby was gone, too," another woman said.

"As well as mine," Molly said.

"Were all of you told this?" Aimee asked. Most of the women whispered "yes" into the darkness.

"That doesn't seem logical to me. How could all of your babies die within days of you ending up here."

"It is because the demons have overtaken our minds, sinful creatures that we are," Molly said. "Sister told us that losing our babies was a punishment from God."

"So when she comes here, we pray for the souls of our babies who are in limbo, and for forgiveness of our grave transgressions. This is our penance."

Aimee could taste the bile in the back of her throat, her pulse quickening with anger. "Listen to me, all of you. I may not work in the service of our Lord, but I understand enough about His goodness and mercy to know that he doesn't take babies from their mothers just because they are struggling. He certainly doesn't kill the innocent. Sister is not only confused about how God operates, she is pure evil."

But Aimee's plea was met with silence. The women had been more indoctrinated than she originally thought, controlled by two misguided women, whose motives were questionable.

She was anxious to meet both the nurse and the nun. If they wanted a fight, they would get one. This time, they wouldn't have an unfair advantage. She wasn't weak, vulnerable or easily manipulated. This time, those two had met their match.

CHAPTER FORTY-FOUR

Aimee was lost in her own thoughts, trying to work through the possibilities of what was to come. Occasionally, one of the women would cry out, which would break the silence, but for the most part, the group quietly sat in the stillness of the dark room, waiting for the lamplight to appear in the crack under the door.

"Listen," Molly whispered. "I think I hear footsteps."

Sure enough, within minutes they heard the sound of the key in the lock.

The nurse placed the lamp on the lone table, bathing the room with light. Aimee squinted, rubbing her aching brows in response to the brightness. "Evening ladies," she said. "I see that you missed your dinner, although why that is so is beyond me." She pushed the tray from outside the door into the room with her foot. Dishes clanked together. She bent low to examine the platter before closing the door. "You," she said, pointing to Molly. "Give everyone a piece of bread and a bit of cheese. The soup is cold. You won't be having that."

Some of the women groaned. Molly retrieved the bread and cheese, carefully handing each woman a fair portion.

"Now then," the nurse said, "let's take care of your medicine so that you can sleep, shall we? You know what to do."

One by one, each of the women lined up with outstretched palms, ready to receive the lone pill. The nurse handed the cup to the first woman. "A small sip," she said, "make sure there is enough for everybody." As she made her way down the row, she carefully handed a tiny white tablet to each. By the time she reached Aimee, who was last in line, she had run out of drugs. She was puzzled.

"Did one of you get two in error?" she asked, and then, began to count. When her lips moved, forming the number nine, she turned to Aimee facing her squarely as she looked her in the eye. "Who are you?"

"I'm Aimee. I am not supposed to be here, so I am going to ask you to please let me leave of my own accord, no questions asked."

The nurse laughed, the sound of it echoing against the walls. "Ladies, how many of you are not supposed to be here?"

The women shifted in line, a few laughed nervously.

"When did Sister bring you in?"

"You don't understand. I was not brought here. I am a nurse as well, and I work in the hospital. I insist that you allow me to leave."

The nurse nodded. "Am I to allow these other women to leave as well?"

Aimee could feel her heart pounding, her blood pressure rising. "Perhaps you should consider that, but right now, let's focus on me. You cannot hold me against my will."

"Is that what you think this is? I assure you that it is treatment. You will receive the same quality of care."

"Which is no quality," Aimee's voice grew loud. "Give me the key and let me go. I can assure you that if you do not, others will be looking for me."

"That's what they all say, my dear. I am afraid that you have become quite agitated, which concerns me, Aimee."

"If you don't release me, you are going to see how agitated I can become." Aimee took a step forward until just a few inches separated her from the other woman.

The nurse smiled. "There, there. Everything is going to be just fine. She grabbed Aimee's wrist, with one hand and removed a syringe from her apron with the other. Aimee struggled, twisting herself away, but not until after the needle had been inserted into her arm.

"What did you do to me?" Aimee screamed.

"For your own protection, my dear," the nurse said before turning to the others. "Back to your beds, ladies. Unfortunately, this one will have to sleep on the floor."

And as though on cue, Aimee fell, unconscious, oblivious to everything and everyone around her.

The nurse walked to the window and slammed it shut, along with the shutters. "Rest well, ladies," she said. "I will let Sister deal with our newcomer in the morning."

CHAPTER FORTY-FIVE

Franklin arrived home at half past eight and was surprised to see that the house was dark. He wondered if Aimee had gone to sleep earlier than usual, but when he searched the bedroom, there was no sign of her. He looked for a note that she might have left for him, but when he found none, he began to worry. Aimee was, above all things, considerate and responsible. Certainly she knew that he would be concerned if she wasn't where he expected her to be.

He decided to walk the five blocks to his mother's house. Perhaps Aimee had gone for an afternoon visit and stayed longer than she had originally planned, he thought.

"Franklin," Angelique said, answering the door, "how wonderful to see you. Come in. Your father and I were about to have a late dinner. Are you hungry? Where's Aimee?"

Franklin's face grew pale. "Is she not here with you?"

"Why, no. Was she supposed to be?"

"I don't know. I just made that assumption. I worked late, and she wasn't home when I got there. It is so unlike her."

"I agree. Have you checked the hospital? Perhaps she stayed with her patients."

"No, but I am headed that way next. It's just that she took the day off, at least I thought she had, so unless she changed her mind, I didn't expect her to be there."

"All women change their minds, Franklin. You certainly know that about the Slater women."

Franklin smiled. It always struck him as funny that after marrying him, Aimee didn't need to change her last name. Aimee Slater remained Aimee Slater. It was hard to explain to people who didn't know them well. "I suppose you are right. I might be over reacting."

"It is perfectly understandable. I over reacted to everything where you children were concerned after Aimee's kidnapping. That experience taught me that you can't ever be too protective when it comes to your loved ones."

"It is a good lesson."

"Your father was late himself working on a research project. We have not yet unbridled the horses. Let me go with you to the hospital."

"But you haven't had your supper."

"I will just eat when we return. You and Aimee can join us. Your father will stay here just in case she shows up looking for you. It could happen, like in one of those silly books about missed encounters that Aida used to love to read. Let me grab my cape."

Franklin had retreated to the stable and had the buggy ready when Angelique joined him. He resisted the temptation to race through the streets, telling himself that when he discovered Aimee, calming some gravely ill man or women, he would laugh at his fears, deem them irrational. But until he held her in his arms and gazed upon her beautiful face, his mind was filled with uncertainty.

They reached the hospital at a quarter to ten, and Franklin immediately headed to the surgical ward. All was still and quiet, with the lone light of the nurses' station illuminating the hall. "Have you seen Aimee?" he asked the nurse on duty.

"No," she said, "but I have only been here for a few hours. "She doesn't normally work the night shift, does she?"

"No, but I thought that something might have kept her here a bit longer. Is there anyone still here who worked during the day? Anybody who might have seen her?"

"Not that I know of, but you might check the other wards."

Franklin turned to Angelique. "I am concerned. This is where I thought she would be, here in surgery. Nothing else makes sense. She wouldn't intentionally do this, so I must believe that she simply got involved in a case and lost track of time."

Angelique took a deep breath and forced a smile. "Let's systemically go through each part of the hospital. You lead the way. If she is here, we will find her."

"Right. This is ward 1, surgery. Let's move on to ward 2."

The nurse in ward 2 had only met Aimee once, when she was first hired. "There are two of us on duty; let me ask Rachel." She returned minutes later. "I am sorry Dr. Slater; Rachel has not seen her either. Wish I could help."

Franklin ran his fingers through his hair. He glanced at the hall clock, it was almost eleven.

"Well, hello, Franklin, what are you doing here this late, especially in this part of the hospital?"

Miranda asked, when they reached the nurses' station in ward 3.

"Miranda," Franklin said, breathing a sigh of relief, "I am so grateful to see a familiar face. Aimee. Do you know where she is?"

"Why no. We had lunch a few days ago, but I haven't seen her since. She's always working days, while I sometimes alternate nights. You look worried. Is she missing?"

"I don't know where she is, so I guess you could say that. I have been looking for the past couple of hours. She wasn't home when I returned. I am trying not to panic."

"That's all very uncharacteristic of Aimee."

Angelique stepped forward and offered her hand. "I'm Angelique, Aimee's mother. I met you at the wedding, Miranda. I know that my daughter is very fond of you."

"I feel the same about her. I don't think I could have survived life in this place without her. What can I do to help you, Franklin?" Miranda asked.

"Help me think of where else to look. We have been through all of the wards and both surgical suites."

Miranda's face grew somber. "Let me check something out, and I will be right back."

She made her way through the beds filled with sleeping patients and into the pantry. She opened the broom cabinet where she had discovered the two keys. Only one hung on the peg. She removed it and returned to Franklin and Angelique.

"I think I know where she might be," Miranda said, her voice quivering.

"Where?"

Miranda motioned to the nearby screen. "I cannot leave the ward unattended."

"Tell me," Franklin pleaded.

"There. The stairs to the third floor. At the end of the hall, there is a room. Something sinister exists behind that door, and Aimee was determined to find out what it was."

"And you let her go?" Franklin was trying to control his anger.

"No," Miranda said as she lit the spare lamp and handed it to Franklin. "Never. We had made a pact to explore it together. You know, safety in numbers. I found the key and told Aimee about it. I guess she thought she could solve the mystery on her own."

"My brave, yet foolish, wife," Franklin said, hurrying toward the stairs with Angelique closely following him.

At the landing, he paused, surveying the scene as the lamp cast eerie shadows on the walls. "Watch your step," he said to

Angelique, pointing to the debris which littered the floor, "looks like this could be a bit dangerous."

Angelique nodded.

Franklin bent to pick up a metal table leg. "Just in case I need it," he said more to himself than to anyone else.

Slowly, they made their way down the hall until they stood in front of the door. He turned the knob, which refused to budge. Franklin knocked. "Aimee?" he called.

There was no answer.

He knocked again, harder. "Aimee?" his voice more urgent.

"She's in here," a soft female voice said.

"Open the door," Franklin ordered.

"We can't," several voices said, in unison.

"Then, stand back."

He handed the lamp to Angelique. "Hold the light. I am going to break the door."

Holding the metal rod in his hand, he swung it with all of his might. The knob moved. He did it again. By the third time, the knob fell with a loud thud at his feet. And then, he kicked the door with the heel of his boot. It swung open, and he hurried inside the room.

"Where is she?" he asked, unable to see who he was addressing in the darkness.

"Come," he called to Angelique, "Bring the lamp."

The women stood wordlessly, like phantoms in their soiled nightgowns. Angelique blinked in disbelief. "What is this place?" she whispered.

One woman stepped forward. "You must be Franklin. I am Serena. Aimee said that you would come. She never doubted it for one minute."

Franklin scanned the room, trying to conceal the panic racing through his mind. Then he saw her, crumpled on the floor. He rushed to her side, gently lifting her head. "Aimee?

Can you hear me?" He lifted her in his arms and turned to the women. "What happened to her?"

"Nurse shot her in the arm with something," Molly said. "I've seen her use it before when somebody gets unruly. She's going to have to sleep it off, but she will be alright."

"Morphine," Franklin mumbled.

"I am afraid this is quite confusing," Angelique said. "Who are you, and what are you all doing here? More importantly, what is my daughter doing here?"

"It is a long story, ma'am," Serena said. "Just know that Aimee here is a hero."

"She almost got herself killed being one," Angelique said.

"Yes, ma'am, but she said that if anybody would understand, it would be you two. She told us that she comes from a family of heroes. Now, I think I understand why."

CHAPTER FORTY-SIX

It was well past three by the time the women had been escorted down the stairs to ward 3. Miranda had managed to get each of them into the bathtub and dressed in a clean gown with an efficiency that impressed even Franklin, who had seen his share of capable nurses. Angelique took turns sitting with each of them, listening to story after story of the horrors they had endured behind the locked door.

"I can't imagine such cruelty," she said to Molly. "I am so very sorry."

Molly smiled, moved by the kindness. "My baby is in heaven, ma'am, so I guess I have my own special angel."

Angelique nodded and swallowed hard. She often felt that way about sweet Josephina who had gone to heaven far too soon. "Yes, you do," she said.

Franklin never left Aimee's bedside, not for one moment. He wiped her forehead with a cool wet cloth and spoke to her softly. Occasionally, he would call her by name, hoping that it would rouse her. At four a.m., she opened her eyes and smiled.

"Franklin," she whispered. "I knew you would come."

"Oh, Aimee," he said, "you scared me half to death. I am far too relieved to scold you, but when you are stronger, you will have to listen to a few choice words."

"And a few from me, too," said Miranda. "How could you be so reckless?"

"I guess I didn't think about the consequences, but in hindsight, I should have waited for you. I did leave you a note."

"What note?"

Aimee sighed. "I left it on the desk with instructions for the charge nurse to give it to you. I suppose you never got it."

Miranda shook her head. "No. I didn't. I don't see it anywhere. I'm sorry."

"Me, too" Aimee said, smiling with relief.

"Here, drink this," Franklin said, offering her some water. "How are you feeling?"

Aimee took a sip. "My head hurts a little, but otherwise, I am not so bad."

"Then, we should get you home."

"Not quite."

"What do you mean?" Franklin asked.

"There is someone I would like to meet, and I need for you and Momma to be with me when I do."

"Now? Who?" Franklin asked.

"You'll see."

"Haven't you had enough excitement for one day?"

"There is just one more piece to this puzzle," Aimee said. "And I intend to find it."

An hour later, Sister tried to place her key in the lock, but found that it was broken, the handle missing. The door was slightly ajar, which she thought troubling. She nudged it with her foot, and it swung open.

She stood stone still as she surveyed the room, a look of disbelief and shock on her face.

"Good morning, Sister. My name is Aimee Slater. This is my mother, Angelique, and my husband, Franklin. Do come in and have a seat. We are very anxious to get to know you."

CHAPTER FORTY-SEVEN

"Is that a rose in your lapel?" Aida asked over dinner one night. "I don't think I have ever seen you wear something like that."

Michel shrugged. "A woman came by the office peddling flowers this afternoon. I felt sorry for her, so I bought one. And yes, it is uncharacteristic of me."

"I think it is rather nice, although it does make you look less like a lawyer and more like an undertaker."

He laughed. "I suppose you might be right," he said, removing the flower and placing it on the table. "You seem much happier these days, my dear. It no doubt pleases me to know that those long days of melancholy are behind you. May I ask what has brought about this change?"

"Time, I suppose," Aida said. That was only partially true. Her volunteer work at the Center for Hope had been fulfilling. And although she had never really thought of herself as a teacher, the fact that within a few short months, the women were able to read simple books and write basic correspondence filled her with great pride. Her life seemed to take on a greater meaning because of this new mission, which was gratifying and gave her purpose.

She had managed to leave the house and return every Tuesday without arousing suspicion, and at Gretchen's request, she added an additional day to her tutoring schedule. Suddenly, that seemed to accelerate the women's progress.

It was a delicate balancing act that she performed, attending to her social duties as Michel's wife and placating her mother-in-law, with whom she had reached an unspoken agreement of polite tolerance. She wondered if she would ever feel completely comfortable in his family's presence or grow accustomed to their stiff adherence to protocol and concern for appearances. She missed the overt affection and constant laughter of her mother's house, which made for a very different atmosphere than the Countess had created.

"I hope that I am also part of that happiness equation," Michel said, reaching for her hand. He lightly kissed her knuckles. "I am so pleased to be in your good graces once again."

"By that you mean in my bed," Aida said.

"I suppose so," Michel said, his eyes meeting hers. "I do hope to expand our family soon. The continuation of our noble family bloodline lies with me."

Aida could feel her blood rising, and she swallowed hard. She would always remember their first child, the one she would never get to hold or watch grow. While her heart had forgiven Michel and hoped for a happy future together, her mind had not forgotten that there was a selfish side to him, one in which he put his own needs first. When he spoke to her that way, she felt that he saw her as little more than a breeding mare. How he confused her!

He could be charming and tender at times, which reminded her of the man she first met, the one who had come to New Orleans and instantly swept her off her feet. She had fallen madly in love with that man. But once they were legally wed, and he could lay complete claim to her, she noticed the change in him. It was subtle at first. He sometimes made biting comments or unusual requests. But then, he became more controlling, while at the same time neglectful. It seemed like such a contradiction in behavior. She had grown accustomed to his apathy, the long absences from home in the name of work. And yet, as much as she hated it, she responded to his kindness, his moments of affection, like a starving dog who is given a bone. She supposed that she cared for him more than she wanted to admit.

She forced a smile. "I share that expectation, Michel. In God's time, it will happen."

"I am always hopeful," he said, offering his hand.

She glanced at the rose, confused by why it held such a fascination, the sight of it triggering some unidentifiable emotion.

"Shall we retire upstairs?"

Aida nodded. She prayed that this time, she would feel that he loved her, too.

CHAPTER FORTY-EIGHT

Aida entered the Center, right on time, to find that Gretchen was waiting for her along with the other women.

"Well," Aida said, "it looks like I have quite a welcoming party today. To what do I owe this honor?"

"Let's see if you still think it is an honor in a few minutes," Gretchen said.

Aida furrowed her brow. "That sounds ominous. You can't fire me, Gretchen. I work for free, remember?"

When none of the women even smiled at the joke, Aida knew that something serious was happening. "Talk to me," she said. "What's going on here?"

"One of the girls is in trouble," Gretchen said.

"Trouble?" Aida asked. "What kind of trouble?"

Gretchen gestured to the wooden table in the middle of the room. "Come. Let's sit. I want the rest of the group to hear this."

"Have you ever met Colleen?" Gretchen asked. "She had only been with us for a few months."

"I don't think so. She wasn't one of the regulars in my class, so I am not sure how our paths might have crossed."

"I thought perhaps you might have seen her, even if in passing. I am sure if you had, you would have remembered her."

"Really? Why is that?" Aida asked.

"She looked like a child, rather fragile looking, and although she told me when she arrived here that she was eighteen, I doubted it," Gretchen said.

"Would that have made a difference?"

"Maybe. I don't believe in putting kids into an adult environment, so I would have probably sent her over to the girls' delinquent home. But I don't know if that would have made a difference."

"What do you mean?" Aida asked.

"She told me her story that first day. It is one of the things that I insist upon. We all have a history, but I need to know the background of any woman I take in here. If there are drugs involved or a love affair with the drink, I want to know it."

"Are the women truthful about their past?" Aida blushed, realizing that she was asking this question in front of the others who were hanging on every word.

"Usually. You know me, Aida. I don't play around. And I don't take too kindly to being lied to. I am willing to help anybody, but I have to know what I am up against. So yeah, honesty is important. But I also reserve the right to turn away anybody whose intentions I question."

"I can see why," Aida said, "but is there a reason why you are telling me about this?"

"Sorry," Gretchen said, "I guess I needed to lay a little foundation here, give you a little background. Three days ago, the police came to the door with a warrant for Colleen's arrest. She is in jail."

"Jail? I thought that they usually turned a blind eye to petty things like prostitution," Aimee said, and then immediately regretted it. She turned to the other women. "My apologies."

"No need to apologize, Aida," Gretchen said. "This conversation is about honesty."

Aida nodded.

"Colleen was arrested for something much more serious than prostitution." There was a hush in the room. Gretchen continued. "I can't say that I am surprised that she got into trouble, given her background. She told me that she was the middle daughter of seven children, who lived in a two room tenement on the outskirts of town. They were poor, but so were lots of other families. However, their misfortunes only became greater when her father went off to work one day and never returned, leaving her mother to support the family in whatever way she could. The kids were made to do odd jobs, delivering coal or newspapers. The girls did ironing for neighbors. But money was a struggle and food was scarce. When she turned twelve, her mother sent her to stay with her uncle who lived here in Harlem. She was told that he would make sure that she got some schooling and learned a trade. That way she could return to the family and help with the financial responsibilities. But it didn't end up being the kind of education her mother had in mind."

"What do you mean?" Aida asked.

"Her uncle immediately sold her to the first man he met who was willing to meet his price."

"Sold her? As in slavery?" Aida asked.

"No, Aida. You do that and it's a one-time transaction. To put a girl on the streets means you have a constant cash flow. And that's what he did."

Aida shook her head. Suddenly, she recognized that her life was worlds apart from that of these women. She was never concerned for her safety or wondered about her welfare, even when Michel made his demands. It was hard to imagine such fear, but it also helped her to understand why she was viewed with such derision when she arrived that first day, waving a donation check. She was fortunate. It pained her to think of how unaware she had been.

"How did she get here?" Aida asked. "To you, I mean?"

"Our mission is well known in the community. We are a safe house. She told me that she had simply run away in the middle of the night to escape his brutality."

"Was that the truth?"

"I thought so, but I now know that there is more to the story."

"More?"

"I suppose that I should clarify, Aida. Colleen was arrested for murder."

"Murder? Of whom?"

"Her uncle, of course. More women kill their pimps than they do lovers or husbands."

It stuck Aida as such an odd comparison. The women in the social circles that she ran with would have fainted dead away just by hearing such a thing. Aida wondered if she had gotten herself into an unseemly situation through this association. She imagined what the Countess would do if she had any idea where her privileged daughter-in-law was at this very moment.

"Is she guilty of the crime?" Aida asked.

"She is," Gretchen said. "But it was self-defense. I saw her this morning. I was only allowed a brief visit with her in the jail. She is afraid."

"Of course, she is. Murder is a capital offense. Does she have a lawyer?"

"She is a poor girl, Aida, with no money to pay for a defense. The court appointed her one, a man old enough to be her great grandfather."

"Which means he is experienced. That could work in her favor."

"I might agree with you, but she said that he came once, told her that he would advise her to plead guilty and that with any luck, the judge would give her a life sentence rather than death. He also said that she should not expect to see him again until the day of the trial."

"Did she explain that it was self-defense, ask him to present her case?"

"Yes, and he refused."

"This is so awful, Gretchen, but I am afraid that I still don't understand what this has to do with me. My husband controls the money, I am afraid, but I should be able to manage to come up with some to help the cause if your intention is to hire a more competent lawyer."

"I am not asking you for money, Aida."

"Then, what are you asking for?"

"You. I am asking for you."

"To do what?"

"To defend her. You said you once hoped to be a lawyer. This is your chance. We want you to represent Colleen," Gretchen finally said. "There couldn't be a better choice."

"But that is not possible. I am not licensed to practice the law; my knowledge is limited."

"Anything is possible," one of the women said. "I can read. Never thought I would. And that's thanks to you. If anybody can save Colleen, you can."

Aida swallowed hard, her mind searching for a way to refuse, trying to think of a plausible excuse. "I will do what I can," she said, and then, wondered if she had completely lost her sense of reason.

CHAPTER FORTY-NINE

"Colleen's life hangs in the balance," Aida said, lifting the heavy bag of books onto the table. She had practically emptied the shelves of her husband's law library, and then filled the spaces with classics and children's primers, hoping that she could return them before Michel realized that they were missing. Most of his case work was done in the large walnut-paneled research room that his firm had spent years furnishing. And since he used that as an excuse for working late so often, she felt confident that her selective borrowing would go unnoticed.

"You are to work in pairs. I will give you a question, and you are to search these books until you find the answer. Is that clear?"

The women nodded. "But what if we can't read the big words or understand things?" one of them asked.

"Ask me if you need clarification on anything. Write down page numbers and the title of the book on the paper I have given you. What we are looking for are examples of other women in Colleen's situation, who were found not guilty by reason of self-defense. If we are able to do that, we may be able to show precedence."

"What does that mean?"

"It is something that the court considers when interpreting the law. If a decision was made under similar circumstances, the judge will often rule that same way."

"Gretchen has gone to see Colleen daily, asking her questions about the way her uncle mistreated her, and details about the night that it happened." Aida was careful not to use words like "kill" or "murder," which were not only emotionally charged, but implied guilt. "I have her notes here. And they are very convincing, if we are able to present them during the trial."

"Why wouldn't we?"

"Because," Aida said, "I am not allowed to speak in court, remember?"

"Then all of this is for nothing," one of the women said. "What's the point if we can't use it?"

"Ah, but we can use it. You will see how in a little while. Now, keep looking. This chatter isn't going to accomplish anything."

The women opened the books and began searching the argument which they had been assigned. Sometimes, one of them would stop and ask a question, but for most of the afternoon, the room remained silent.

Aida smiled. This was more powerful than any lesson she might have fashioned. These women had a vested interest in the outcome of the trial. They were trying to save one of their own, and they were highly motivated.

At half past three there was a timid knock on the door. "Ah," Aida said, "right on time."

The women looked up just as Aida escorted a young man into the room. "Ladies, this is Mr. Reeves. He is here to help us."

He removed his hat and held it in his hands, nervously fingering the brim. "Hello," he said, but nothing more.

"Please," Aida said, "come in and have a seat. We will show you what we have so far."

She gathered up the papers on the table and began reading her summary. When she had finished, she looked at him squarely in the eye. "So what are your questions for me?"

"I am not sure," he said. Aida's confidence began to wane.

"How is he supposed to help us? He looks barely old enough to be out by himself." one of the women asked. The others laughed. It was a legitimate question and one which Aida had just asked of herself.

"He is a lawyer, and I have retained his services." That part was true, but just barely. Joseph Reeves had graduated from law school that spring and had been admitted to the bar only two weeks earlier. Gretchen got his name from a friend of a friend, who knew his uncle. When she had questioned if he had ever tried a case, she learned that this would be his first. But because of that, he worked cheaply, which made him the only option.

"Why?"

"Mr. Reeves will be addressing the court."

"If you say so."

She had hoped that he would make up for his lack of experience with enthusiasm. This case could help his career, she reasoned, but Aida quickly learned that his lackluster personality matched his knowledge of the law. She sighed. Had she been allowed into legal study, she would have been properly prepared and vested, and she would have saved Colleen. Of that she was certain. Instead, she had to settle on orchestrating this puppet show, where he spoke while she provided the script and pulled the strings. It was unnerving, but she tried not to think of that.

Two hours later, he tipped his hat and bid them goodbye, promising to return the next day. The advantage to being his only client, Aida thought, is that they got his full attention.

CHAPTER FIFTY

Aida was exhausted. She had a difficult time sleeping at night as she analyzed Colleen's defense over and over in her mind. Right after Michel left for work, she was off to Harlem to meet with the women and Joseph Reeves to discuss their trial strategy. She wasn't feeling well most days, her stomach protesting at the mere thought of food. Nerves, she assumed was the cause, and she hoped that her husband hadn't noticed her rather significant weight loss.

Soon, she figured, the trial would be over and life would return to normal. The women would no longer require her regular tutoring, having successfully mastered legal research. The idea of them becoming law clerks made her smile, and she couldn't help but wonder what Michel would have thought of the whole thing. He wouldn't have approved, of course, deeming her actions as inappropriate, "slumming" as he liked to call anything which had to do with anyone outside of their very restricted social class.

Perhaps when the trial was over, she would concentrate her efforts on creating a real library for the women, she thought. And on her weekly visits, she could teach what she knew about finances and budgeting. She could conduct mock job interviews, too, so that they would know how to handle them when the opportunity arose. She had become quite fond of the women, and her presence at The Center made her feel needed, as though the investment of her time made a difference.

Michel had a big case of his own to prepare for, which kept him busy. She often caught him daydreaming, his brow furrowed as though he was working through some complicated legal argument. "A penny for your thoughts," she would offer, and he would laugh in response.

"Sorry, my dear, I don't mean to be so distracted."

"Perhaps I can help. I do love a good legal argument, you know," she would say.

"Don't you worry your pretty little head about such things," he would respond, ending that idea once and for all. And although she would have loved for him to have shared what he was working on, just because he knew how much she wanted to practice the law, he made it clear that he intended to keep his professional life and home life separate.

Aida and Michel fell into the rhythm of their separate lives. Sometimes, she would arrive home only minutes before she heard the sound of his carriage, and hurriedly position herself in the library or alert cook to prepare to serve dinner. She reminded herself that she needed to proceed with caution since if he returned home, and she was not there, her absence would be hard to explain.

So one afternoon, when she looked at the clock at The Center and realized how late it was, she hurriedly summoned her driver, praying that she would get home in time. Settling back into the seat of the carriage, she looked out the window at the crowded streets. Gretchen had been right: Harlem was an ever-changing community and yes, she had become a part of that change.

She studied the buildings which had once been abandoned, but were given new life as shopkeepers transformed them into viable businesses. New apartments were being constructed, which would mean neighborhoods would grow. It had been fascinating to watch.

There was a diversity to the population, which created an interesting tapestry, she thought. And she liked to people-watch on her way home, wondering what secrets each person held close, for as she had come to understand, everyone lived duel lives, one public, and the other, private.

She was so preoccupied that she almost didn't notice the familiar silhouette as he walked along the sidewalk. Somehow, her brain was unable to process what her eye could clearly see, and as she watched with a detached interest, she could not comprehend that indeed, it was he. She observed the scene play out from her carriage window in stunned silence as her husband embraced a tall red head, dressed in a sparkly blue gown. He paused to whisper in the woman's ear, and she laughed in response before placing her hand in his. Seconds later, they disappeared into a bar, as the sound of jazz music filled the air.

CHAPTER FIFTY-ONE

"Where are the women who occupied this room?" the nun asked, her voiced filled with indignation.

"In a place where they are safe," Aimee replied, "no thanks to you."

"I beg your pardon? They were perfectly safe here, protected and carefully monitored. I personally made certain that their overall treatment proceeded as smoothly as possible."

"Which is why you will be held responsible for the consequences of your actions," Aimee said.

"Consequences?" the nun asked, her voice becoming louder, the irritation growing. "If anything I should be thanked for keeping them safe, and for keeping their loved ones safe from them as well."

"So is that why they were hidden away in a deserted room in this hospital where no one was likely to discover they were here?" Aimee asked.

"It was the only suitable place, a decision that was made rather quickly when the need arose."

"With whose permission?" Franklin asked. "I have worked here for many years now, and I am in tune with administrative decisions in regard to facilities. Under whose authority were you given approval to use this room?"

The nun shrugged. "I don't think I am obligated to share that with you."

"Is it because you can't?" Franklin asked.

For a fleeting second, Angelique felt sorry for the woman. Aimee and Franklin's justifiable outrage only made her defensive. Emotions were running high and tempers were flaring, which never made for a productive conversation, especially with so many unanswered questions. She wanted the truth, and that would take a bit of finesse to get it.

"Sister," Angelique said. "My daughter Aimee is a nurse here and stumbled across the room and these captive women quite by accident. It is her very nature to help others, which is why she felt compelled to try to rescue them. But in the process, she was locked into this room herself. I am merely grateful that we were able to find her in time."

"And injected with morphine by your nurse, I might add," Franklin said. "She could have very well killed my wife; at which point someone would have had hell to pay."

The nun made the sign of the cross, her lips moving in a whispered prayer.

"Franklin," Angelique said, "this is getting us nowhere. Let's allow sister to explain herself, shall we?"

Franklin scowled and Aimee folded her arms, but then, both sat on the edge of the bed, their eyes fixed on the nun.

"Now then, Sister," Angelique said. "This situation raises many questions, suspicions about intent and mistreatment. You understand that, don't you?

The nun nodded.

"We are going to sit and listen as you explain this to us. Then, there will be questions and perhaps a call to the constable. Holding people against their will is a crime."

"If that is what I was doing, then, I would expect to be held accountable. As God s my witness, my intentions were pure. I meant only to help."

Aimee couldn't resist the urge to ask the obvious question. "How did you think you would help these women by taking their babies and locking them away? Have you no heart, no sense of human decency?"

"Aimee," Angelique said, "let her finish with her explanation. There will be time to ask whatever you want in just a few minutes."

"Proceed," Angelique said. "We want to give you an opportunity to speak."

"For many years, I have assisted families in the Diocese from time to time, aiding in delivering babies and such. Sometimes, I have been called in to teach young mothers how to tend to their infants or to aid with breast feeding when the milk didn't come so easily. I had grown close to one such family two years ago. In some ways I thought of the woman as a daughter I would never have of my own."

She paused, wiping a tear from her eye.

"Go on," Angelique said.

"She had a particularly difficult time in the months preceding the child's arrival. I noticed that she was struggling even more after the baby girl was born."

"Struggling?" Aimee asked.

"Emotionally, I mean. It was as though giving birth had taken the light right out of her eyes. She cried most of the day and took little to no interest in the newborn. I tried to call on the family as often as I could, reciting prayers with her, helping with the care of the baby while I was there, but nothing seemed to bring her comfort. Her husband was worried about her, and so was I.

At the end of the second week following the delivery, I made my regular visit to the house. It was the middle of the afternoon, but she sat in a darkened room with the shutters closed, the curtains drawn. When I went to take the infant from her, I was shocked to see what had happened."

The nun began to cry. "That sweet little baby lay dead in her arms. Her little lifeless body cold.

I asked her what had happened, and she told me that the voices said that she should take the baby's life to spare her having to grow up in a cruel world. She put a blanket over the infant's head and smothered the breath right out of her."

"Oh, Lord help us. That's horrible," Aimee said. "What a terrible tragedy for this family. But what did she mean about the voices?

"I wondered the same thing. In the end, I figured it could only be the work of Satan, who seeks to destroy. She was possessed by demons, no doubt, robbed of the sanity that made her human."

Angelique nodded. "It might seem that way, certainly. No rational mother would do such a thing. I can't imagine anything more devastating. But I am afraid that I don't see how that incident relates to these women we discovered here tonight."

"There is an obvious correlation," the nun said. "The husband, so distraught over his wife's insanity and the death of his newborn child, asked me to take her away so that she would never hurt herself or another again."

"That's when you brought her here?"

"I did. I felt responsible. I had to do what I could. Another sister, one who once worked in the hospital, told me about this room. I thought that it would be temporary until I could find someplace more suitable for her, but in time, there were other women who suffered from the melancholy. Their families reached out to me, and I didn't want to see another baby die, so I moved the mothers here. Some, were able to leave in time, return home. Others, like the first one, passed from the grief, I suppose."

"And their infants?" Aimee asked. "Most of the women I met in that wretched room were told their babies had died. Is that true?"

The nun hung her head. "No."

"Repeat that." Aimee commanded.

"No. They didn't die. Some were simply turned over to the church by husbands who felt ill equipped to raise a child alone. But there were a few, I took upon myself to remove from the home, convincing the families that everyone would be better off."

"Why was that?"

"Some circumstances were not so good, which is why I was called in to begin with. Sometimes, there were many other children already living there, with little money to buy food to fill their little stomachs. Some of the men drank, which certainly made me question leaving a baby in their care. My objective was always the same, to be certain that these children had the best possible chance of having a decent life."

"In other words, you played God," Aimee said.

"No," Sister said, "I did God's work."

"That's a matter of opinion," Aimee said, trying to control her anger.

Angelique swallowed hard. "I have one more question, and this is an important one."

"I have told you all that I know," Sister said. "It is my true confession. But I will answer you as best I can."

"Where were these children taken once you removed them from their homes?"

"The Bishop has a protocol for placement. Most, if not all were taken to the Countess Maria Children's Home."

Aimee gasped. Angelique's face grew pale. She struggled to breathe as though suddenly all of the air had been sucked out of the room. Her chest ached.

"Do you know what this means?" Franklin asked. All three women looked at him, each with their own set of answers.

CHAPTER FIFTY-TWO

"Mother," Aimee, whispered, searching for some words of comfort to offer. "I am so sorry." She could have never imagined that her discovery of the room at the end of the hall would have somehow been tied to the orphanage. It seemed like a rather painful twist of fate, and yet, it meant a glimmer of hope for the women who had lost their babies. The possibility that somehow the broken families could be reunited was nothing short of a miracle.

"I had no idea," Angelique said, her voice filled with emotion. "And yet somehow I feel responsible, that perhaps I contributed to the tragedy that these women had to endure."

"You are not responsible. She is." Franklin said, pointing to the nun who stood riveted to the spot, her face expressionless.

"Sister,' Angelique said. "We must determine how to right this wrong. Did you keep records of the families that you helped, the babies that were placed with us? Do you think that the Bishop may have them as well?

The nun nodded. "I have a little book with notes I took after each home visit. I recorded the birthdates of the children, as well."

"That's a start," Aimee said.

"I have the archives of placement at the orphanage," Angelique added. "The Bishop will have the third piece of the puzzle."

"But may I humbly request a favor?" Sister asked.

Aimee frowned. "That seems a bit presumptuous, don't you think? You certainly weren't granting favors to those women you locked away."

"I will understand if you refuse," Sister said. "I just wonder if it was necessary to mention my involvement to the Bishop."

"It might be difficult to mention you by name since we don't know it. Ironically, none of the women who you claimed to be so close to knew you by anything other than your title." Aimee said.

"It's Sister Mary Grace," the nun whispered.

"Well, there's a start," Aimee said.

"Do you fear the Bishop's displeasure or the repercussions of your actions?" Angelique asked. "The answer to that is obvious, I suppose."

"Certainly. He will have to report this to Mother Superior, who has entrusted me to carry out the work of the convent. I have been a member of this order since I was sixteen. It is all I know. What if I am asked to leave?"

"That's a possibility," Aimee said, "one that you might have considered earlier."

"I am afraid that I have overstepped my authority. I know that I did. There will be grave consequences for me; I should expect nothing less," Sister said.

"Penance perhaps?" Aimee said. "Isn't that what you told the women your so-called treatment was meant to be? I think it only fair that you accept whatever punishment may befall you whether the sentence is in a civil or spiritual court of law."

Sister swallowed hard. "I understand, but truly, I only did what I thought was right. My heart was not filled with malice."

"Now you know how misguided you were," Angelique said. "If you help us, turn over your book, I will make that known to the Bishop as well. That may work in your favor in terms of leniency."

Sister nodded.

"So come," Franklin said, "let's leave this dreadful room. I am expected to be at work in an hour after a night with no sleep."

"I am off to see the Bishop," Angelique said. She turned to the nun. "I expect for you to meet me outside of his office in an hour with your book. What I say to him depends on it."

"I will honor my word," Sister said.

"And the women?" Aimee asked. "What shall we do about them? Franklin and I will see to it that they are able to remain at the hospital until they have fully recovered, but then what is to become of them?"

"We hope that they will be able to return to their homes, and we will work tirelessly to reunite them with their children, especially those in our care, but ultimately, that will be for them to decide," Angelique said. "We can give them back one thing among the many that they have lost."

"What's that?'

"Freedom," Angelique said. "Precious freedom."

CHAPTER FIFTY-THREE

Angelique paused on the sidewalk outside of the hospital, trying to process the events of the past twelve hours. It had been almost overwhelming, the panic over Aimee's disappearance, coupled with the discovery of those poor women who had been locked away by a misguided nun. She whispered a prayer, asking for guidance as she spoke to the Bishop. She had no concrete solutions to offer, no real way to help, and that bothered her as well. But she knew she had to try.

Aimee suddenly appeared at her mother's side. "I am so glad that I found you. I was worried that you were already on your way."

"No," Angelique said, "I suppose I am trying to summon a bit of courage first. It won't be easy to share this with the Bishop."

"Which is why I want to go with you," Aimee said.

Angelique smiled. "Truly? I could use the moral support, so yes, I would love to have you join me."

"I'd like to offer more than that."

"Yes?"

"I have a proposition for the Bishop."

Angelique raised an eyebrow. "Well, now you have aroused my curiosity. Shall we discuss it first or am I to be equally as surprised?"

"I am interested in what you might think, of course, since this actually would be a partnership with you. There was no time to discuss it with Franklin, who I hope will be in agreement."

"A partnership? Now I am even more interested. Come, let's sit in the carriage, and you can tell me what is on your mind."

"I want to become a midwife," Aimee said once they had settled. "It has become more and more evident that my dreams of becoming a doctor will be deferred until the country becomes open to the idea that women are capable of practicing medicine. That could take years, but realistically, it could never happen for me."

Angelique nodded. "It is truly unfair. I have witnessed your knowledge and compassion. You would be an amazing physician."

"But I can't put my life on hold, waiting for the door of opportunity to open. It is time that I make my own destiny and hopefully do some good in the process."

"So far, I like what I am hearing, but your idea is still rather vague. You certainly don't need my help to become a midwife."

"No, but I would like your help to open a home for unwed mothers, who require a place to live during their confinement through the time when they give birth. So many of these women place their babies up for adoption. The transition into the Countess Maria Orphanage would be seamless."

"I had dreamed of such a place a few years ago. The need exists. It is far greater than you might imagine."

"I know what I have seen at Charity. Young girls in labor who desperately require help. It is not our responsibility to aid them post-partum and many are without homes, rejected by their families. Often, they are released onto the streets with a newborn they are ill-equipped to care for. Maternal health is a real issue, one rarely addressed."

"It is a growing concern. I acknowledge that. We have babies left on the doorstep of the orphanage more often than I'd like. It always saddens me that anyone has to begin life that way. But I think of the poor mothers, too."

"Ah yes, the mothers. I had no idea that the need for aftercare was so urgent. I learned a great deal from those women as we sat together in the darkness," Aimee said. "Ultimately, I would hope to expand the practice to include any woman who has recently given birth and whose situation necessitates a safe house, a place where she and her newborn can be cared for in circumstances like those women we encountered today. I won't use the word sanitarium or asylum because I don't believe that they are any more insane than you and me. And I think that you agree."

"If losing their babies and then being locked away didn't make those poor women go crazy, I can't imagine that anything would. I think you might be right. The affliction seems to be temporary, an adjustment after childbirth."

"Exactly, which means the facility would provide a brief place of respite, a chance to talk to other women who are experiencing the same overwhelming emotions."

"It all sounds wonderful, Aimee," Angelique said, "but quite ambitious."

"Which is why I want to go with you. The situation is dire. This is a plausible solution. And I want the Bishop to fund it."

"Then let's see if we can make that happen. You and I are quite the team. The poor Bishop has no idea what he is up against. Given the right cause, we can be most persuasive. And Aimee?"

"Yes?"

"Thanks for being my daughter. You make me incredibly proud."

"I suppose that we did listen to all that you tried to instill in us after all."

Angelique reached over to give Aimee a hug, "Who could ask for anything more?"

CHAPTER FIFTY-FOUR

Sister Mary Grace was waiting outside the iron gate that led to the courtyard behind the cathedral and the Bishop's office. With a trembling hand, she gave Angelique the book containing the records of the women who had spent months locked away in the secret room on the third floor of the hospital.

"Please remember," she whispered, "my intention was to do no harm."

"Then perhaps you should come with us to speak with the Bishop," Aimee said.

The nun shook her head. "I will be in prayer. My fate lies in God's hands."

Angelique nodded before turning to enter the Bishop's office. She knew they had no appointment and that quite possibly, she would be unable to see him, so as she announced her name to the clerk, she was surprised to hear the Bishop's voice as he appeared in the door.

"My dear Mrs. Slater," he said. "I am so happy that you decided to follow up on our previous conversation. I am anxious to discuss my proposal with you."

Angelique offered a weak smile. "That will have to wait, Your Excellency. I have more pressing matters that require your attention, I am afraid."

"Then, come into my office. This is your daughter, is it not? One of the twins?"

"How nice of you to remember," Angelique said. "This is Aimee."

"We met at my sister's wedding. It seems like such a long time ago," Aimee said.

"Or just yesterday," the Bishop said with a laugh. "The years do pass quickly. Please sit and tell me the nature of your visit."

They took their places on the chairs opposite his massive desk. "I am afraid that there has been a terrible wrong, a virtual crime committed by a member of the religious community under your jurisdiction. I thought that it was necessary that we report it to you," Angelique said.

The Bishop leaned forward; his face grew somber. "That sounds serious and most disturbing. I assume that you will tell me the details of what has happened?"

"Perhaps my daughter Aimee should provide those. She was, after all, the one who uncovered the situation."

"Proceed then, Aimee," the Bishop said.

Aimee told of the mysterious room at the end of the hall in the unoccupied part of the hospital. She described the haunting cries of the women held there and how she was able to gain access. And then, she explained how she discovered the poor mothers, frightened and neglected, locked away from their families, robbed of the babies that they had just birthed.

The Bishop listened attentively "That is a sin before the eyes of God. How does such a thing happen?" he asked.

Angelique opened the book. "A nun, Your Excellency. Sister Mary Grace. These are her notes, with the dates and names of those families she thought that she was helping, but inevitably destroyed."

"May I see it?"

"Of course," Angelique said, handing the volume over to him. "This is the evidence, which I leave to you. I trust you will know how to proceed."

"I will speak to Mother Superior, of course, and we will determine the best course of action in terms of discipline."

Angelique nodded. "But there is a larger, more pressing issue, one which I take very personally."

"Which is?" he asked.

"These women were told that their babies had died, but I have learned that they were placed with me at the orphanage. It is my greatest desire to reunite these mothers with their children if at all possible. The information needed to do so lies with Sister Mary Grace and the details in that book."

"I understand. Rest assured Mrs. Slater that I will have my staff on this as soon as possible. We will move heaven and earth if necessary to restore what these women have lost. You have my word on it."

"I am so grateful, Bishop. In the meantime, we will suspend all adoptions from our nursery until after you have completed your investigation."

"That seems like a prudent course of action. I am hopeful that we can right these wrongs. And please know how much I appreciate what you have done here today. Both of you."

Aimee cleared her throat. "Your Excellency, Sister Mary Grace was misguided, there is no doubt about that, but the need that she saw remains. So many women must face childbirth alone because they are unmarried."

"Which is the mark of their sin," the Bishop said.

"But God forgives," Angelique said, "and so must we. Surely, you believe that as well."

"These women need help," Aimee said.

"It is not the place of the church to help them," the Bishop said, his voice firm.

"I think that the church is the perfect place to provide this kind of shelter and solace. It is most certainly God's work," Aimee said.

"But the idea of it is scandalous," The Bishop said. "A home for unwed mothers?"

"Didn't Our Lord teach us compassion?" Aimee asked. "Isn't all life sacred, especially the unborn?"

The Bishop cleared his throat. "What would you propose?"

"A facility for them to live during their confinement, one that would provide a safe environment into which those babies can be born," Aimee said. "The church could aid in placement if the mothers choose adoption. Equally as important, we could provide a place of respite and healing for new mothers suffering from the post-partum melancholy that Sister recognized. Her intentions were good, even if her methods were all wrong."

"When you say 'we,' I assume that you are referring to yourself and your mother, of course."

"If you will provide the needed funding, then, yes, we will see to it that it comes to fruition."

The Bishop smiled. "Mrs. Slater, I can see that your daughter is as persuasive as you were when you began the orphanage."

"I take that as a compliment, Your Excellency."

"There is a home that the Diocese just acquired that is rather close to you. We had discussed using it as a seminary for young men entering the priesthood, but I think I can justify pressing it into service for these women. I make you no promises, but if the council agrees, then, you will have my blessing and may proceed."

"Thank you, Bishop," Aimee said. "You have no idea how many lives you are about to change." The thought made her smile, for she included her own in that statement.

"Mrs. Slater?" the Bishop added. "My original proposal involved asking you to become the Director of all of the church-run orphanages in the Diocese. You have proved to me that you have a way with the children that is divinely ordained. Plus, your administrative skills are excellent. I had looked forward to a partnership with you. As usual, you have outwitted me."

"Not at all, your Excellency. I would never presume to do such a thing." Angelique said. "We are still partners, all three of us. We have just taken off in a different direction, one which will expand our mission. I hope that you agree, this is by God's appointment."

"And He works in mysterious ways," Aimee added.

CHAPTER FIFTY-FIVE

The rumbling in the pit of Aida's stomach was hard to ignore, and she took a deep breath, willing herself not to be sick. In that moment, she thought that if God was merciful, He would simply take her, allowing her to escape the heartbreak of her husband's disloyalty. In the peaceful slumber of death, there is no deceit, she thought, for it delivers what it promises, the end of life. Betrayal, however, destroys hope. It can only happen if you love.

She considered that idea. How she had loved Michel and how great were her expectations for their life together. He had been on his best behavior during their courtship, charismatic and kind. She quickly became infatuated, lost in the young girl fantasies of true love and happily ever after. But the reality had been quite different. She had tried to ignore his unresponsiveness, forgive his absences from home. She held onto the rare moments of tenderness between them as though they were a lifeline. But she had been foolish, and she knew it. Their marriage was nothing more than a pretense, for the sake of appearances and his good name. And that hurt almost as much as his disloyalty.

By the time the carriage reached their home, she still had no answers. She longed for her mother, whose advice had always been invaluable during the particularly difficult times in her life. But this was a situation that she would have to analyze on her own, a problem that only she could solve. She wondered if she could separate her emotions from logic and chart a path for her future, one that included happiness and peace of mind.

The clock in the hall chimed, marking the hour. Aida wondered how much time she had before Michel returned, and if she would be able to look upon his face with anything other than distain. She climbed the stairs to the bedroom they shared and although it was far too early, she changed into her dressing gown. The waistcoat that he had worn the previous day hung on the wooden valet. She lightly fingered it, the stiffness of the collar, the impeccable seams sewn by a talented tailor. He thought himself to be a gentleman, no doubt, and yet, he had proved to have the morals of an alley cat. She wondered what his fine and fancy friends might have thought of his questionable choices, his secret life on the seedy side of town. She reached into the outer pocket and discovered a lace handkerchief that most certainly belonged to a woman, the strong scent of lavender clung to it, permeating the air with its thick sweetness. Aida's stomach lurched in protest. She searched the other pockets. There was a small flask of a thick green liquid. She opened it and smelled. "Absinthe," she whispered, recalling her own brief dance with the green fairy on their honeymoon. Was he partaking of it regularly, she wondered? She raised the bottle to her lips. She imagined her mother's disapproval, calling such cheap indulgences unladylike. But then, she remembered the serenity she felt when she had tried it.

"Just this once," she whispered as she took a small sip. Within seconds, a warmth filled her body and a sense of calm replaced her fear. She stumbled to the bed. I will rest for a bit, she thought, and then, worry about what will happen next when I wake. The anxiety faded away as her thoughts turned to fields of flowers and as she ran through them, their fragrance intoxicating, she fell into a deep sleep.

CHAPTER FIFTY-SIX

Sunlight flooded the room and Aida woke with a start. She rubbed her temples and licked her dry, chapped lips. She was surprised that she had slept through the night. The events of the previous afternoon nagged at her, torturing her with the reality of the current state of her life. If nothing else, the absinthe had provided her with a merciful respite, albeit a temporary one.

Perhaps she should take the rest of the bottle, she thought, just in case she needed it on some future sleepless night. So when she spied his waistcoat, still hanging in the same spot, she tiptoed across the room, reached into the pocket and carefully removed the flask, tucking it away in an empty hatbox. She hoped that he would look for it and dared him to ask her if she had taken it. If it provided her with occasional relief, let him go without. The thought of it brought her a bit of comfort.

She sat at her dressing table and brushed her hair before repining it into a neat bun. Her face was pale, she thought, as she pinched her cheeks. She wondered if she was coming down with something. Then, she laughed out loud. Her heart had been broken over and over again during the course of her marriage. If she was sick, it was from sadness. She had just put on her day dress when she heard the front door close. She assumed it was Michel, leaving for the day, and then, breathed a sigh of relief. Until she was strong enough to confront him, she was glad to avoid being in his presence.

Besides, the women at the center were counting on her. Colleen's trial was only a month away and there was still so much ground to cover if Joseph Reeves was to present a reasonable defense on her behalf. Aida's life at home may have been empty and unfulfilling, but she had found a purpose, an order to her days, even if the distraction was only temporary.

By mid-afternoon, she had written the opening argument, outlining Colleen's home life, the struggles and obstacles that led to her being sent to her uncle. She painted a picture of a poor abused young women, forced into a form of sexual slavery, with no recourse and no means of escape. She described the uncle's ill temper, especially when he had been drinking, the moments of fury that often became violent. Finally, she told of how on one such occasion, Colleen feared for her life, so much so that she stabbed him with a kitchen knife in self-defense. She read it aloud as the women sat in stunned silence, and when she was done, they applauded. Joseph Reeves stood, shouting "bravo." In that moment, she felt that she had accomplished what she had hoped, to show the judge and jury that everyone deserves a fair trial, even the less fortunate.

"I have these notes for the closing. Here is the list of questions for each possible witness as well as those for Colleen's testimony," Aida said.

"We are going to show them," one of the women said, her crimson lips making her look more like a clown than a seductress.

Aida tried not to think of the irony that she spent her days with prostitutes while wondering if her husband spent his evenings with them as well. These women were reformed, of course, hopeful for a better life, but as she quickly learned, old habits die hard. She often wondered how many of them eventually returned to a life on the streets.

The soup that Gretchen served for lunch was the first thing that Aida had eaten in twenty-four hours. She hadn't thought much about food, especially with her nervous stomach, but after just a spoonful or two she was unable to eat another bite.

"Are you ill?" Gretchen asked. "There is no color in your face."

Aida shrugged. There was no way that she could share all that had transpired in her life just since yesterday, nor would she. They thought that she had an enchanted life, married to Prince Charming with whom she lived in a beautiful castle. But as she well knew, appearances can be deceiving, and in reality things are often far different than they seem to the casual observer.

"I haven't slept well, lately," Aida said. "I think I worry far too much about the outcome of this trial than I care to admit."

"We all do," one of the women said. "But without your guidance, I don't know where we would be."

"I agree with that," Joseph Reeves said. "I would have never imagined that my first trial would be a capital one, with life or death hanging in the balance. But I am grateful that you have entrusted me with the responsibility. I have learned more from you, Aida, than I did in law school. I may not have experience, but you have given me a voice, and I will do my best to represent Colleen."

"I know you will," Aida said. "I am so pleased, too." She paused. "Pardon me. I am feeling rather dizzy."

Gretchen rushed to her side, just as Aida fainted, catching her before she fell to the ground.

Joseph carried her to the threadbare sofa, while one of the women returned with smelling salts.

"What happened?" Aida mumbled, her eyes fluttering as she struggled to regain consciousness.

"You fainted," Gretchen said.

"That's so strange," Aida mumbled. "I have never done so in my life."

"Perhaps it is fatigue and worry, as you claim," Gretchen said, "but I have another idea."

"Truly, it is nothing. I am just under the weather," Aida said.

"That may be so, but I have a hunch that you are pregnant."

"Pregnant?" Aida whispered. That possibility had never entered into her mind. But then, she began to do the mental calculation, the moments she had lain with Michel and the months that had passed without her regular cycle. Her heart raced in response. As much as she longed for a child, wanted motherhood more than anything, the timing couldn't have been worse.

"Is it likely?" Gretchen asked. She could be direct, although it was one of the things that Aida liked about her. So many of the women in her social circle, acquiesced to the opinions of others as though they waited for some subtle signal before nodding in agreement. They never challenged their husbands or anyone else, for that matter, nor would they have asked such a question of another woman out of some misplaced notion of perceived propriety and proper place.

Aida nodded. "Yes. I suppose it is. I have been so preoccupied with my work here, coupled with Colleen's trial, that I hadn't kept track of my time of the month as I should have."

"How far along might you be?" Gretchen asked.

Again, the question was blunt, and Aida hesitated before answering, but she had spent so much time in the presence of these women that she felt certain that they regarded her as a friend. It was asked out of concern, rather than curiosity. She shrugged. "Three months, I think. Perhaps closer to four."

"Then, you must stay home from this point on. We have your notes and the research that we have all gathered. You leave us in the capable hands of Mr. Reeves."

He stepped forward, his face turning crimson. His discomfort over discussing such delicate issues. obvious. "Mrs. Slater," he said. "If you are with child, then I think that you have been given wise advice. I feel confident that I will be able to finish the work that we began, and I have no doubt that I will be prepared for trial when the day arrives."

Aida swallowed hard. Colleen's defense had been her project, her chance to practice the law, even from this unlikely place. She wanted to be in court on opening day of the trial and each one thereafter until the judge pronounced a not guilty verdict. She wanted to share in the victory with these women, to see that justice prevailed. A part of her needed it.

She sat in silence for a long while before speaking. "If God has seen fit to bless us with a child," Aida said, "then I must do my absolute best to protect it."

"That much is certain," Gretchen said.

"Do you hope for a boy or a girl?" One of the women asked.

"I hope for a healthy baby." Her eyes filled with tears. She had known the joy of impending motherhood before, felt the life growing in her womb. But she also knew what it felt like to have those expectations dashed, the dreams broken. She couldn't imagine having to endure such a loss again. Gretchen was right: she needed to stay home.

"I have one request," Aida said.

"Certainly," Gretchen said. "You have done so much for all of us here. Anything you ask."

"Let me give you my address. Send a note to me following the trial. I must know the outcome."

"I will come myself," Gretchen said. "I will bring Mr. Reeves with me. We will give you a complete account of every moment."

Aida shook her head. Their presence in her home would be hard to explain to her mother-in-law, who would most certainly become meddlesome once she learned of Aida's condition. Her husband, always so unpredictable, would be irate if he learned of her daily trips to Harlem. Only because of his absence from home had she been able to conceal it from him. It was time for her to part ways with the Center for Hope and the women who lived there. "I am afraid that won't be possible," Aida whispered.

Gretchen forced a smile, but the awkwardness was obvious. She nodded. In that moment, while much was unspoken between them, each clearly understood the other.

And Aida wept.

CHAPTER FIFTY-SEVEN

"Are you feeling poorly, my dear?" Michel asked when he arrived home and peeked into the bedroom. "I am surprised to see that you have retired so early."

Aida shrugged.

He seemed oblivious to her lack of interest. "You were sound asleep when I got home last night. I didn't want to wake you this morning. You seemed so peaceful."

Aida forced herself to smile, although she loathed him with every fiber of her being. He crossed the room and moved to the edge of the bed, where he sat. When he reached for her hand, it took every bit of self-control on her part, not to reach out and slap him. She took a deep breath.

"I seem to have a little headache. Perhaps it is the change of weather. The rest does appear to help, though."

"Then, I will leave you to it. Cook can bring you a tray if you are hungry."

Aida shook her head. The nausea was unrelenting. Just the mere thought of food made her stomach even more queasy. "Maybe later," she said.

"I will be in the library if you need me," he said.

His solicitous behavior confused her, after so many months of indifference. She also thought it odd that he was home early. On most nights it was well after dark when she heard his footsteps in the front hall.

"I do hope that you will recover quickly," he added. "May I remind you that my parents are coming for dinner tomorrow night? I know that you will do your best to be the gracious hostess."

She wanted to scream, to throw something at his smug face. His motives were clear: they had not entertained his family in quite some time, and he needed her to play nice, to continue the charade that theirs was a perfect marriage, a model for other young couples. She needed no reminder that for him, appearances were everything.

"Ah, yes, tomorrow," Aida said. "I had forgotten all about it." And she had. "I will make certain that cook has a special menu prepared."

"I knew that I could count on you," he said, taking a small bow before leaving the room. "I will return at bedtime."

Aida pretended to be fast asleep when she saw the lamplight under the door. She had hoped that he would simply choose the guest room instead, but when she felt his weight on the mattress as he slid into bed, she turned her back to him and prayed that he wouldn't touch her.

The next morning, he appeared with a cup of tea and a piece of toasted bread on a tray. "I know that you haven't eaten," he said, "I thought perhaps the tea might be more palatable than coffee."

Aida sat up in bed and reached for the cup. "Thank you," she whispered, taking a sip. There were two very different sides to her husband. This one was warm and caring, and for a moment, she allowed herself to forget the images of him with his arm around his Harlem mistress. But everything that Michel did was calculated, driven by his own self interests. It is what made him a good lawyer, shrewd and cunning, but it made him a lousy husband, one who was also the father of her unborn child.

"I will see you tonight," he said. "My parents will be here at 7. Can we say dinner at half past?"

Aida nodded. She said no more.

At six, Aida smoothed her hair and donned her second best gown. She pinned the cameo broach to her bodice and glanced in the mirror. I am presentable, she thought. It had already taken most of her energy to get herself out of bed and dressed for an evening that filled her with dread. She hoped that she would be able to survive the meal without being sick at the dinner table.

Michel arrived at home fifteen minutes before his parents knocked at the door, and he opened the door widely, welcoming them a little too enthusiastically in Aida's opinion.

"Come in," he said, "I am so glad to see you."

"Likewise," the Count said, embracing both of them.

They retired to the parlor for a pre-dinner glass of wine. Aida took hers, but placed it on the coffee table where it remained untouched. Just the thought of drinking it made her stomach flip.

"My dear," The Countess said, "I haven't seen nearly enough of you lately. What on earth do you do to occupy your time?"

She wanted to say that she made daily visits to Harlem where she has been working on the legal defense of a prostitute accused of killing her pimp, who also happened to be her uncle. It might have been fun to watch her mother-in-law's reaction. But instead, she smiled sweetly. "I stay busy, Countess. I don't know where on earth the day goes. I hardly turn around, and it is dinner time."

"Aida has done a fine job of making this our home," Michel said. "We look forward to filling the place with the laughter of children."

He reached for her hand, but she pulled it away. She wondered if anyone noticed.

"That is our wish for you, too," the Count said.

When cook announced dinner, they all made their way to the dining room. The china and silver glistened in the candlelight. "What a lovely table you have set," the Countess remarked. It seemed rather insincere, but Aida accepted the compliment.

The men discussed politics over dinner. Aida moved the chicken and rice around on her plate without eating a bite. The Countess listened with rapt attention, hanging onto every word. Occasionally, she would interject something mindless like, "That's interesting" or "most fascinating." Aida was bored to tears.

Afterwards, pie and coffee were served in the parlor. Aida glanced at the clock and wondered how much more of the evening she would be expected to endure. She had not decided when to tell Michel about the pregnancy. Since she had already considered this her baby, not his, she wondered if she would wait until she was no longer able to conceal the growing bump under her gown. That didn't seem prudent, but the idea of having a bit of control over when she would reveal her condition did bring her some comfort. She hated being powerless.

She had given some serious thought to leaving him straight away, buying a one-way ticket to New Orleans and returning to her loving family. They would happily help her raise the child and perhaps, she thought, in due time she could find love again. But she was a smart woman, and she understood that the limits placed on her gender weren't just restricted to voting privileges. Women were legally non entities when it came to divorce. In a court of law, the ruling always favored the man, especially when it came to property rights. A family like Michel's had power and position, which extended far beyond New York City. She feared that they would use that influence to take her son or daughter away, arguing that they should be lawfully granted parental rights. No, she had considered all of the possibilities when it came to her marriage and as much as she hated it, until this baby was born healthy and she could devise a plan, she was stuck in a marriage of convenience.

But she was also clever enough to play the game, wield her power, if necessary.

"Count and Countess," Aida said. "We wanted to wait until after dinner to share a bit of news with you."

Michel narrowed his eyes and looked at her. He was well aware of how crafty and unpredictable she could be. At one time, that thrilled him, but now, it simply filled him with dread. Would she tell them of his long absences or the trouble in their marriage, he wondered? Would she announce that she was leaving him or that he was to fund some wild scheme? What was this news and why did he have no knowledge of it? "My dear," he said, and then stopped short, unsure of what to say next.

"Michel," Aida said, "I am sorry. Perhaps you would like to tell them."

His face turned red. He was humiliated, caught unaware by her words. He tried not to stammer. "No," he said. "You should continue."

"Well then," Aida said, clapping her hands. "We are going to have a baby."

"My dear, Aida," the Countess said, rising to embrace her daughter-in-law. "That is such wonderful news. I have hoped for this for such a long time."

"Congratulations, son," the Count said, shaking Michel's hand.

Aida turned and fixed her gaze on her errant husband, who sat in stunned silence. "It is indeed the happiest of days," she said. "Isn't it, Michel?"

CHAPTER FIFTY-EIGHT

Angelique's heart leapt with joy as she reread the letter from Aida. "A baby," she whispered. "I can't imagine anything more wonderful."

Andrew was in his study, deep in concentration. She paused at the door watching him as he examined the maps spread out across his desk. Occasionally, he would stop and record some observation he had made.

"Are you busy?" Angelique asked, hesitant to interrupt him. "You have been hard at work since dinner."

"Never too busy for you, darling."

"You seem to be occupied by some serious task," Angelique said. "You know, I probably don't mention this enough, but I am incredibly proud of you. Not only have you earned your position as Dean of Science at the university, but the research you have done is groundbreaking."

"I hope so. I think that when the Army Signal Corp was able to issue its first hurricane warning a few years ago, I felt that I had come full circle."

"Think of the lives you have saved through your efforts, the lives yet to be saved. Hard to imagine that you began your career as a young man with a few simple tools and a note pad."

"On a resort island, of all places," he added. "That bit of providence allowed me to meet the most fascinating woman in the world, one whom I am still honored to call my wife."

Angelique smiled. "I hope that you will be equally as honored to call me "Grandma.' "

He removed his glasses and stood to embrace her. "Really? Is it true? Which of our daughters is expecting?"

She held up the letter. "Aida. This just came in the mail."

"So late?"

"It was delivered next door by mistake. I just got it. Good news often seems delayed, doesn't it?"

"I never thought of that, but perhaps it is true." Andrew's face grew serious. "Do you think she will be alright, I mean, considering all that she endured the first time?"

"I hope so. There is always a risk of such things, of course, but we will think positive. Aida is a smart woman, and she will protect this baby with all that she has."

"Of course. I know that she will. I just wish that she lived closer. New York might as well be on the other side of the world. From what I gather, her husband's family can be rather stiff and formal. I wonder how much support she will get?"

"It pains me, too. A woman needs her mother when she is about to give birth and certainly in the days which follow. I am going to do my best to convince her to spend the last few months of her confinement here with us. With Aimee now being a midwife, I can't imagine a better person to help her through it, perhaps even delivering her baby."

"Indeed. Aimee is quite the young woman," Andrew said. "I never thought that my daughter would be running a home for unwed mothers, but she is doing remarkably well. I was impressed with the facility and how warm and inviting it was. Certainly, it has provided a safe haven for desperate women in their time of need."

"It has been more successful than I might have imagined. The Bishop is pleased, which means he will continue to advocate for funding. But more importantly, we are able to help so many."

"Aimee is much like you, I think. She has your compassionate heart."

"And Aida?" Angelique asked.

"Aida has your tenacity. She is strong."

"Both girls are smart like their Poppa," Angelique said, offering her hand to Andrew.

He lightly kissed her palm. "I miss our talks, the quiet moments together. They happen so rarely these days. Forgive me if I have been busy, preoccupied by work."

"My days are full as well," She said. "Jubilee writes that things are going well at the plantation. The times of unrest seem to have passed, which is a relief, but I still have the books to balance. And then, there are the responsibilities at the orphanage."

"How did we get so busy?"

"It just happens, I think. We have constructed these hectic lives for ourselves, but in the process, I think we have forgotten that we were supposed to also build one together."

"That statement is a bit sobering. Are we growing apart or just growing older?" Andrew asked.

"I think it is a bit of both. The years pass so quickly, that I find it hard to believe that here we are, with grown children, about to become grandparents."

"I do still adore you, my darling, as much as I did the day I married you," Andrew said, "perhaps even more since my love for you has grown exponentially."

Angelique laughed. "You do love those science words."

"I suppose I do, but in this case, it is an appropriate term."

"Do you ever think about those dreams we had as newlyweds, the places we wanted to go in the land of someday?"

"All the time. Perhaps we should think about pursuing some of those dreams. Where shall I take you, my love?"

She shrugged. "I have thought about France. For a long time, I wouldn't have even considered it, since that's where

Jean Paul had ultimately planned to take Aimee. But I do think I'd like visit the place where my ancestors lived before they ended up in America."

"Then, we should plan it. Time waits for no one. And soon, you will be filling your days with the laughter of grandchildren and will have no interest in anything other than them."

"I suspect that Aimee and Franklin will start a family soon as well. I can't imagine anything more wonderful than to watch my children's children grow."

"Our legacy."

"Indeed. You know, I have kept a journal since I was a young girl."

"Really? Are there any secrets in those pages that I might want to know about?"

"Much of it is nonsense, my silly observations about life. But some is more serious, the chronicling of my days before and after I met you. I want to remember it all, every single moment."

"What a lovely thought, darling. The years pass and those memories fade. Someday, your words will be important to our children, and now, our grandchildren. I would love to know more about my late parents, wouldn't you?"

"Oh, yes! I have never thought of myself as a writer, but perhaps I might become one. Not in the literal sense, of course, but just to document that family history. I already have so much of it scribbled in various places. I just need to compile things, organize the accounts to make it ultimately more readable."

"My darling, I know that if you decide to become a writer, then you will be a good one. Once you have taken on a task, you are unstoppable."

Angelique blushed. "This is a simple little project, Andrew. I am not building a pyramid."

Andrew stood, wrapping his arms around her. "But even the ancient Egyptians understood that which you leave behind makes you immortal, especially the written word."

"I suppose that is true. So now, I have a mission to accomplish, although this will be more fun than work. Perhaps by the time Aida's baby is able to walk, I will have it finished."

"There you go, a goal with a timeline."

"Thank you, Andrew. For always being there with words of encouragement."

"Just as you have done for me."

Angelique stood on her tip toes to kiss him. "I think I will retire now. Don't work too late."

"I won't."

"Promise?"

"Always."

Angelique pulled the ivory comb from her hair, which fell in soft curls around her shoulders. There were a few grey hairs mixed in with the raven strands, but she was still a handsome woman, with a timeless beauty that captivated men and exasperated women. Her steel blue eyes sparkled in the lamplight.

Andrew is right, she thought. There were stories, tales of the grand adventures that her grandmother had once told her, the family sagas of both good times and bad. And she had accounts of her own life that often seemed more like a grand work of fiction than fact. Certainly, there was the deep culture of Louisiana, much of which had been erased in the years following the war. Hers was a rich heritage, one that she hoped to pass along to this baby yet to be born.

"Tomorrow," she whispered. "Tomorrow, I begin."

CHAPTER FIFTY-NINE

SPRING, 1879

"You must rest, my dear," the Countess said, fluffing the covers and placing another pillow behind her daughter-in-law's head.

"I am so very tired of being in bed," Aida replied. "I think I shall go mad if I am forced to lie here yet another day."

"You will do no such thing," the Countess said. "Many women with your history have had to make a similar sacrifice for the health and well-being of their unborn child. When the baby arrives with all of his fingers and toes, you will be glad that you did so as well."

Aida laughed, "You do know that you always use the pronoun 'he,' right?"

"Perhaps it is wishful thinking on my part. But I do so hope that it is a boy, for your sake."

"For my sake?"

"Well, certainly both my husband and Michel are keen to continue the family name. But you will soon see that being a mother, especially of a son, brings with it certain advantages."

"Advantages? Like what?"

"There is power in giving birth to an heir, Aida. You, my dear, are smart enough to know how to use it."

Aida considered the idea and tried not to laugh at her mother-in-law's naïveté. The women in the de la Martinique family had no power at all, except perhaps for Countess Maria, and she, of course, had long gone to live with the angels. No, theirs was a patriarchal clan, a fact which had become painfully obvious to Aida within a few weeks of her wedding to Michel.

"Perhaps you and I define that differently, Countess. My life with my husband has shown me that while he is allowed to do as he pleases; I am expected to defer to his wishes. I can't imagine that motherhood would change that for me."

The Countess moved to sit on the edge of the bed. "Aida, I don't presume to know what goes on between you and Michel. But every marriage has its challenges. You are a very headstrong young woman, which is no doubt why my son fell in love with you, but sometimes, you have to put your pride aside for what is good for the relationship."

Aida could feel her pulse quicken. Her mother-in-law was of a different generation and therefore, embraced a different way of thinking. But she couldn't help but wonder if even the complacent Countess could ignore her feelings if she was presented with the obvious signs of her husband's infidelity.

"Michel has been unfaithful to me, Countess," Aida said, a little more bluntly than she had planned. Actually, she had no intention of sharing this bit of sordid history with her mother-in-law, and she blamed her straightforwardness on a momentary lapse in judgement. She fully expected the woman to rush to her son's defense, dismissing Aida's accusations in the process, but she did the opposite.

"Do you think that you are the first women of a noble family to experience such a thing, Aida? I took you to be a woman of the world, and as such, should understand that titled men seem to periodically take such liberties. Perhaps you may recall that we talked about this ages ago when you first married my son."

Aida shrugged. There had been so many of those tedious conversations in the early days, when the Countess thought that she was in charge of Aida's training. She hated living with her in-laws, the lectures on decorum, the mind-numbing dinners with boorish guests. Oh, she had tolerated it then out of obligation, but she would not be lectured in her own home.

"So are you implying that you have looked the other way, accepted similar behavior from the Count?"

The Countess swallowed hard and nodded. "Yes, my dear. I suppose that when I was a young bride it upset me greatly, his long absences from home, the tell-tale signs of where he had been. But I grew to understand that we must often give something to receive something in return."

"I am afraid that I don't see your point. Secrets destroy a marriage."

"Or strengthens it. Look around you, Aida. You live in a fine house, sleep in a soft bed. You have servants to cook and clean for you. Marriage to Michel has made that possible."

Aida was prepared to object, but there was a bit of truth to what the woman had said. She had taken her life of privilege for granted, assuming that she would always have the finer things in life. It was pure folly on her part to think that without her husband's wealth and position, she would have been able to create such an existence for herself as a working woman. Her mother had been an exception, but even her success had been due, in part, to the generosity of others.

"It is not the life I wanted for myself," Aida said.

"But it is the life that you chose," the Countess said. "If it is any consolation to you, bear this in mind: your husband may leave every morning, but he always returns home. You, and soon, this child, will always be his true North. And no other woman will ever have that power."

Aida thought of this for a moment. Perhaps fatherhood would change Michel. Relationships, like people, are dynamic. And anything is possible.

"Oh, and by the way," the Countess said, handing her a sealed envelope. "This came for you earlier today by messenger. I almost forgot to give it to you."

Aida took a deep breath. Colleen's trial had begun two days ago. She expected the verdict to be delivered at any moment and hoped that Gretchen wouldn't forget her promise to let her know as soon as possible. "Thank you," she whispered.

"I will leave you to it, then," the Countess said. "And do take a little nap if you can."

But before her mother-in-law had closed the bedroom door behind her, Aida had ripped open the envelope. Inside was a single sheet of paper with two words written boldly in the middle of the page. "Not Guilty."

Suddenly, overcome by emotion, Aida burst into tears.

CHAPTER SIXTY

Aida was pleased to have been a part of Colleen's victory. She may not have been a practicing lawyer, but constructing the defense's case had been an enjoyable challenge. Justice was ultimately served, which didn't always happen for those with little power or money. Aida vowed that when the baby was born, she would return to her work with the women at the center, and she would bring the child with her.

She wanted, more than anything, to raise her son or daughter to understand that the world is made of many different kinds of people and that all were created equal. She thought back on that afternoon when she lectured the women about the Declaration of Independence. It was more than just a document to her. Certainly, being born with Michel's noble last name would mean certain advantages, but she would never let those turn her offspring into someone who was spoiled or willful. The Count and Countess might view themselves as superior to the rest of the world, but she didn't and neither would anyone she raised. If anything, she wanted her child to understand that because of the family's social and economic position, much would be expected of him or her. And it was an opportunity to do good, to make a difference.

The days of her confinement seemed interminable. Her mother-in-law visited daily, fussing about and issuing stern warnings whenever Aida tried to get out of bed. Instead of helping, that seemed to make the time even more difficult to endure. She tried to read, but few books held her interest. Neither did needlepoint. She wished she had friends who might have come to call, entertaining her with their idle gossip, but the social scene in New York had little appeal to her, and as a result, she had formed no close ties. It might have been fun to walk about the fancy shops on Madison Avenue, she thought, buying a layette for the baby, but that was out of the question, too, an honor that she reluctantly yielded to her mother-in-law. For the time being, her life was relegated to the four walls of her bedroom, where she was predictability bored to tears.

She rarely saw Michel, who had permanently moved into the guest room, although on more than one occasion, she heard him stagger up the stairs well past midnight. Most of the time, his absence was a relief rather than a cause for concern, but occasionally, she longed for the early days of their relationship, when he was loving and attentive. Impending fatherhood hadn't made him a better husband. She had, in fact, stopped wishing for anything more than their current arrangement.

Aida had already decided that she would pursue the things that made her happy, work for causes that allowed her to make a difference. They would continue to live separate lives until she had decided once and for all to leave him for good. After the baby was born, she would devote her time and energy into raising a decent human being. Maybe in a few years, law school might be a possibility. Her dreams had simply been deferred, she reminded herself.

The first sign of spring had Aida longing to welcome the changing season. How lovely it would be to sit outside for a bit, to feel the sun on her face, she thought. She had even considered sneaking out into their tiny backyard, but then, imagined her mother-in-law catching her there. It wouldn't be worth having to endure the lecture. Instead, she crossed the hardwood floor in her bare feet, threw back the curtains and opened the window wide. The room was suddenly filled with light and a gentle breeze wafted through the air. She took a deep breath, trying to identify the sweet smell. "Roses," she whispered, spying the first blooms of the bush which climbed up the wall of the neighbor's house. She thought of the flower that Michel had worn in his lapel. She was reasonably certain that she had conceived the child that night. The memory made her smile.

Aida hadn't quite reached the bed when she felt it, an unmistakable twinge deep inside of her belly. She inhaled and slowly exhaled, willing it to go away. Carefully, she slipped under the covers and lay perfectly still for what seemed like an hour. When the pain failed to return, she breathed a sigh of relief, attributing the whole thing to her overactive imagination. Birds chirped outside the window. Their chatter was not altogether unpleasant, she thought, as she drifted off to sleep.

She woke two hours later. The sunset was magnificent, illuminating the sky with vibrant hues of pink and purple. Even from the limited view that her bed provided, she could see the reflection of the colors, which made her smile. Such moments were rare and meant to be relished. She wondered how many more twilights she would need to count before her baby would finally make his or her appearance. At least a hundred, she figured.

Cook appeared with the dinner tray and when Aida sat up in bed, she felt it once more, the unmistakable ache that comes with a contraction. "Too soon," she whispered.

"Ma'am?" cook asked, and Aida simply smiled.

"Nothing. Just a little uncomfortable, that's all," Aida said. "Has my mother-in-law come yet today?"

"She was here a while ago. Came to check on you. Said that you were sleeping, and she didn't want to disturb you."

"I suppose I took quite a nap."

"You needed it. Good for the baby. Shall I get you something?" Cook asked.

"No," Aida said. "I'll be fine."

"I will be here for another hour. Going to fix the Viscount's evening meal before I leave. You have that bell by your bed," cook said. "Ring if you need me."

Aida nodded, repositioning herself to accommodate the tray. "Thanks. Dinner looks wonderful."

"Eat it all. You need to keep up your strength."

Aida had taken a bite of the potatoes when the tightening in her stomach returned once more. She pushed the dinner tray aside and watched the clock on the nearby fireplace mantle. "Hold on, little one," she whispered. "It is not yet your time."

She concentrated on her breathing, willing her body to relax. The pain gripped her again. She glanced at the clock. Five minutes had passed. Aida closed her eyes and said a prayer. "God help me," she said out loud, her voice echoing in the empty room. Once again, the ache began slowly as it built into a crescendo. How long between them, she wondered? The clock confirmed her fears, exactly five minutes apart.

Her heart beat wildly, and she imagined that of her unborn child in synchrony with her own. "Not again," she whispered. "Please God, not again." As the tears flowed, she reached for the bell, ringing it with all of her might.

CHAPTER SIXTY-ONE

By the time cook reached the top of the stairs, Aida was moaning, the pain unrelenting as one contraction followed another. "Help me," she pleaded.

"Ma'am, what would you have me do?"

Aida wanted to throw something at her, to yell and scream at the top of her lungs. Instead, she took a deep breath. "Is there anyone else in the house?"

"The maid."

"Send her to get my mother-in-law. Tell her to come quickly and to alert the doctor."

"I can do that, ma'am."

"Put a pot of water to boil. We will need it soon, I am afraid."

"Yes, of course."

"Please hurry."

Aida could hear cook's footsteps as she hurried down the stairs followed by the muffled sounds of voices in the kitchen.

"Please, baby," Aida whispered, "fight for your life. If I lose you, then, I will surely die as well."

She closed her eyes, begging God for mercy. But before she had finished her prayer, she was seized by the grip of another labor pain, and all she could do was lie there, giving into it.

It seemed like hours had passed before the Countess entered the darkened bedroom. She lit the lamp and then closed the window, drawing the curtains tight before turning to her daughter-in-law.

"I came as quickly as I could, my dear. What is happening here?"

"The baby," she stammered. "It is coming now."

She examined Aida's face, etched with pain. Beads of sweat formed on her brow. "Are you sure? It is far too soon."

Aida nodded. "The doctor? Is he coming?"

"He was not in. I left word for him to come here straight away, but that may not happen for quite some time."

"I don't have time," Aida said. "If this baby is coming now, you will have to deliver it."

The Countess grew pale. "I am no midwife, Aida. I have only had one child of my own. I don't know if I can. We need help."

Aida was in no position to placate her pampered mother-in-law. "Get cook. Bring blankets and the hot water. I have no idea how to do this either, but I have no choice and neither do you."

The Countess opened her mouth to protest, but then, changed her mind and left the room as instructed.

Aida tried not to push as the urgency became stronger with each contraction. By the time the two women had returned with blankets and the pot of boiled water, the baby's head had crowned.

"I see him," the Countess said.

In an instant it was over as cook moved in to catch the baby emerging from Aida's body.

"It's a girl," she announced. "And so very tiny."

Frantic with fear, Aida yelled, "Is she breathing?"

"I can't tell."

"Pat on her back," the Countess said.

"I don't know how," cook said.

Aida opened her mouth to scream, but no sound came out. "Please, baby girl. Breathe," she pleaded.

The maid appeared at the door. "The doctor has come," she said.

"Show him in, right away," the Countess barked.

The bedroom looked like the scene of some heinous crime. Blood and soiled towels were strewn about. There, in the middle of the bed lay a lifeless infant. Aida was rocking back and forth, crying uncontrollably. The doctor quickly moved to where she lay and scooped the baby up in his arms. He turned her over and gently tapped her once, then again, harder.

His face grew grim. He blew softly into the newborn's face.

"She is turning blue," the Countess whispered.

The doctor repeated the process several times and then stopped, shaking his heard. "I am sorry," he said, "but there is no life in this child."

Through the still of the night the calm was punctuated by Aida's screams which echoed through the house until hoarse and exhausted, she was no longer able to make a sound.

✳✳✳

Michel returned home far too late in his mother's opinion, but she resisted the urge to question him, knowing that the responsibility of telling him about the loss of the baby fell to her. She understood that there would be no easy way to do so, but when she met him at the door in her blood splattered gown, it was as though he knew by instinct what had transpired in his absence. He opened his mouth to speak, but seemed to have no words to say, and instead collapsed into the closest chair, his head in his hands, repeating "no, no, no," over and over again.

The Countess did her best to console him, but his grief was palpable. Even as a child, he didn't cry when he skinned his knee or broke a favorite toy, but here he sat as a grown man, sobbing uncontrollably.

"There will be others," The Countess said. "You are both so young. Time has a way of healing such disappointments."

He shook his head. "I don't think so. Not after having lost two."

"It is in God's hands, son."

Michel shrugged, wiping away the tears with a fine silk handkerchief. "You should go home, Mother," he said. "Change your clothes. I am going to bed. Perhaps sleep will release me from this nightmare."

He turned away to slowly climb the stairs.

The Countess stood in silence for a long time. How odd, she thought, he never once asked about Aida.

CHAPTER SIXTY-TWO

Aida had fallen deep into the abyss. It was a place where she had resided once before, a place where mothers with empty arms dwelled and sadness occupied every waking moment.

She had no idea how many days or weeks had passed since that terrible night when her baby daughter was lost forever, but that made no real difference to her. Cook brought her food, which she rarely touched. The maid came to change the sheets on her soiled bed and coax her into a clean nightgown. But she spoke to no one.

"There is a letter from your mother," the Countess said, on her daily visit.

Aida shrugged.

"I will place it with the others, although at some point, you should at least open them and read them. I know that she is worried. Michel did send her a telegram with the sad news. Do you think that perhaps you might want to visit her? That did seem to cheer you up last time."

The words "last time" reverberated in Aida's mind, reminding her that in all probability, she would never have a child of her own. She began to cry once more, the dam of emotion breeched.

"My dear, you simply must try to move past this," the Countess said. "Your life is not over."

Aida nodded as she pulled the covers around her.

"I will be back to check on you tomorrow," the Countess said, offering a weak smile.

When Aida heard the carriage pull away, she reached into the drawer of her dressing table until her fingers found the object she sought. She carefully opened the bottle and took a small sip of the absinthe, waiting to feel the familiar warmth throughout her body. Within minutes, she was asleep.

She woke with a start, the sound of muffled voices coming from downstairs. Normally, she would have cared less, but she could hear her husband's voice and that of another woman. Curiosity overtook her. Tiptoeing into the hall, she stood stone still in a spot where she had a clear view of the front door. The woman she had seen with Michel so many months earlier was gesturing wildly as though to punctuate the conversation. There was no mistaking the tall redhead, the one who had embraced her husband in broad daylight. Aida shifted her position to get a better look and then gasped. The woman was visibly pregnant and relatively far along in Aida's estimation. She bit the back of her hand to keep from crying out. How much more could she take, she wondered?

"I am carrying your baby," Aida could hear the woman saying. "What do you intend to do about it?"

"I intend to do nothing but to ask you to leave my home immediately," Michel said.

"And if I refuse?"

"I will have the constable come and physically remove you."

The red head laughed. "Please do. I would love to tell him about your bastard."

Michel's face turned red. "The child is not mine, and you will have a difficult time proving otherwise."

"We shall see about that."

"I have asked you to leave."

"Perhaps your wife might want to know about this turn of events. Is she here? I would love to meet her."

Michel took a step toward the woman. "Leave my wife and the rest of my family out of this." He reached into his pocket. "Here. I know that all you are after is money. Take it and be gone."

She placed the gold coins into her pocketbook. "As you wish. But consider this a down payment. I expect you to support this baby, who will be here any day now."

"Don't expect anything of me, madam," Michel said, closing the door behind her.

Aida reached for the vase on the nearby table and held it high above her head. She could throw it at him and with any luck, reach her target. But then, she reconsidered as she gently set it down and returned to her bedroom. She slowly exhaled. For the first time in weeks, anger replaced grief.

CHAPTER SIXTY-THREE

Aida could hear the sweet sounds of spring. As the earth awakened from its long winter nap, she considered that she, too, was trying to reclaim her life. For so long, she could only think about the oppressive sadness that had left her paralyzed, unable to do more than exist. Much like a caged bird that has suddenly been given its freedom, the prospect of building a life for herself was daunting. The open sky called to her, and yet, she wondered if she was still able to spread her wings and fly.

Aida read each of her mother's letters before sitting down to reply. She longed to be with her family once again, away from the charade of her marriage to Michel. Although she had already determined that she would leave him, she seemed unable to take the first step toward her independence. Soon, she told herself and then turned her attention elsewhere.

She reached for the flask of absinthe. A drop, maybe two, remained. As much as she hated to admit it, the liquor had been a constant companion during those interminable days of sorrow. She had come to understand that sometimes, the pain is so deep that it doesn't even hurt. But perhaps, that numbness had come from the contents of her hidden bottle. It was a possibility. And although she knew that she could quit when she so desired, she assured herself that she needed just a little more time. Tomorrow always presented an opportunity to try again.

Aida reached for her purse. She had a few coins left, enough for another bottle. Her mother-in-law's visits were far less frequent, but she could probably manage to get a bit of money from her when she came to call. The situation was not yet urgent.

The maid would be coming in to tidy up within the hour, she thought, and perhaps she could get her to run the errand. But as the sun broke through the window, bathing the room with light, Aida changed her mind. It would do me a world of good to get out, she thought, as she moved to the armoire to choose a dress to wear.

Moments later, she examined her reflection in the mirror. The green linen gown hung on her thin frame. Her face was gaunt, dark circles framing her steel blue eyes. She hardly recognized herself. "Just this last time," she whispered.

She tied the ribbon of her bonnet under her chin and made her way down the stairs. She stopped at the front door, pausing to catch her breath. I have been in the bed far too long, she thought, and then, willed herself to the curb where thankfully, she discovered the carriage and the driver hitching the horses to a nearby post.

"Can you take me to Harlem?" Aida asked.

He tried to conceal the look of alarm on his face when he saw her altered appearance. "Madame?"

"Harlem," she repeated. "I need to visit the apothecary."

He nodded. "Perhaps you might want one nearby?"

For a moment she had considered it, but then, realized that she would be easily recognized so close to home. She knew of a reputable place frequented by some of the women from the center. Perhaps if she felt strong enough, she would stop there for a visit. It mattered not to her if the driver told Michel. His opinion was of little value to her now.

She sat back and enjoyed the ride through the city. It had been so long since she had left the house, gone out among people, that she felt her spirits lift a little. She was almost disappointed when the carriage pulled in front of the apothecary, and the driver moved to help her out. But then, remembering her mission, she took a deep breath and entered the storefront.

"May I help you Madame?" the man behind the counter asked.

Aida cleared her throat. "I have recently had a most distressing personal tragedy, the stillbirth of my child. I am afraid that it has left me feeling melancholy, as you might well imagine, and I was hoping that perhaps you could help me by prescribing something to take the edge off."

He nodded. "I can make you a tonic, which will be quite therapeutic."

"I would greatly appreciate it. Perhaps, you might also have a small bottle of absinthe?"

He shook his head. "You might try the saloon on the next block. We stopped carrying it for medicinal purposes six months ago."

Aida tried to disguise her disappointment. She certainly didn't intend to enter a saloon in Harlem. Her mother would have lectured her for a week if she found out that she had. Besides, she was determined to hold fast to the last shred of dignity that she had left. Perhaps the tonic would serve the purpose. Hopefully, she rationalized, if she could put the absinthe aside, she could gather the courage needed to leave New York and her disloyal husband.

The man returned with a small bottle, which he wrapped in brown paper and tied with a string. Her hands shook as she counted out the coins and placed them on the counter. "Madame," he said. "Be forewarned. This is a powerful potion, meant to be used sparingly and as needed. I caution you to limit your consumption. Understood?"

Aida nodded. She made her way to the door and stood on the sidewalk, surveying the street for her carriage. It took a moment for her eyes to adjust to the bright light, and she squinted, trying to identify the form of a woman speaking to her driver.

In Aida's mind, the scene seemed to play out slower than in real time as the woman turned and smiled, her fiery red hair glistening in the sun. She held a bundle in her arms, a tiny infant.

For a moment, Aida was confused.

"You are Michel's wife, are you not?" the woman asked, taking a step forward.

Aida stood in silence, her brow furrowed in confusion as though the words were spoken in some foreign language and completely incomprehensible.

"I recognized the carriage. His carriage. And of course, the driver. I thought perhaps he had come to pay me a visit, but now I get the pleasure of meeting you," the woman said, as though it was some wonderful surprise, a delightful social encounter.

"Who are you?" Aida asked, although she was well aware of the answer.

"My name is Rosalie, but you may call me Rose."

Aida thought that was a bit of irony, but made no comment. She looked at the baby snuggled close to the woman's ample bosom. The longing for a child of her own was deep, the envy palpable.

"This is my son, Michel."

Aida turned and leveled her eyes on the woman. Suddenly, she had become defensive, tasting the bitter bile in the back of her throat. She steeled herself for what was to come. "Michel? It seems an odd choice. That isn't a very common name."

"This is not a common child. He is, of course, your husband's son."

This was the showdown, the day of reckoning, and Aida had to determine what course to take. She fingered the bottle she held in her hands. How she wanted just one sip, something to calm her, help her to think clearly. Instead, she laughed.

"So you think you are the first woman who has tried to pin their illegitimate offspring on my husband?" Aida asked. It was a lie, of course, but she was determined to hold her own, not give into the fear and anxiety. The sound of her racing heart echoed in her ears, her stomach churned.

"I know your husband very well, Madame. And yes, I am reasonably certain that I am not the first. But perhaps I am the first to present you with this," and she loosened the blanket which bound the newborn, freeing his little legs and feet. "Look closely," she said.

Aida protested, shook her head, and swallowed hard. She watched, transfixed, as the baby squirmed, kicking in the air. Tears welled in her eyes. Then she gasped. The infant had six tiny toes on each foot.

She thought of that afternoon after her honeymoon when she had confided the deformity to Aimee. How they had laughed at his aristocratic mark, a trait that most of the men in the de la Martinque family bore. Suddenly, it didn't seem the least bit funny.

Aida struggled to catch her breath, the world spinning around her as she fell to the sidewalk, wrapped in a cloak of darkness and despair.

CHAPTER SIXTY-FOUR

The color drained from the driver's face as he quickly moved to Aida's side. He carefully scooped her into his arms and gently placed her on the seat in the carriage.

"Off with you," he said to the redhead. "I must get the missus home, right away."

Rose nodded and took a step back, but smiled with satisfaction as they drove away.

Aida woke to a pounding in her head, as she rubbed her temples. It took her a moment to remember what had transpired, but the memory returned with unmistakable clarity. The old woman's warning from so many years ago echoed in her mind.

"Rose," she whispered. "It was not a flower, but a person." It seemed like a dreadful twist of fate, one which nagged at her.

She surveyed the room. Mercifully, she was alone. However, the voices outside of her bedroom door confirmed what she already imagined. Michel and his mother were trying to decide what to do with her. She remained still, holding her breath to better hear the conversation.

"I am afraid that she has gone completely mad," Michel said.

"What happened?" the Countess asked. "I came as soon as I could."

"She took off to some sordid apothecary in Harlem, looking for drugs, I presume. The driver gave me this." He held up the bottle as though presenting evidence in a court of law. "I had no idea that she had become so desperate, but I think it just proves that she is not of sound mind."

"You need to give her some time, son," the Countess said. "She has recently suffered a great loss."

"Do you not think that I suffered the same loss, Mother?" Michel asked.

Aida winced, stung by his indifference. He was utterly self-absorbed, with little concern for her feelings.

"It is more difficult for a woman. Surely, you realize that," the Countess said.

Michel shrugged. "I intend to find a place for her, one where she will be safe, unable to hurt herself. Perhaps then, I can begin to live a normal life as well. Come, let me discuss my plans with you."

Aida wiped away a tear with the back of her hand. She quietly slipped from the bed and tiptoed across the room to the armoire as she carefully opened the carved walnut doors, then removed the satchel. There would be no time to pick and choose what to bring with her, and so, the fancy ball gowns remained as she quickly folded several practical day dresses. Reaching for her jewelry box, hair brush, hand mirror and a pair of shoes, she added them in as well. She fingered the tiny white batiste baby dresses that she had tucked away in anticipation of the birth of her child, and removing the one on top, slipped it into the bag. Satisfied that she was ready, she donned her cloak and stood tall. Today, she thought, is my independence day, as she slowly made her way down the staircase.

Michel and the Countess seemed surprised to see her when she appeared in the parlor where they were having a cup of tea.

"Aida dear," the Countess said, rising to greet her. "you must not be out of bed. You need your rest."

Michel narrowed his eyes, and then spied the satchel. "Are you going somewhere?' he asked, his voice dripping with sarcasm.

Aida was unsteady on her feet, but she willed herself not to stumble. She raised her chin in defiance. "Believe it or not, Michel. I am perfectly sane. You will not be sending me anywhere. In fact, I am prepared to leave on my own accord right this very minute."

Michel laughed. "Your actions prove how very fragile your mental state has become."

"On the contrary. This is the soundest decision I have made in a very long time."

"Mother," Michel said, addressing the Countess. "I give you my wife, a poor wretched creature who has completely lost her faculties. What a disappointment she has become."

Aida took a deep breath and narrowed her eyes. She could feel the years of frustration, anger, and betrayal welling up inside her like a volcano on the verge of erupting. She had held back for so long, deferring to her husband and swallowing her feelings, while failing to say what was on her mind. Michel had ultimately turned her into one of those fragile dependent women, the kind that she despised. Her misplaced loyalty had, in fact, cost her dearly, and it was a price she was no longer willing to pay.

"While you are describing how weak-willed I am, perhaps you might want to talk about about your illegitimate son, whose mother, I dare say, is of a questionable moral character."

"Truly, Aida, you are delusional," Michel said.

"I think perhaps that descriptor applies to you, I have met Rose and her son, whom you will not be able to deny."

Michel snickered, but his confidence was shaken. "I don't believe you."

"It matters not to me if you do," Aida said, tying the ribbon on her bonnet.

"You cannot connect me to that woman."

"Unfortunately, I can," Aida said, turning to face him squarely. "The child's feet bear the distinguishing characteristic of the de la Martinque family. He will be impossible to deny."

The Countess gasped.

"I have no doubt that this woman will soon surface in order for her son to claim his rightful place in the family," Aida added. She knew that his arrogance, his unending pride, made this his most vulnerable spot.

Michel's face grew pale.

"She doesn't strike me as the type of woman who would fade into the background. Wouldn't you agree, Michel? I suspect that she will want what is best for her child, and that means a title," Aida said.

"This cannot be true," the Countess said, sinking into a nearby chair.

"I can imagine that your fancy friends will be quite impressed with the redhead from Harlem, the mother of the heir to your fortune," Aida said.

There was a long pause, the space in the room filled with silence.

"What do you want, Aida? Name your price." He did not protest or beg her forgiveness. Oddly enough, he seemed reconciled or perhaps too arrogant to admit his transgression.

Regardless of his motivation, she seized the opportunity. "A ride to the train station and a first class ticket to New Orleans. Divorce me or not, it matters little. You have nothing I would ever want. I will be returning to my family, the people who love me. You may have robbed me of my past, but you won't take away my future."

Michel nodded. "As you wish. I won't attempt to persuade you otherwise. I will summon the driver. And your things? You have this one small bag."

"Have the maid pack my trunk and send it to me at my mother's house. If it is an inconvenience to you, then, don't bother. I would rather dress in rags than don another expensive frock and be in your presence." She had won.

The Countess stood and opened her arms to embrace Aida. "This is painful for me, Aida. I had come to think of you as the daughter I always wanted. I know that our relationship has been strained at times, but you were always important to me. I want for you to know that. Be happy and be true to yourself. That truly is my wish for you."

As the carriage pulled into the station, Aida thought of her mother-in-law's parting words. And for the first time, she thought that she finally understood the woman's heart.

CHAPTER SIXTY-FIVE

"I thought I knew him," Aida said, grateful to be sitting in her mother's kitchen. "The man I first met and the man I married were very different. I fell in love with his wit and intelligence, his kindness and compassion. Those qualities evaporated into thin air within months of our wedding. As silly as it seems now, I thought he was my soulmate."

"Your soulmate won't break your heart, Aida. That much I know."

"You are right, of course."

"It is unfortunate," Angelique said. "I had hoped that you would have found complete happiness with Michel, the kind that lasts forever."

"So did I. In hindsight, I should have waited a while before I agreed to marry him, gotten to know him more fully. I was blinded by infatuation, in a rush to get on with life."

"Ah, but people who are in love often make impulsive choices. It isn't your fault. We think we know those we care for so deeply. But I don't know if we ever really know someone else."

"If that is true, then how on earth can we find happiness in any relationship, if all that we see and experience is just an illusion?" Aida asked.

"I suppose that is a matter of faith. We all yearn for a knowledge that we will be loved, no matter what. It is the most basic human need."

"Michel certainly didn't love me unconditionally. That much I know. He loved himself far too much. I embraced the fantasy of what I thought our life together might be. Reality was far different."

"But you weren't wrong to believe, honey. He was your first love, your first real experience with a true emotional connection. There is a certain amount of magic to that."

"And naiveté."

"Love often blinds you to the truth of what is right before you. Let's face it, we make the decision every day to care for someone, regardless of whether or not we get what we need in return. But after a while, that one-sidedness erodes the foundation of a relationship. He truly was a selfish man, Aida."

"But I am not some giddy school girl, and this wasn't a teenage crush. We were married. I believed in him. In us."

"Of course you did. Certainly, you are not the first young woman to have her heart broken by someone she trusted."

"That doesn't make it hurt any less. How quickly he changed from the man I adored into a stranger."

"Sadly, the marriage was not as you thought it would be. When we deny the truth about something so dark and toxic, it only enlarges it, gives it more power. Once we can see a situation for what it really is, it no longer has the power to poison us. Acceptance is not resignation."

"What do you mean?"

"You must give yourself the grace to work through the sadness during this challenging time in your life. You have to feel the emotions, even if you think you are going to die in the process. But you won't. You will live, and you will move forward with a greater appreciation and renewed perspective. Life goes on, Aida. I know that much for sure."

"I suppose that you understand this all too well, having lived through those awful years yourself."

"Unfortunately, yes. But you, too, have endured so much."

"I suppose the prospect of having a child is what kept us together. The deep hurt of that loss is still very real."

"It is a burden that you will carry all the days of your life, Aida. I am so very sorry."

"Sometimes, I wonder if it is all too much to bear."

"We all suffer, Aida. It is one of the truisms of being human. When it comes, we are given a choice. If you run, it chases you, torturing you with feelings of rage and sadness. But if you turn toward it, face it, it steps back and opens up to show us that pain is really a way to be transformed."

"I don't see how that is possible."

"But it is. When you have had to fight for your own survival, you build strength. Everything, even a bad moment, is an opportunity to grow. This is your time to plant seeds in your life. Nurture them, and you will see the fruit of your labors."

"I'm afraid that I don't quite understand."

"Do you remember the day of your graduation when you questioned the choices I had made?"

Aida blushed. "I was a foolish young girl then. You have done a great deal with your life, Momma. Those children in the orphanage and now the young women at the birthing center have been saved by your efforts."

"But I also had limits placed upon me which you don't have. Think about the opportunities that await you. How will you change the world, my daughter?"

"I don't know."

"Then, your first task is to discover what your mission will be. There is something that you were ordained to do, something that will bring you great joy and personal satisfaction. Look inside of your heart for that is where you will find the answer."

"It is all so overwhelming at this point."

"Most important things are. It becomes a matter of balancing expectations with reality. We keep trying, even if we know that we may fail or face heartbreak. We do it because we must."

"I understand. And you are right, of course. It is just going to take time."

"That's the one thing that is on your side, Aida. I just want you to be happy."

"Right now, that feels like a very lofty goal."

"Just remember," Angelique said, "happiness isn't in someone else, in a job or a goal met. It is within us, and there is the secret, Aida. We give life to joy."

"I hope that you are right."

"I know that I am. It is not in what you achieve, but in who you have become. And Aida, you have become a remarkable young woman."

Aida rose to embrace her mother. It was good to be home, she thought, knowing that there was no better place to begin her life again.

CHAPTER SIXTY-SIX

SUMMER, 1880

Andrew hoped that Angelique would be pleased with his surprise, a planned itinerary for a month- long tour of France. It had taken him quite some time to plot out the trip since he wanted the places they visited to be significant. And so, when he succeeded in getting a sneak peek at her journal, particularly the story of her great grandmother's life, he made a note of the towns that were mentioned and then studied the map to figure out the best route to take.

He had also managed to get the time off, a sabbatical of sorts, and he had hoped that perhaps a visit to the Sorbonne would prove to be professionally beneficial for him as well. All that remained was for him to book the tickets aboard the steamer, and although he had planned to do that before he told Angelique, he figured that it might be wise to discuss it with her. She seemed to be busy with the orphanage and the women's home, and when she wasn't working, she was writing. But he had to admit that he, too, was preoccupied most days. More often than not, they were like two ships passing in the night, a reality that pained him. Their recent talk had made him even more aware of the need for some quality time together.

He admired her tenacity, her zest for life. But he particularly appreciated her kind heart. Of course, her benevolence had exacted a price. It kept her occupied, a fact that he became painfully aware of once the children had moved away. Yes, he thought, this trip would be their chance to reconnect, while giving Angelique an opportunity to walk the streets of her ancestors. He hoped that she would be pleased with the proposal.

"A moment of your time?" he asked, happy to find her alone in the study that afternoon.

"For you? Always." Angelique said, putting down her pen.

"You are certainly taking this writing project seriously, aren't you?" he said, pointing to the open book on the desk.

"I suppose so. Once I started, I just seemed to have one idea after another. This feels important to me, Andrew. I remember hearing the stories of my grandmother and great grandmother, the tales of their lives in France. And as I write, I have become lost in the history of those who lived before me. And then, it occurred to me that I have my own adventurous story to tell."

"You most certainly do."

"Someday, I will have a granddaughter or two."

"Or a grandson."

"Well, yes, of course, but I do like to think of them reading my silly little stories and truly getting to know me."

"I would like to think that you will be here to read them aloud to your future progeny, but I understand what you mean. And I think it is a beautiful thing to do. In fact, it is what has motivated my little surprise."

"Surprise?" she asked, clapping her hands. "I do so love surprises."

"I hope that you will be pleased with this one." He handed her several sheets of paper, along with a map.

"What's this?"

"It is our travel plans."

"Do we have travel plans?"

"I hope that we will. I confess that I did read one of your journals, the one about the ancestral homes in France. Those places sparked this itinerary. I want to take you there; let you see your homeland as they did."

"Truly? When?"

"As soon as possible. I have arranged to have the time away from the university. All I need to do is book our passage across the Atlantic. Think of the romantic starlit nights on the sea. What do you say?"

"I say absolutely, although I need a bit of time to make arrangements. You know how I tend to fret, especially over the children. But I leave much of my responsibilities in Aimee's capable hands. Now that Aida is back home and has taken over some of the administrative duties for both institutions, I have a little more freedom than I once had."

"Perfect. I am so relieved."

"Did you think that I might not agree, darling?" Angelique asked.

"I had hoped that you would. But I sometimes wonder where I fit in that busy schedule of yours."

Angelique moved to him, wrapping her arms around his neck. "But you are always my first priority."

Andrew smiled. "Sometimes, it doesn't feel that way, but thanks for the reassurance."

"We are different, no doubt, but we always find a way to remain in love, don't we?"

"That we do."

Aida appeared at the door. "You two are so sweet, and I hate to interrupt, but a messenger just brought this note for you, Momma. I think it is from the orphanage."

"Thanks, honey," Angelique said. She opened it and as she began to read, her face grew somber.

"Trouble?" Andrew asked.

"I am afraid so. I must go there, right away."

"What is it?"

"Some of the children have been taken ill."

"Shall I go with you?" Andrew asked.

"No, you stay. It could be nothing at all."

Or it could be something big enough to derail our plans, Andrew thought. And he hoped that he was wrong as much for himself as for the children.

CHAPTER SIXTY-SEVEN

Andrew summoned the carriage. Their New Orleans house was relatively close to the orphanage, and on temperate days, Angelique would often walk there, enjoying the fresh air, but there was an urgency to reach the children as soon as possible and so, she hurried out the door, tying the ribbon under her bonnet as she paused on the porch.

Franklin was attending to the sick as she arrived, and she breathed a sigh of relief. He had already segregated those who were ill into a separate dormitory and was instructing the staff on how to care for the sickest among them.

"I came as soon as I heard," Angelique said, moving to the bedside of a young boy who cried out in pain. "Thank you for coming, Franklin."

"Of course. Fortunately, I was already here, checking on things at the clinic. You know that you and the children are of utmost importance to me."

"And for that, I am grateful," Angelique said. "What do you think this is?" she asked, mentally counting the number of occupied beds.

Franklin took a deep breath. "I fear that it is yellow fever," he said. "These children display many of the symptoms."

Angelique's shook her head. "Are you sure?"

"No, of course not, but I have seen this before at the hospital. I think my educated guess is correct."

"What do we do? There are twelve of them now. Could there possibly be more?"

"That's a question that will be answered over the next few days."

"What has caused it? Is it something we did wrong?"

"I don't think so, Mother. This seems to be one of those diseases that shows up periodically, especially during the summer months. If we knew why, we would know how to prevent it. What concerns me is the potential for an outbreak."

Angelique furrowed her brow. "That's a frightening possibility."

"Indeed it is, but it is far too soon to panic."

"What can I do?" Angelique asked.

"Some of the children have nausea; others, head and back pain. They are all running a temperature. Cold compresses help some, especially if we can break the fever. But many are displaying chills."

"I will send to the laundry for more towels."

"Blankets, too, if you have them."

Angelique nodded.

"And mother?" Franklin said. "If it is what I suspect, it is going to get worse."

"Please don't say that."

"I feel that I must warn you. There will be bleeding."

"Bleeding?"

"From the eyes, mouth, ears. It can be quite gruesome at the end."

"What are you trying to tell me, Franklin?"

"You must prepare yourself for what may come. Some of the children may die."

Angelique shook her head. "Not on my watch. I will be here day and night, if need be, but I will stay with these children. They think of me as their mother, and I won't let them fight this alone. In the meantime, do we have medicine that I can administer? Surely, you don't expect me to stand by and watch them suffer?"

"I understand your concern. Right now, we must do what we can. Give them plenty of water and continue with the cool baths. I have some elderberry syrup at the clinic that I will send over."

"Anything else?" Angelique asked.

"Just pray."

"I have been doing that since I got word. May God protect these innocent babes, who have already endured so much in their short time on this earth."

"One more thing."

"Yes?"

"Pace yourself. You will do nobody any good if you work yourself to the point of exhaustion."

"I won't leave until I know that the children are safe, Franklin. There is a couch in my office, if I need it. Besides, I wouldn't be able to rest at home, anyway. I will send your father word that I will be here for a while."

"I know that nothing I can say will change your mind."

"Good. We agree on that."

"I'll check in with you on my way to and from the hospital. In the meantime, I suggest dividing the staff into shifts, so that someone is here the entire time. I will see if Aimee knows of any nurses who are able to volunteer for a few hours."

"I know that she is so busy with the women's home, but perhaps she can lend a hand, too. She is particularly good with the children."

Franklin nodded, but made no further comment. He had no intention of allowing his wife to enter a yellow fever ward, not in her delicate condition. Although he wanted to shout their happy news from the rooftops, he knew that Aimee would have never forgiven him if he had spoiled the surprise. Besides, today was not a day for a celebration. There was always tomorrow, and he knew that the expectation of a new baby would bring great joy, especially to their mother.

CHAPTER SIXTY-EIGHT

Angelique was tired. Her shoulder ached. Dark circles ringed her eyes and her face was pale. For three days and nights, she had kept watch over the sick children, wiping their feverish brows and coaxing them to take small sips of lemon water. People had come and gone, some staying for an hour or two, others, for longer periods of time, but after a while, she barely noticed who was there with her as she moved from bed to bed.

Franklin had visited twice a day as promised to examine each of the children, and at the end of the second day when several of them appeared to be improving, he cautioned Angelique not to become overly optimistic.

"It often happens with the fever. Some will have a brief period of remission and recover, but for others, the disease returns quickly and with far greater severity," he had said.

Just as he had predicted, seven of the children did seem to get better right away. Angelique was delighted, convinced that the worst was over. But by the morning of the fourth day, the remaining five only grew worse. She and the volunteer nurse tended to them well into the night.

Although she said that she had no favorites among the children, Angelique was partial to a young girl of six named Melanie, who waited at the door to the dining room every morning when she joined them for breakfast, her blonde curls bouncing to and fro as she clapped her hands and shouted,

"Welcome Momma." And now, she lay in a sick bed, fighting for her life.

Angelique felt helpless as she pulled the wooden chair to her bedside and studied Melanie's ashen face, contorted in pain. She gently wiped the girl's brow, a droplet of blood staining the white cloth a crimson red. Angelique swallowed hard, afraid that if she allowed the tears to flow, she would be unable to stop them. She said a prayer.

"She seems to be getting worse," Angelique whispered to the nurse. "Is there nothing else we can do?"

"I know of nothing that we have not yet tried," the nurse said. "All we can do is hope and say a little prayer."

Angelique forced a weak smile, her eyelids heavy from exhaustion.

"You are tired, Miss Angelique," the nurse said. "I promised Franklin that I would make sure that you got a bit of rest tonight. You know that you can't continue like this."

"But I must be here," Angelique said. "What if I am needed?"

"What if you get sick yourself? Who will take care of you then? I am afraid that I must insist. You are right; you are needed, and you won't be of any use to these children if you collapse."

Angelique didn't have the energy to argue. She nodded. "Perhaps for an hour or so. Will you send for me if something happens?"

"Yes," the nurse said. "Of course."

By the time Angelique had reached her office, she barely had the energy to walk across the room to the sofa. Her chest felt tight as she lay down and before she could finish her prayer, she was sound asleep.

At daybreak, Franklin tiptoed into the room, holding a steaming cup of black coffee. "Momma," he whispered.

Angelique's eyes fluttered, and she licked her lips. "What time is it?" she asked, still groggy from sleep.

"It is a little after six. I brought you some coffee."

"I didn't intend to sleep so long. I must get back to the children."

Franklin nodded. "In due time. Drink this first."

Angelique reached for the cup and took a tentative sip. "Have you been in to check on them?"

"I have," Franklin said. "I got here an hour ago to relieve the night nurse."

"Thank you for that. She has been a godsend. I guess I am disappointed that Aimee couldn't help. I always feel that we are all well taken care of when she is around."

"I am certain that if she could be here, she would be. She has had some rather pressing demands at the women's center, with one particularly difficult labor and delivery. She knew you would understand." It was only a half truth, but he always hated lying to Angelique.

"And what about the children? Any change? Has Melanie's fever broken?"

Franklin took a deep breath. "I am afraid that I have some distressing news to share."

Angelique shook her head. "Please, Franklin, no bad news."

"Melanie passed away a few minutes after I arrived. She never woke, just stopped breathing as she slept peacefully. Mercifully, she didn't suffer."

Angelique could feel the tightness in her chest return as she began to cry. "That beautiful little angel truly is one now," she said, her voice cracking with emotion. "She was so precious. My heart is broken."

"I know it is. This is a terrible disease that is no respecter of persons. I have seen it take the weak and the strong."

"But an innocent child?"

"They are often the most vulnerable."

"I don't know how you do this, Franklin. How do you watch people die every single day?"

"The same way that I see people survive, recover from some mighty devastating illnesses and injuries. We do what we can to help the sick, but ultimately, God decides these things. Remember? You taught me that."

Angelique nodded, wiping away the tears with the back of her hand. "It's still painful and difficult to accept."

"But it also makes life precious. There are seven children eating porridge in their beds right this very moment. Four others are still fighting, although I am confident that two of them have turned a corner and will fully recuperate. They need you. This orphanage is filled with those who need you."

"You are right, of course, Franklin. Let me splash a bit of water on my face. I am sure that I look frightful. Perhaps I should have breakfast with those who are well this morning."

"That's a great idea. Let them see that you still care for them."

"Of course I do."

Franklin kissed the top of her head. "It will be good for you, too."

"Look," Angelique said, pointing to the window. "The sun is up. I can hear the laughter of the children. You are right, Franklin. While yesterday was filled with tragedy. Today is another day. That brings us all hope."

"Indeed it does."

CHAPTER SIXTY-NINE

Angelique rubbed her shoulder. The squeezing pain had become a constant companion, and at times, it was so severe that she struggled to catch her breath. She had lived with the discomfort for years, forgetting about it when it went away. But those moments of respite seemed fewer and farther between.

She steadied herself against the kitchen sink. Today, her entire family would be gathered around her table, and she had no time for such inconveniences.

"It sure does smell good in here," Aida said, entering the kitchen. "What can I do to help?"

"Everything is ready. I just need to get it all into the dining room and call everyone in to eat."

When they had taken their places and after Andrew had said grace, Franklin cleared his throat. "Aimee and I have news to share. We wanted to wait until we were all together."

"Well now, we are certainly curious," Andrew said.

"Do tell," Aida said.

Franklin reached for Aimee's hand. "We are going to have a baby."

Angelique clapped her hands. "Oh, my goodness. After so much sadness at the orphanage, this is especially wonderful." She rose to embrace her daughter. "I am happy for you, for the whole family, really."

"Now you understand why I couldn't come to help," Aimee said.

"Certainly," Angelique said. "Your priority right now is your health. That's my grandchild you are carrying, you know."

"Our grandchild," Andrew corrected.

Aimee smiled. She glanced at her sister, who remained quiet. "Sissy. I hope that this isn't too painful for you. I know how much you wanted a child of your own."

"Yes, of course, I did," Aida said. "But I also imagined a fairy tale life with Michel. I envisioned the perfect little family, but our relationship was far from perfect. You and Franklin are different. You are going to have everything you ever dreamed of, and I get to be a part of that. I am going to be quite the doting aunt, just you wait and see."

"I am counting on it," Aimee said.

"I suppose that working with these young mothers who have little to no support has made me truly appreciate the family that I have," Aida said.

"We are all very blessed to have each other," Angelique said, winking at Andrew. "I love you all, and I am going to show you just how much by serving you the most amazing dessert I made this morning. Let's celebrate!"

"I have already spied the cake," Aimee said.

"You rest, Momma," Aida said. "You look a little pale. I am sure that you will enjoy entertaining the men. We will bring coffee and cake in to you once Aida and I have cleaned things up a bit.

"Thanks you girls. Normally, I might protest, but I suppose I am a little tired. Now that the crisis at the orphanage has passed, I can breathe a sigh of relief, but those long days and nights have caught up with me, I think."

"I have a strong feeling that you are going to have a girl. At least that's what I am hoping for," Aida said as she and Aimee stood shoulder-to-shoulder washing the dishes.

"Secretly, I am, too, although I know that like any man, Franklin wants a boy. I am just hoping that the child is healthy." Aimee's face turned crimson red. "Oh, Aida. I am so sorry. I don't mean to hurt your feelings."

"You haven't. I don't want for you to feel like you can't be yourself around me or express your concerns. Having a baby is a miracle, Aimee. You should rejoice in that. Besides, in some crazy way, my experience with Michel has taught me that my heart is quite resilient. I am tougher than I ever thought myself to be. We both are."

Aida nodded. "We get that from our mother."

"Indeed we do. She is the strongest person I know."

"And we are her legacy."

"And Franklin."

"And this new baby."

Aida and Aimee laughed in unison.

"I have a bit of news of my own," Aida said.

Aimee dried her hands on a towel and turned to face her sister. "I'm listening."

"I have been accepted into law school."

"Really? Where? Here in New Orleans?"

"No. In Chicago. The university there has been accepting women into their school of law for over a decade. Now that women are allowed to argue in any federal court, I can return here to set up my practice and spoil my niece or nephew, of course."

"I am so pleased. It sounds like you have a solid plan."

"I do, Aimee. For the first time in my life, I am in control of my own destiny, not dependent upon somebody else to provide for my happiness."

"Because that never works, does it?"

"No. I always considered myself so independent, and yet I readily gave up my power to a man, allowed my womanhood to be trampled."

"Most women, do, Aida. When marriage vows include obeying our husbands, we have little recourse for determining our own fates."

"But you did. I always thought that I had you beat when it came to choices. I was wrong."

"Franklin is unusual. He was raised by our parents, who are both pretty progressive. Let's face it: we both had misguided ideas about life when we were younger. Experience makes you wise. Don't you think?"

"I do. I have finally come to understand that happiness never lies in someone else. That is far too great a burden to place on another human being, and it always leads to disappointment. It isn't in what we own or what we accomplish, although that might sound strange coming from me. No, true contentment is within us. That's the secret: we give life to our own joy."

"You are started to sound like Momma. That's pretty profound."

Aida giggled. "That's because I am quoting her. But yes, it is pretty insightful. Besides, I have goals that will bring me great satisfaction. I figure that's pretty close to being happy."

"You have a point. So what are your plans?"

"I feel very strongly about the rights of women."

"You always have."

"We were very fortunate, Aimee. We were given an education, which gave us a bit of control over our own destiny."

"I suppose so."

"I know that to be true. I thought myself to be oppressed until I met the women in Harlem who had little recourse but to sell their bodies because they had no other way to support themselves."

"But you taught them to read. That gave them a future."

"I hope so. I often think of the women, wonder what became of so many of them. I suppose I will never know."

"But that's what happens when you give such a precious gift. You aren't always there to see them enjoy it. Certainly, I feel that way as well. But the fruits of your labors last forever. That's pretty amazing."

"But you and Mother have done much more to help the cause than I have. The orphanage is teaching young girls to be brave and smart. The women's home is a godsend to those in need. You are making a difference."

"And you will, too"

"Which is why I want to connect my law practice to both places, to be your partner. I want to represent women who need legal protection, like Colleen, the woman in Harlem."

"That was quite a story, Aida. I must admit, that was pretty daring of you, all things considered."

"I didn't see any other option if I wanted to live with my conscience."

"Which is why your idea sounds like a perfect fit."

"Of course, I will continue my work in the suffrage movement. Until we are allowed to vote, we will have no power or voice. I fight for us, of course, but I also now fight for my niece."

Aimee laughed. "You seem pretty confident about this little one."

"Time will tell."

"Give me a hug, Sissy," Aimee said. "I am so proud of you."

"I am proud of both of us," Aida said. "Momma raised us right."

Angelique suddenly appeared at the door of the kitchen. "Did I hear my name mentioned? I hope that you are speaking fondly of me."

"Always, Momma," Aida said.

"Have you girls forgotten about that cake?" Angelique asked.

"No," Aida said. "It is my fault. We got involved in conversation."

"Then join us. And bring the cake."

"We are coming," Aimee said. "Aida has some news of her own to share. This is a happy day, a happy day indeed."

CHAPTER SEVENTY

"I am worried about Momma," Franklin said on the way home. "She looks unwell."

"Unwell? What do you mean? Certainly, she has pushed herself between the orphanage and the women's home. I know that she worries about the plantation, too. She is accustomed to doing so much, which isn't as easy for her as it once was."

"I don't think that this is simple fatigue, Aimee. She is pale and far too thin. When she doesn't think anybody is looking, she rubs her shoulder as though she is having quite some discomfort. I am concerned."

"She is getting older, Franklin. As much as I hate it, that's a fact. Perhaps she is simply experiencing the aches and pains of aging."

"You might be right, but I think I will stop by the house on the way to the hospital tomorrow just for my own peace of mind. I am afraid I have seen far too many cases that appeared to be nothing, but were in reality something far greater. You have, too."

Aimee nodded. "I suppose that it is easy to take the health of our parents for granted, but in this case, I hope that you are wrong."

"So do I."

***

The moon was full, illuminating the room with a bright light that cast shadows upon the walls. Angelique wondered how long she had lain there, unable to sleep, listening to the sounds of the night. Her arms and legs felt leaden, which made shifting her position difficult. The tightening in her chest returned, and she focused on the regular cadence of her beating heart. Each night, when she whispered her prayers, she thanked God for her strong body, the vessel for her immortal soul. And yet, she knew with an alarming certainty that it was failing her. She wondered how much time she had left, and that filled her with a sense of urgency.

"Andrew," she whispered.

He groaned and turned over, oblivious to her voice.

"Andrew," she repeated.

"Hmmmm?" he finally answered, the sleep leaving him confused.

"I want to go home."

He reached out to her, pulling her close. "You are home."

"No. I mean to Chauvin. I must go there. It is a special place to me. I grew up on that land and so did our children."

Andrew laughed. "You must be dreaming."

"No, I am not. This is important."

"Do we need to go tonight?"

"No, but tomorrow. First thing."

"This must be significant to you since you rarely leave your responsibilities here."

"We always return to what matters, Andrew. Promise me."

"I promise. But until then, can we go back to sleep?"

"Of course. Sorry that I woke you." Angelique took a deep breath and exhaled slowly. Tomorrow, she would be at Chauvin. Tomorrow, she would be alright.

CHAPTER SEVENTY-ONE

"I don't think that your mother is well," Andrew said when Franklin appeared at the door early the next morning. "She has been up since dawn packing for what appears to be an extended stay at Chauvin."

"Really?"

"Yes. For some reason, she has some pressing desire for a visit there."

"Well, it is the family home and a thriving business. She doesn't get there nearly as often as she'd like," Franklin said. "Perhaps that's her motivation."

"I don't think so. She knows that it's in good hands. I think it is something deeper."

"Let me talk to her."

Franklin found Angelique in the bedroom, folding dresses and placing them in the large wooden trunk. "Poppa said that you two are going away for a while."

Angelique nodded, "To Chauvin. I need to dig in the rich black soil, breathe in the country air. I want to sleep in my big bed with the windows wide open. I want to see Jubilee."

"Understandable. How are you feeling?"

"Excited. I am looking forward to being home."

"No. I mean physically. Does your shoulder still hurt?"

She narrowed her eyes. "How did you know?"

"I am a doctor, Mother. I have been trained to observe people. Would you allow me to examine you?"

"For what? It is just a bit of rheumatism."

"Or angina."

"You mean my heart?"

"I do."

"You are wrong, Franklin."

"Then, you won't mind letting me take a look." He pulled his stethoscope out of the leather bag. "Do it for me, for my peace of mind."

She nodded, sitting on the edge of the bed. He leaned over, placing the instrument against her chest, first in one place and then another as he listened. "Take a deep breath." She did as he instructed. "Now cough."

His face became somber.

"What is it?" Angelique asked.

"It is just a clinical observation, but your heart is beating erratically. Surely, you are aware of that?"

"Sometimes."

"I think that you have been through some difficult moments, especially lately. That does take its toll. I am concerned that perhaps there isn't enough blood going to your heart. That could be serious. Right now, you need to rest."

"So a trip to Chauvin is just what the doctor ordered, right?"

He smiled. "Yes, Mother. It would do you a world of good. You should take Aida with you and I am sure that Aimee would love to join you in a few days. It would be nice for the three of you to have some time together."

Angelique smiled, revealing the tiny wrinkles around her eyes. "What a wonderful doctor you are! Sounds like just what I need to get better."

"Then, I will leave you to your packing. Remember to rest."

"I will."

"And Momma?"

"Yes, Franklin?"

"I love you. Thanks for taking me in so many years ago. You truly changed my life."

"While I appreciate the sentiment, it seems like you are saying goodbye."

"Not at all, although you will be at Chauvin for a while, I assume. I just wanted you to know how I feel."

"Well, then, it is mutual. You have changed mine as well, son. I love you right back." She opened her arms to embrace him.

He always admired the ever-present kindness in her eyes, perhaps now more than ever.

CHAPTER SEVENTY-TWO

Angelique wrapped the threadbare shawl around her shoulders. She had others, fancy silk ones with delicate embroidery, tucked away in the dresser, but this was her favorite. It reminded her of the day she bought it, on a sunny afternoon in Charleston, when she and Cousin Lilly had shopped the upscale shops along Market Street. That seemed like a lifetime ago. She shivered as the wind whipped between the oaks, the camellia blossoms barely visible in the moonlight.

"May I join you?" Andrew said, moving to close the window. "You appear to be in deep thought."

"Just thinking of how grateful I am to be here."

"I am glad that we were able to make the trip. The girls seem to be enjoying it."

"Being together has been wonderful. I rarely get this kind of time with them. It has been special. Today, we walked the fields. I had hoped for a few remaining blackberries to make a cobbler with, but all of the bushes were bare. It is far too late in the season, I suppose. Winter is almost upon us."

"Sounds like a nice day, anyway."

"It was. And how was yours?"

"Productive. I seem to be able to think more clearly out here in the country. I am working on some interesting projects."

"That's the magic of Chauvin, Andrew. I am glad that you aren't bored."

"On the contrary."

"Good. That makes me heart happy."

"And that's what I live for. You look tired, darling."

"I suppose I am. I hate having so little energy these days. Am I getting old?"

"No, darling, certainly not in my eyes. You will always be that beautiful young woman I met when I stumbled into the auction at your house and bid on that blue and white china clock."

"Ah, fate. I still love that clock, by the way. And you."

"And I love you right back. Promise me that you won't overdo it. The whole idea of his trip was to give you some much needed time to relax. You should rest now."

"I am. Will you sit with me for a while?"

"It would be my pleasure," he said, reaching for her hand. "I hope that you are feeling better soon."

"I suppose that I wasn't paying attention to my health."

"It is because you always put everyone else first. But you always do seem to be happiest when you are here. I am hopeful that this visit will lift your spirits."

"I know that it will. We have places to see, right? I am looking forward to our trip to France. I can only imagine the places we will see. It is all very exciting, isn't it?"

"It certainly is, and it pleases me that you think so, too. I may have to renegotiate the time away from work, but I am not concerned about that aspect."

Angelique smiled. Her eyes were weary. "It will be a second honeymoon."

"If I recall, we never had the first one."

"Well, then, it is never too late."

"We have been together for almost twenty-seven years," he said, reaching for her hand. "Such a very long time."

"A beautiful tapestry of moments woven together in love."

"That's rather poetic, my darling."

"Perhaps I am a little more introspective that usual tonight."

He pointed to the open book on her desk. "Have you been writing?"

"I have. It seems to have become part of my evening ritual. I had so many memories tucked away, filed in some untouchable corner of my mind. Much of this is our romance, Andrew, but there are others. It is like the voices of the past spoke to me, refusing to be silenced, demanding that their stories be told."

Andrew laughed. "That sounds like you have been visited by ghosts."

"I guess I have, although these phantoms are very friendly."

"I hope that you will share them with me. I would enjoy reading your words."

"Of course I will. I would love to revisit some of these moments with you. I am very close to finishing, although certainly, the future is yet unwritten. That's what makes it exciting, I suppose."

Andrew reached for her hand. "There will be many more volumes to write."

She nodded. "About our grandchildren, for sure. I am filled with such anticipation! And you and I will have other new adventures, I hope."

"You can count on it."

Angelique yawned.

"You are tired." He pulled back the blankets. "Climb into bed and get some sleep. I will be here."

"Your presence is always comforting to me. It always has been. I love you, Andrew."

"I love you, my darling. I hope that you always find security in my arms. We have been through many highs and lows together, haven't we?"

"And loved each other through each and every one of them. Life takes time to live, to somehow unfold its truth, and yet, in retrospect, it all seems to happen in the blink of an eye. Such a contradiction."

He kissed her palm. "You are, as always, a wise woman."

She smiled, closing her eyes.

Angelique's mind drifted as it often did, to the sounds of the fiddler playing as dancers twirled across the ballroom floor. She tapped her foot to the rhythm of the music. The voices of the Countess and Monsieur Muggah seemed so real, so very close, that she could hear their conversation. She walked onto the wide veranda and looked out at the wide expanse of the Gulf. Andrew was on the beach, studying his meters and gauges. She waved in recognition.

Fat blue butterflies filled the air. Her three children ran through the rows of sugar cane with Jubilee chasing after them, their squeals of laughter echoing in the wind. She blew them a kiss.

She entered the dining hall of the orphanage, taking Melanie's small hand in hers. The children greeted her, then bowed their heads in prayer before breakfast. Her heart was full.

Life is but a momentary breath, she thought. We inhale deeply, taking in all that it has to offer us, and for an instant, we realize true completeness. And then, we empty our lungs, giving back to the world all that is within us. This is the rhythm of existence, a task which we accomplish hundreds of times each hour.

To Angelique, it all seemed like one big miracle, even the trials. Like the fish who swim in the shallow waters, we navigate our way through the tides and currents until we reach our ultimate destination, the calm of the open sea. No one is born with a knowledge of how to do this, she thought, but we must try, each in our own way, until we find the harmony that stills our minds and soothes our souls. These were the certainties that life had taught her, the wisdom of experience, gathered by exploring the complicated territory of her own heart. She was grateful for the lessons, having earned each and every one of them. They were hers forever. There was a stillness, followed by an overwhelming sense of peace. Suddenly, the weight lifted and only joy remained.

Her eyes searched the heavens. There in the clouds was sweet Josephina, her tiny arms outstretched in a warm embrace. Behind her stood Hannah. Her mother and father were there, waiting. Angelique smiled. The wind blew through her raven hair and her heart opened wide. This is the most basic truth, she thought: in the end, love wins; it transcends everything, even death. She wished that she could tell Andrew, share this final certainty with her children. But it was theirs to discover, and she would be there, waiting to show them the way. She exhaled for the last time.

Angelique was free. She was going home.

EPILOGUE

"It feels a bit intrusive going through Momma's things like this," Aimee said.

"Remember how she would lock the door to her bedroom to keep us out?' Aida asked.

"Well, we were a bit nosey when we were young. I can imagine that she didn't want her fine bonnets and gowns ruined by our sticky fingers."

Aida sighed. "I still can't believe that she is gone. There is an emptiness that will never be filled. My heart feels like it is broken."

"Mine, too. This is one of those moments when it is hard to think or breathe, where everything has just stopped. All I want to do is go back in time and hug her once again."

"Or have a quiet chat over a cup of tea. But as much as we might wish it, that's not possible."

"I know, but I can't help but feel that way. The pain is palpable for all of us. She was the glue that held our family together. It is like when one of the pillars of a building is destroyed: you wonder how long it will remain upright. She was the support for our family What will we do without her wisdom and guidance?"

"I don't know. It is difficult and scary."

"She has always been there for us. Always."

"Poor Poppa. He has lost the love of his life. He hasn't moved from the study since the funeral. He seems lost. I worry about him."

Aimee wiped away a tear. "I worry about him, too. You don't stop loving someone just because they die."

"That much is true. And yet, we are left with this patchwork of experiences we once shared, so many of them."

"Those are our memories, Aida. And I hope that we have absorbed enough of them to keep her alive within each of us."

"But memory can be slippery. We sometimes forget because the person is no longer of this world. I do hope that we are able to hold onto them because I know it will be comforting."

"In truth, life will never be the same for Poppa or for any of us," Aimee said. "And this baby will never know how special she was."

Aida wrapped her arms around her sister. "I know, and I am so sorry. But you do know that Momma will live on through the next generation. Don't overlook that."

"You are right, of course. I am hoping for a girl. Franklin and I have thought about naming her Angelique."

"That would be a beautiful tribute."

Aimee rose to retrieve another box. "I am very much aware of her presence, aren't you?"

"Yes, for sure. I think it is because we are surrounded by that which meant something to her. These were her treasures. But I do think that we should try to finish this up for Poppa's sake. I can imagine that it would be painful for him to have to deal with it. It is as though each item speaks."

"That's an interesting way to put it, but yes, you are right. However, I must admit that it is fascinating to see what she kept through the years. Here is the brooch we gave to her when we graduated. The butterfly. She was so proud of that. And these sapphire earrings. I don't ever remember seeing her wear them."

"Oh, my," Aida said, "Look at this mask. Perhaps it was used for Carnival."

"How odd. There's a tintype made into a brooch. Look closely: I do believe that it is Uncle Gaston, I mean, Jean Paul. It certainly seems like his face. I wonder why she kept it? That had to be such a difficult memory for her."

"Although he was certainly a part of her history, I think we can just toss that token."

"Let me do the honors," Aimee said, opening her hand to receive the pin.

"Wait. What's this?" Aida asked, removing a small trunk from the bottom of the armoire. "It certainly is heavy."

"It is filled with books," Aimee said, opening the box, "all written by Momma, it seems."

"Here," Aida said, handing one to Aimee. "Read it."

Three hours later, the girls sat on the floor, surrounded by the volumes. "She wrote it all for us, so that we would know every bit of her history. I just read her account of the storm. Listen to this:

> *I could not sleep. The heat was oppressive in the confined quarters of the Star and the smell of unwashed bodies was unbearable. Hunger and thirst gnawed at my insides. It was difficult not to give in to the utter wretchedness, the ever-present despair. As quietly as possible, I tiptoed out of the cramped space, careful not to rouse anyone. A bit of fresh air on the deck would clear my head, I thought. At least I hoped that it would. How I longed for a respite from the misery.*
>
> *The moon illuminated the predawn sky as I gazed up at the stars, trying to remember the names of the constellations that Andrew had so carefully pointed out to me weeks earlier. Those moments of joy we shared as our romance was just beginning were among the sweetest I had ever known, and I locked away those memories deep within my heart. Regardless of what fate awaited us, we had experienced moments of great tenderness and abiding love. I tried to*

remember that some people never get that in an entire lifetime.

Clouds slowly drifted by, their clean white puffiness in stark contrast to the filth and muck which surrounded us. At times, I questioned if God lived there, high above the haze. Was that His heavenly home? More importantly, I wondered if He heard our collective petitions, the pleas for mercy and pity, as the desolation and misery grew stronger with each passing hour. With a child-like faith, I began to pray, begging to be released from another night of uncertainty and anguish, asking for guidance and protection for my beloved, and finally, thanking the Lord for sparing our lives. I am reminded that there is always something for which to be grateful. I have witnessed the tragic loss of so many who were not as fortunate to have survived, including my dear friend the Countess. We were spared, tossed about by the tempest, but saved from the certain death in churning waters and raging wind.

The morning sun appeared just below the horizon, casting a red and orange glow as it slowly moved into view, ushering in a new day. I surveyed the landscape; buzzards flew overhead, diving into the rotting animal corpses that still littered the beach and beyond. It made me tremble. I often wonder if I will ever be able to wipe the images of death and destruction from my mind's eye, the pictures so firmly implanted in my brain. Will they return to me in my dreams, the nightmare appearing over and over again? I pray that someday this experience will be a distant memory and that I will be stronger, living each day of my life in joy. Then, I will truly be a survivor.

"I don't think I fully understood all that she and Poppa endured on that island."

"Neither of them spoke much about it, I suppose. Most people find it difficult to revisit that kind of traumatic experience. But she wanted us to know, which is why she wrote about it in such vivid detail."

"There is one about your kidnapping. It is pretty powerful, Aimee. You will want to read that one right away."

"I don't know if I can."

"I understand. But it might help you to know just what she experienced during that difficult time."

"I suppose. This truly is incredible."

"Isn't it? What a treasure Momma has left us. She truly left something rather significant behind."

"Besides us, you mean?"

"Funny, Sissy. You must admit, this is pretty special. What a rich heritage we have!"

"It's truly priceless. I love this one: *'My grandmother once told me of a mighty oak in a forest called the tree of the beloved. Couples would visit there to lie under its shady branches and carve their initials in the trunk. And legend had it that if you kiss the person who is your one true love while standing under that massive tree, blossoms begin to magically sprout. She had managed to talk her young beau into taking her on a hunt for it, promising him a picnic lunch of fried chicken and biscuits. And after they had eaten, she looked deeply into his eyes and leaned forward for a kiss. Within minutes, pink flower petals fell like rain upon them. My grandmother smiled, placed her hand in his, and told him that someday she would be his wife. And indeed, six months later, she was.'* Isn't that amazing?"

"It's lovely and so romantic."

"I have a thought. How about a book? We could publish these as one volume from beginning to end. It's her story." Aida said. "I think that it would appeal to a reading public, don't you? The world should know her as we did."

"How would we accomplish that? Neither of us have any idea of where to begin, having no experience with such things. It seems like a daunting task."

"I will be in law school soon. I can search for a connection in publication who can guide us through the process. Shouldn't be that difficult. Her life was truly remarkable. Momma has shown us that there are many sacred places a person visits on their journey from birth to death."

"Indeed. She has taught us about the grace and beauty of the human experience."

"She certainly did. Every single day of her life. I say we do it."

"It certainly would be a way to honor her. She deserves that."

"We would need a title. What shall we call it?"

"How about *Angelique's Legacy*?"

"That's perfect! *Angelique's Legacy*. For indeed, that's exactly what it is."

AUTHOR'S NOTES

I must admit, I truly considered *Angelique's Peace* to be the final chapter in the saga. In the three years since the publication of that book, my dance card has been filled with medical appointments and chemotherapy infusions as I have arm-wrestled the cancer demon. I shifted my writing efforts to the blog, which grew into the two *Ovacoming* books. Chronicling the moments of that experience as I fought for my life seemed important, and I wrote with an urgency to remember every bit of raw emotion. But during those many months of confinement, I also found myself thinking of Angelique as her siren song gently called me back into the world I had created for her. I began to imagine what might have happened to the Slater family in the years following the death of the villainous Jean Paul. And I soon began to realize that there was more story to tell. But I also questioned if I was up to the task of telling it.

The phenomenon of chemo brain is not a myth, but a real physiological response to the challenging treatment that cancer patients undergo. I like to call it "chemoamnesia," because it does contribute to forgetfulness. (I also wanted to coin my own word.) It particularly affects critical thinking and language usage. And so, the idea of writing an entire novel seemed totally daunting and completely overwhelming. Besides, I thought, I owed it to readers to pen a compelling finale to the series, not some mediocre drivel. In other words, it had to be good. Quite frankly, I was a little afraid to try as I recited a litany of excuses.

Eventually, I managed to write the first sixteen chapters of the book, but then, I began to second-guess every single word. I doubted myself. And so, out of sheer frustration, I shoved it in a drawer, unsure if I would ever revisit it.

And then, the world suddenly stopped.

Spring of 2020 brought with it the threat of the Corona virus and folks like me, with a weakened immune system, went into quarantine. During the first few days of sheltering-in-place, I cleaned closets and rearranged my sock drawer. I cooked dinner every single night. But the excitement of those domestic chores quickly lost their appeal, and out of sheer boredom, I began to think of Angelique again. With lots of quiet time and no pressure to produce a final manuscript, I reread the beginning of the book with a fresh set of eyes. And slowly, I reentered Angelique's world. How I missed her!

And so, I give you this, the final installment in the series. I hope that you have enjoyed it. And thanks for the support that I have received from so many of you. Your emails have been comforting during this challenging season of my life. God willing, there will be more books in my future. I am thinking about a prequel, the story of Angelique's grandmothers. She did, after all, leave all of those journals behind, right? And in truth, her legacy has become mine.

Many thanks to my beta readers. I am so grateful for their help.
Jane Daugherty
Ruth McClelland

Additional titles by Paula W. Millet:

Angelique's Storm
Angelique's War
Angelique's Peace

Cosigning a Lie

Ovacoming
Still Ovacoming

Follow her blog at www.paulamillet.com
Email: paulawmillet@gmail.com

Manufactured by Amazon.ca
Bolton, ON

34200415R00181